TURN ON THE LIGHTS!

All the lights. Then sit back and indulge as fifteen masters relate bone-chilling tales of the occult and horror.

Yes, sit back, relax, and indulge in hours of ghoulish pleasure as the finest practitioners of the art relate stories of ghosts, demons and monsters—

THE THINGS THAT GO BUMP IN THE NIGHT

MODERN MASTERS of HORROR

Edited by FRANK COFFEY

MODERN MASTERS OF HORROR

Published by arrangement with Coward McCann & Geoghegan

ISBN: 0-441-53507-0

First Ace Printing: September 1982
Published simultaneously in Canada

Manufactured in the United States of America

2 4 6 8 0 9 7 5 3 1

MODERN MASTERS of HORROR

Contents

Introduction ✷ Frank Coffey 9
The Monkey ✷ Stephen King 13
The New Tenant ✷ William Hallahan 57
In the Cards ✷ Robert Bloch 67
Clay ✷ George A. Romero 83
A Cabin in the Woods ✷ John Coyne 105
Makeup ✷ Robert R. McCammon 123
The Small World of Lewis Stillman ✷ William F. Nolan 145
The Siege of 318 ✷ Davis Grubb 161
The Champion ✷ Richard Laymon 175
The Power of the Mandarin ✷ Gahan Wilson 183
Horror House of Blood ✷ Ramsey Campbell 203
Absolute Ebony ✷ Felice Picano 221
The Root of All Evil ✷ Graham Masterton 247
Julian's Hand ✷ Gary Brandner 265
The Face ✷ Jere Cunningham 279

Introduction

And much of madness
and more of sin
and Horror—the soul of the plot.

Poe, *The Conqueror Worm*

What is horror fiction? And why in the world are we, the readers of the 1980s, eating up horror fiction like marijuana smokers devouring a plate of fresh baked brownies?

An interesting question. Consider the following: the word "horror" is defined by *Webster's New World Dictionary* as "the strong feeling caused by something frightful or shocking; shuddering fear and disgust; terror and repugnance, etc." (The "etc" here is particularly worrisome: Just what does Webster have in store for us?)

Why deliberately seek out "disgusting, repugnant things"? Just why do we like to be scared? I think the key is the words "strong feeling."

In our highly technical world we are inundated with vivid, shocking facts, figures and pictures. The radio and TV bombard us each day with more "real horror" than our grandfathers encountered in a year. During the Vietnam war America was deluged with bloody, grisly pictures—which we watched while eating dinner in front of the tube. Intellectually we knew what we were seeing was real—and altogether terrible. But, on the other hand, weren't they just images on the screen? Like "The Untouchables"? Or "The FBI"? When an hour was up wouldn't it be over and couldn't we change channels to "Star Trek"?

No. We couldn't switch Vietnam off. We can't turn off

muggings and rape today. So we repress our fears about these crimes and the people who commit them.

We know our world is a hostile place. We cannot escape that conclusion. Yet we do not carry our apprehension nakedly with us; we couldn't function if we did. Instead, our fears are hidden, quietly stored away from conscious recognition, the universal baggage of contemporary Americans.

The horror story recognizes dread, which seems such an inevitable, even necessary part of our psychological baggage, by creating metaphorical evils that symbolically embody our fears. Through the monsters and psychic ghouls of occult fiction we can vicariously work out the fears inside us which might otherwise fester and grow into bogeymen.

Horror fiction is one method of dealing with our dread of the real life hobgoblins who slither through the troubled, unsettled America of the eighties. As we read horror stories we can meet our fears; we can overcome them as our heroes and heroines overcome or succumb to some horrific madness; we can have courage; we can *do* something—or try to; we are afraid—but in heroic fashion we conquer our own fear and, with the hero, fight an implacable foe. And even if the hero loses we always win.

Stephen King, perhaps our most successful horror writer, has said that writers of the supernatural are "tuning forks for the fears of a society." King, whose creepy *The Monkey* leads off this anthology, believes that occult stories are most successful in "unsettled times."

And because these are indeed "unsettled times," horror stories, novels and movies will continue to be successful. The horror boom is not temporary, like the Pet Rock or the Hula Hoop craze; it is not a fad that "will die any day now" as one publisher predicted to me almost five years ago; it is rather a genre that accurately reflects the very real, very primitive fears extant in our society.

Despite the real evils they symbolize, occult stories are fun. Almost everyone likes to be scared—*if* he or she is sure there's no real threat, as on a roller coaster. I'd rather writhe in delicious, thrilled expectation of the bloody hand about to pop from behind the creaking, slowly opening door—and then laugh at myself for being scared—than stew in my own psychological juices. It's healthier, and more fun, to work the dread out through fiction.

And writers of the occult, for all their horrible creations, are usually fun people—the opposite of the image of the typical writer: a lugubrious fellow brooding over his typewriter ribbon in contemplation of mankind's unutterably melancholy future. This capacity for humor, often black, makes for books and stories that are enjoyable to read. And that's the whole point.

So, dear reader, enjoy the following stories of unimaginable terror, base impulses and inhuman decadence. Remember that they are merely a way of applying psychological balm to your quivering psyche, that they are, after all, merely *stories*. Still . . . it might be best not to read them alone, especially at night—for the night holds the unknown. And the night does not belong to us.

FRANK COFFEY

STEPHEN KING

The Monkey

When Hal Shelburn saw it, when his son Dennis pulled it out of a mouldering Ralston-Purina carton that had been pushed far back under the attic eaves, such a feeling of horror and dismay rose in him that for one moment he thought he surely must scream. He put one fist to his mouth, as if to cram it back . . . and then merely coughed into his fist. Neither Terry nor Dennis noticed, but Petey looked around, momentarily curious.

"Hey, neat," Dennis said respectfully. It was a tone Hal rarely got from the boy anymore himself. Dennis was twelve.

"What is it?" Petey asked. He glanced at his father again before his eyes were dragged back to the thing his big brother had found. "What is it, Daddy?"

"It's a monkey, fartbrains," Dennis said. "Haven't you ever seen a monkey before?"

"Don't call your brother fartbrains," Terry said automatically, and began to examine a box of curtains. The curtains were slimy with mildew and she dropped them quickly. "Uck."

"Can I have it, Daddy?" Petey asked. He was nine.

"What do you mean?" Dennis cried. "*I* found it!"

"Boys, please," Terry said. "I'm getting a headache."

Hal barely heard them—any of them. The monkey glimmered up at him from his older son's hands, grinning its old familiar grin. The same grin that had haunted his nightmares as a child, haunted them until he had—

Outside a cold gust of wind rose, and for a moment lips with no flesh blew a long note through the old, rusty gutter outside. Petey stepped closer to his father, eyes moving uneasily to the rough attic roof through which nail heads poked.

"What was that, Daddy?" he asked as the whistle died to a guttural buzz.

"Just the wind," Hal said, still looking at the monkey. Its cymbals, crescents of brass rather than full circles in the weak light of the one naked bulb, were, perhaps a foot apart, and he added automatically. "Wind can whistle, but it can't carry a tune." Then he realized that was a saying of his Uncle Will's, and a goose ran over his grave.

The long note came again, the wind coming off Crystal Lake in a long, droning swoop and then wavering in the gutter. Half a dozen small drafts puffed cold October air into Hal's face—God, this place was so much like the back closet of the house in Hartford that they might all have been transported thirty years back in time.

I won't think about that.

But the thought wouldn't be denied.

In the back closet where I found that goddamned monkey in that same box.

Terry had moved away to examine a wooden crate filled with knickknacks, duck-walking because the pitch of the eaves was so sharp.

"I don't like it," Petey said, and felt for Hal's hand. "Dennis c'n have it if he wants. Can we go, Daddy?"

"Worried about ghosts, chickenguts?" Dennis inquired.

"Dennis, you stop it," Terry said absently. She picked up a wafer-thin cup with a Chinese pattern. "This is nice. This—"

Hal saw that Dennis had found the windup key in the monkey's back. Terror flew through him on dark wings.

"Don't do that!"

It came out more sharply than he had intended, and he had snatched the monkey out of Dennis's hands before he was really aware he had done it. Dennis looked around at him, startled. Terry had also glanced back over her shoulder, and Petey looked up. For a moment they were all silent, and the wind whistled again, very low this time, like an unpleasant invitation.

"I mean, it's probably broken," Hal said.

It used to be broken . . . except when it wanted to be fixed.

"Well you didn't have to *grab*," Dennis said.

"Dennis, shut up."

Dennis blinked at him and for a moment looked almost uneasy. Hal hadn't spoken to him so sharply in a long time. Not since Hal had lost his job with National Aerodyne in California two years before and they had moved to Texas. Dennis decided not to push it . . . for now. He turned back to the Ralston-Purina carton and began to root through it again, but the other stuff was nothing but shit. Broken toys bleeding springs and stuffings.

The wind was louder now, hooting instead of whistling. The attic began to creak softly, making a noise like footsteps.

"Please, Daddy?" Petey asked, only loud enough for his father to hear.

"Yeah," he said. "Terry, let's go."

"I'm not through with this—"

"I said let's *go.*"

It was her turn to look startled.

They had taken two adjoining rooms in a motel. By ten that night the boys were asleep in their room and Terry was asleep in the adults' room. She had taken two Valiums on the ride back from the home place in Casco. To keep her nerves from giving her a migraine. Just lately she took a lot of Valium. It had started around the time National Aerodyne had laid Hal off. For the last two years he had been working for Texas Instruments—it was $4,000 less a year, but it was work. He told Terry they were lucky. She agreed. There were plenty of software architects drawing unemployment, he said. She agreed. The company housing in Arnette was every bit as good as the place in Fresno, he said. She agreed, but he thought her agreement was a lie.

And he had been losing Dennis. He could feel the kid going, achieving a premature escape velocity, so long, Dennis, byebye stranger, it was nice sharing this train with you. Terry said she thought the boy was smoking reefers. She smelled them sometimes. You have to talk to him, Hal. And *he* agreed, but so far he had not.

The boys were asleep. Terry was asleep. Hal went into the bathroom and locked the door and sat down on the closed lid of the john and looked at the monkey.

He hated the way it felt, that soft brown nappy fur, worn bald in spots. He hated its grin—"*That monkey grins just like a nigger,*" Uncle Will had said once, but it didn't grin like a nigger, or like anything human. Its grin was all teeth, and if you wound up the key, the lips would move, the teeth would seem to get bigger, to become vampire teeth, the lips would writhe and the cymbals would bang, stupid monkey, stupid clockwork monkey, stupid, stupid—

He dropped it. His hands were shaking and he dropped it.

The key clicked on the bathroom tile as it struck the floor. The sound seemed very loud in the stillness. The monkey grinned at him with its murky amber eyes, doll's eyes, filled with idiot glee, its brass cymbals poised as if to strike up a march for some black band from hell, and on the bottom the words MADE IN HONG KONG were stamped.

"You can't be here," he whispered. "I threw you down the well when I was nine."

The monkey grinned up at him.

Hal Shelburn shuddered.

Outside in the night, a black capful of wind shook the motel.

Hal's brother Bill and Bill's wife Colette met them at Uncle

Will's and Aunt Ida's the next day. "Did it ever cross your mind that a death in the family is a really lousy way to renew the family connection?" Bill asked him with a bit of a grin. He had been named for Uncle Will. Will and Bill, champions of the rodayo, Uncle Will used to say, and ruffle Bill's hair. It was one of his sayings . . . like the wind can whistle but it can't carry a tune. Uncle Will had died six years before, and Aunt Ida had lived on here alone, until a stroke had taken her just the previous week. Very sudden, Bill had said when he called long distance to give Hal the news. As if he could know; as if anyone could know. She had died alone.

"Yeah," Hal said. "The thought crossed my mind."

They looked at the place together, the home place where they had finished growing up. Their father, a merchant mariner, had simply disappeared as if from the very face of the earth when they were young; Bill claimed to remember him vaguely, but Hal had no memories of him at all. Their mother had died when Bill was ten and Hal eight. They had come to Uncle Will's and Aunt Ida's from Hartford, and they had been raised here, and gone to college here. Bill had stayed and now had a healthy law practice in Portland.

Hal saw that Petey had wandered off toward the blackberry tangles that lay on the eastern side of the house in a mad jumble. "Stay away from there, Petey," he called.

Petey looked back, questioning. Hal felt simple love for the boy rush through him . . . and he suddenly thought of the monkey again.

"Why, Dad?"

"The old well's in there someplace," Bill said. "But I'll be damned if I remember just where. Your dad's right, Petey—those blackberry tangles are a good place to stay away from. Thorns'll do a job on you. Right, Hal?"

"Right," Hal said automatically. Pete moved away, not looking back, and then started down the embankment toward the small shingle of beach where Dennis was skipping stones over the water. Hal felt something in his chest loosen a little.

* * *

Bill might have forgotten where the old well had been, but late that afternoon Hal went to it unerringly, shouldering his way through the brambles that tore at his old flannel jacket and hunted for his eyes. He reached it and stood there, breathing hard, looking at the rotted, warped boards that covered it. After a moment's debate, he knelt (his knees fired twin pistol shots) and moved two of the boards aside.

From the bottom of that wet, rock-lined throat a face stared up at him, wide eyes, grimacing mouth, and a moan escaped him. It was not loud, except in his heart. There it had been very loud.

It was his own face, reflected up from dark water.

Not the monkey's. For a moment he had thought it was the monkey's.

He was shaking. Shaking all over.

I threw it down the well. I threw it down the well, please God don't let me be crazy, I threw it down the well.

The well had gone dry the summer Johnny McCabe died, the year after Bill and Hal came to stay at the home place with Uncle Will and Aunt Ida. Uncle Will had borrowed money from the bank to have an artesian well sunk, and the blackberry tangles had grown up around the old dug well. The dry well.

Except the water had come back. Like the monkey.

This time the memory would not be denied. Hal sat there helplessly, letting it come, trying to go with it, to ride it like a surfer riding a monster wave that will crush him if he falls off his board, just trying to get through it so it would be gone again.

He had crept out here with the monkey late that summer, and the blackberries had been out, the smell of them thick and cloying. No one came in here to pick, although Aunt Ida would sometimes stand at the edge of the tangles and pick a cupful of berries into her apron. In here the blackberries had gone past ripe to overripe, some of them were rotting, sweating a thick white fluid like pus, and the crickets sang maddeningly in the high grass underfoot, their endless cry: *Reeeeeeee—*

The thorns tore at him, brought dots of blood onto his bare arms. He made no effort to avoid their sting. He had been blind with terror—so blind that he had come within inches of stumbling onto the boards that covered the well, perhaps within inches of crashing thirty feet to the well's muddy bottom. He had pinwheeled his arms for balance, and more thorns had branded his forearms. It was that memory that had caused him to call Petey back sharply.

That was the day Johnny McCabe had died—his best friend. Johnny had been climbing the rungs up to his treehouse in his backyard. The two of them had spent many hours up there that summer, playing pirate, seeing make-believe galleons out on the lake, unlimbering the cannon, preparing to board. Johnny had been climbing up to the tree house as he had done a thousand times before, and the rung just below the trapdoor in the bottom of the tree house had snapped off in his hands and Johnny had fallen thirty feet to the ground and had broken his neck and it was the monkey's fault, the monkey, the goddam hateful monkey. When the phone rang, when Aunt Ida's mouth dropped open and then formed an O of horror as her friend Milly from down the road told her the news, when Aunt Ida said, "Come out on the porch, Hal, I have to tell you some bad news—," he had thought with sick horror, *The monkey! What's the monkey done now?*

There had been no reflection of his face trapped at the bottom of the well that day, only the stone cobbles going down into the darkness, and the smell of wet mud. He had looked at the monkey lying there on the wiry grass that grew between the blackberry tangles, its cymbals poised, its grinning teeth huge between its splayed lips, its fur rubbed away in balding, mangy patches here and there, its glazed eyes.

"I hate you," he had hissed at it. He wrapped his hand around its loathsome body, feeling the nappy fur crinkle. It grinned at him as he held it up in front of his face. "Go on!" he dared it, beginning to cry for the first time that day. He shook it. The poised cymbals trembled minutely. It spoiled everything good. Everything. "Go on, clap them! Clap them!"

The monkey only grinned.

"Go on and clap them!" His voice rose hysterically. "Fraidy-cat, fraidy-cat, go on and clap them! I dare you!"

Its brownish yellow eyes. Its huge and gleeful teeth.

He threw it down the well then, mad with grief and terror. He saw it turn over once on its way down, a simian acrobat doing a trick, and the sun glinted one last time on those cymbals. It struck the bottom with a thud, and that must have jogged its clockwork, for suddenly the cymbals *did* begin to beat. Their steady, deliberate, and tinny banging rose to his ears, echoing and fey in the stone throat of the dead well: *jang-jang-jang-jang—*

Hal clapped his hands over his mouth, and for a moment he could see it down there, perhaps only in the eye of imagination . . . lying there in the mud, eyes glaring up at the small circle of his boy's face peering over the lip of the well (as if marking its shape forever), lips expanding and contracting around those grinning teeth, cymbals clapping, funny windup monkey.

Jang-jang-jang-jang, who's dead? Jang-jang-jang-jang, is it Johnny McCabe, falling with his eyes wide, doing his own acrobatic somersault as he falls through the bright summer-vacation air with the splintered rung still held in his hands, to strike the ground with a single bitter snapping sound? Is it Johnny, Hal? Or is it you?

Moaning, Hal had shoved the boards across the hole, getting splinters in his hands, not caring, not even aware of them until later. And still he could hear it, even through the boards, muffled now and somehow all the worse for that: it was down there in stone-faced dark, clapping its cymbals and jerking its repulsive body, the sounding coming up like the sound of a prematurely buried man scrabbling for a way out.

Jang-jang-jang-jang, who's dead this time?

He fought and battered his way back through the blackberry creepers. Thorns stitched fresh lines of welling blood briskly across his face and burdocks caught in the cuffs of his jeans, and he fell full-length once, his ears still jangling, as if the monkey had followed him. Uncle Will found him later, sitting on an old tire in the garage and sobbing, and he had thought Hal was crying for his dead friend. So he had been; but he had also cried in the aftermath of terror.

He had thrown the monkey down the well in the afternoon. That evening, as twilight crept in through a shimmering mantle of ground-fog, a car moving too fast for the reduced visibility had run down Aunt Ida's Manx cat in the road and gone right on. There had been guts everywhere. Bill had thrown up, but Hal had only turned his face away, his pale, still face, hearing Aunt Ida's sobbing as if from miles away. (This on top of the news about the McCabe boy had caused a fit of weeping that was almost hysterics, and it was almost two hours before Uncle Will could calm her completely.) In Hal's heart there was a cold and exultant joy. It hadn't been his turn. It had been Aunt Ida's Manx, not him, not his brother Bill or his Uncle Will (just two champions of the rodayo). And now the monkey was gone, it was down the well, and one scruffy Manx cat with ear mites was not too great a price to pay. If the monkey wanted to clap its hellish cymbals now, let it. It could clap and clash them for the crawling bugs and beetles, the dark things that made their home in the well's stone gullet. It would rot down there in the darkness and its loathsome cogs and wheels and springs would rust in darkness. It would die down there. In the mud and the darkness. Spiders would spin it a shroud.

But . . . it had come back.

Slowly, Hal covered the well again, as he had on that day, and in his ears he heard the phantom echo of the monkey's cymbals: *Jang-jang-jang-jang, who's dead, Hal? Is it Terry? Dennis? Is it Petey, Hal? He's your favorite, isn't he? Is it him? Jang-jang-jang—*

"Put that *down!*"

Petey flinched and dropped the monkey, and for one nightmare moment Hal thought that would do it, that the jolt would jog its machinery and the cymbals would begin to beat and clash.

"Daddy, you scared me."

"I'm sorry. I just . . . I don't want you to play with that."

The others had gone to see a movie, and he had thought he would beat them back to the motel. But he had stayed at the home place longer than he would have guessed; the old, hateful memories seemed to move in their own eternal time zone.

Terry was sitting near Dennis, watching "The Beverly Hillbillies." She watched the old grainy print with a steady, bemused concentration that spoke of a recent Valium pop. Dennis was reading a rock magazine with the group Styx on the cover. Petey had been sitting cross-legged on the carpet, goofing with the monkey.

"It doesn't work anyway," Petey said. *Which explains why Dennis let him have it,* Hal thought, and then felt ashamed and angry at himself. He seemed to have no control over the hostility he felt toward Dennis more and more often, but in the aftermath he felt demeaned and tacky . . . helpless.

"No," he said. "It's old. I'm going to throw it away. Give it to me."

He held out his hand and Petey, looking troubled, handed it over.

Dennis said to his mother, "Pop's turning into a friggin' schizophrenic."

Hal was across the room even before he knew he was going, the monkey in one hand, grinning as if in approbation. He hauled Dennis out of his chair by the shirt. There was a purring sound as a seam came adrift somewhere. Dennis looked almost comically shocked. His copy of *Tiger Beat* fell to the floor.

"Hey!"

"You come with me," Hal said grimly, pulling his son toward the door to the connecting room.

"Hal!" Terry nearly screamed. Petey just goggled.

Hal pulled Dennis through. He slammed the door and then slammed Dennis against the door. Dennis was starting to look scared. "You're getting a mouth problem," Hal said.

"Let *go* of me! You tore my shirt, you—"

Hal slammed the boy against the door again. "Yes," he said. "A real mouth problem. Did you learn that in school? Or back in the smoking area?"

Dennis flushed, his face momentarily ugly with guilt. "I wouldn't be in that shitty school if you didn't get canned!" he burst out.

Hal slammed Dennis against the door again. "I didn't get canned, I got laid off, you know it, and I don't need any of your shit about it. You have problems? Welcome to the world, Dennis. Just don't you lay off all your problems on me. You're eating. Your ass is covered. At eleven, I don't . . . need any . . . shit from you." He punctuated each phrase by pulling the boy forward until their noses were almost touching and then slamming him back into the door. It was not hard enough to hurt, but Dennis was scared—his father had not laid a hand on him since they moved to Texas—and now he began to cry with a young boy's loud, braying, healthy sobs.

"Go ahead, beat me up!" he yelled at Hal, his face twisted and blotchy. "Beat me up if you want, I know how much you fucking hate me!"

"I don't hate you. I love you a lot, Dennis. But I'm your dad and you're going to show me respect or I'm going to bust you for it."

Dennis tried to pull away. Hal pulled the boy to him and hugged him. Dennis fought for a moment and then put his face against Hal's chest and wept as if exhausted. It was the sort of cry Hal hadn't heard from either of his children in years. He closed his eyes, realizing that he felt exhausted himself.

Terry began to hammer on the other side of the door. "Stop it, Hal! Whatever you're doing to him, stop it!"

"I'm not killing him," Hal said. "Go away, Terry."

"Don't you—"

"It's all right, Mom," Dennis said, muffled against Hal's chest.

He could feel her perplexed silence for a moment, and then she went. Hal looked at his son again.

"I'm sorry I badmouthed you, Dad," Dennis said reluctantly.

"When we get home next week, I'm going to wait two or three days and then I'm going to go through all your drawers, Dennis. If there's something in them you don't want me to see, you better get rid of it."

That flash of guilt again. Dennis lowered his eyes and wiped away snot with the back of his hand.

"Can I go now?" He sounded sullen once more.

"Sure," Hal said, and let him go. *Got to take him camping in the spring, just the two of us. Do some fishing, like Uncle Will used to do with Bill and me. Got to get close to him. Got to try.*

He sat down on the bed in the empty room and looked at the monkey. *You'll never be close to him again, Hal,* its grin seemed to say. *Never again. Never again.*

Just looking at the monkey made him feel tired. He laid it aside and put a hand over his eyes.

That night Hal stood in the bathroom, brushing his teeth, and thought: *It was in the same box. How could it be in the same box?*

The toothbrush jabbed upward, hurting his gums. He winced.

He had been four, Bill six, the first time he saw the monkey. Their missing father had bought a house in Hartford, and it had been theirs, free and clear, before he died or disappeared or whatever it had been. Their mother worked as a secretary at Holmes Aircraft, the helicopter plant out in Westville, and a series of sitters came in to stay with the boys, except by then it was just Hal that the sitters had to mind through the day—Bill was in first grade, big school. None of the baby sitters stayed for long. They got pregnant and married their boyfriends or got work at Holmes, or Mrs. Shelburn would discover they had been at the cooking sherry or her bottle of brandy which was kept in the sideboard for special occasions. Most of them were stupid girls who seemed only to want to eat or sleep. None of them wanted to read to Hal as his mother would do.

The sitter that long winter was a huge, sleek black girl named Beulah. She fawned over Hal when Hal's mother was around and sometimes pinched him when she wasn't. Still, Hal had some liking for Beulah, who once in a while would read him a lurid tale from one of her confession or true-detective magazines ("Death Came for the Voluptuous Redhead," Beulah would intone ominously in the dozy daytime silence of the living room, and pop another Reese's Peanut Butter Cup into her mouth while Hal solemnly studied the grainy tabloid pictures and drank his milk from his Wish-Cup). And the liking made what happened worse.

He found the monkey on a cold, cloudy day in March. Sleet ticked sporadically off the windows, and Beulah was asleep on the couch, a copy of *My Story* tented open on her admirable bosom. So Hal went into the back closet to look at his father's things.

The back closet was a storage space that ran the length of the second floor on the left side, extra space that had never been finished off. One got into the back closet by using a small door—a down-the-rabbit-hole sort of door—on Bill's side of the boys' bedroom. They both liked to go in there, even though it was chilly in winter and hot enough in summer to wring a bucketful of sweat out of your pores. Long and narrow and somehow snug, the back closet was full of fascinating junk. No matter how much stuff you looked at, you never seemed to be able to look at it all. He and Bill had spent whole Saturday afternoons up here, barely speaking to each other, taking things out of boxes, examining them, turning them over and over so their hands could absorb each unique reality, putting them back. Now Hal wondered if he and Bill hadn't been trying, as best they could, to somehow make contact with their vanished father.

He had been a merchant mariner with a navigator's certificate, and there were stacks of charts back there, some marked with neat circles (and the dimple of the compass's swing-point in the center of each). There were twenty volumes of something called *Barron's Guide to Navigation*. Cockeyed binoculars that made your eyes feel hot and funny if you looked through them too long. There were touristy things from a dozen ports of call—rubber hula-hula dolls, a black cardboard bowler with a torn band that said YOU PICK A GIRL AND I'LL PICCADILLY, a glass globe with a tiny Eiffel Tower inside—and there were also envelopes with foreign stamps tucked carefully away inside, and foreign coins; there were rock samples from the Hawaiian island of Maui, a glassy black—heavy and somehow ominous—and funny records in foreign languages.

That day, with the sleet ticking hypnotically off the roof just above his head, Hal worked his way all the way down to the far end of the back closet, moved a box aside, and saw another box behind it—a Ralston-Purina box. Looking over the top was a pair of glassy hazel eyes. They gave him a start and he skittered back for a moment, heart thumping, as if he had discovered a deadly pygmy. Then he saw its silence, the glaze in those eyes, and realized it was some sort of toy. He moved forward again and lifted it carefully from the box.

It grinned its ageless, toothy grin in the yellow light, its cymbals held apart.

Delighted, Hal had turned it this way and that, feeling the crinkle of its nappy fur. Its funny grin pleased him. Yet hadn't there been something else? An almost instinctive feeling of disgust that had come and gone almost before he was aware of it? Perhaps it was so, but with an old, old memory like this one, you had to be careful not to believe too much. Old memories could lie. But . . . hadn't he seen that same expression on Petey's face, in the attic of the home place?

He had seen the key set into the small of the monkey's back, and turned it. It had turned far too easily; there were no winding-up clicks. Broken, then. Broken, but still neat.

He took it out to play with it.

"Whatchoo got, Hal?" Beulah asked, waking from her nap.

"Nothing," Hal said. "I found it."

He put it up on the shelf on his side of the bedroom. It stood atop his Lassie coloring books, grinning, staring into space, cymbals poised. It was broken, but it grinned nonetheless. That night Hal awakened from some uneasy dream, bladder full, and got up to use the bathroom in the hall. Bill was a breathing lump of covers across the room.

Hal came back, was almost asleep again . . . and suddenly the monkey began to beat its cymbals together in the darkness.

Jang-jang-jang-jang—

Hal came fully awake, as if snapped in the face with a cold, wet towel. His heart gave a staggering leap of surprise, and a tiny, mouselike squeak escaped his throat. He stared at the monkey, eyes wide, lips trembling.

Jang-jang-jang-jang—

Its body rocked and humped on the shelf. Its lips spread and closed, spread and closed, hideously gleeful, revealing huge and carnivorous teeth.

"Stop," Hal whispered.

His brother turned over and uttered a loud, single snore. All else was silent . . . except for the monkey. The cymbals clapped and clashed, and surely it would wake his brother, his mother, the world. It would wake the dead.

Jang-jang-jang-jang—

Hal moved it, meaning to stop it somehow, perhaps put his hand between its cymbals until it ran down *(but it was broken, wasn't it?)*, and then it stopped on its own. The cymbals came together one last time—*Jang!*—and then spread slowly apart to their original position. The brass glimmered in the shadows. The monkey's dirty yellowish teeth grinned their improbable grin.

The house was silent again. His mother turned over in her bed and echoed Bill's single snore. Hal got back into his bed and pulled the covers up, his heart still beating fast, and he thought: *I'll put it back in the closet again tomorrow. I don't want it.*

But the next morning he forgot all about putting the monkey back because his mother didn't go to work. Beulah was dead. Their mother wouldn't tell them exactly what happened. "It was an accident, just a terrible accident" was all she would say. But that afternoon Bill bought a newspaper on his way home from school and smuggled page four up to their room under his shirt (TWO KILLED IN APARTMENT SHOOT-OUT, the headline read) and read the article haltingly to Hal, following along with his finger, while their mother cooked supper in the kitchen. Beulah McCaffery, 19, and Sally Tremont, 20, had been shot by Miss McCaffery's boyfriend, Leonard White, 25, following an argument over who was to go out and pick up an order of Chinese food. Miss Tremont had expired at Hartford Receiving; Beulah McCaffery had been pronounced dead at the scene.

It was like Beulah just disappeared into one of her own detective magazines, Hal Shelburn thought, and felt a cold chill race up his spine and then circle his heart. And then he realized the shootings had occurred about the same time the monkey—

"Hal?" It was Terry's voice, sleepy. "Coming to bed?"

He spat toothpaste into the sink and rinsed his mouth. "Yes," he said.

He had put the monkey in his suitcase earlier, and locked it up. They were flying back to Texas in two or three days. But before they went, he would get rid of the damned thing for good.

Somehow.

"You were pretty rough on Dennis this afternoon," Terry said in the dark.

"Dennis has needed somebody to start being rough on him for quite a while now, I think. He's been drifting. I just don't want him to start falling."

"Psychologically, beating the boy isn't a very productive—"

"I didn't *beat* him, Terry—for Christ's sake!"

"—way to assert parental authority. . . ."

"Oh, don't give me any of that encounter-group shit," Hal said angrily.

"I can see you don't want to discuss this." Her voice was cold.

"I told him to get the dope out of the house, too."

"You did?" Now she sounded apprehensive. "How did he take it? What did he say?"

"Come on, Terry! What *could* he say? 'You're fired'?"

"Hal, what's the *matter* with you? You're not like this—what's *wrong?*"

"Nothing," he said, thinking of the monkey locked away in his Samsonite. Would he hear it if it began to clap its cymbals? Yes, he surely would. Muffled, but audible. Clapping doom for someone, as it had for Beulah, Johnny McCabe, Uncle Will's dog Daisy. *Jang-jang-jang, is it you, Hal?* "I've just been under a strain."

"I *hope* that's all it is. Because I don't like you this way."

"No?" And the words escaped before he could stop them; he didn't even want to stop them. "So pop a few Valiums and everything will look okay again, right?"

He heard her draw breath in and let it out shakily. She began to cry then. He could have comforted her (maybe), but there seemed to be no comfort in him. There was too much terror. It would be better when the monkey was gone again, gone for good. Please God, gone for good.

He lay wakeful until very late, until morning began to gray the air outside. But he thought he knew what to do.

* * *

Bill had found the monkey the second time.

That was about a year and a half after Beulah McCaffery had been pronounced dead at the scene. It was summer. Hal had just finished kindergarten.

He came in from playing with Stevie Arlingen and his mother

called, "Wash your hands, Hal, you're filthy like a pig." She was on the porch, drinking an iced tea and reading a book. It was her vacation; she had two weeks.

Hal gave his hands a token pass under cold water and printed dirt on the hand towel. "Where's Bill?"

"Upstairs. You tell him to clean his side of the room. It's a mess."

Hal, who enjoyed being the messenger of unpleasant news in such matters, rushed up. Bill was sitting on the floor. The small down-the-rabbit-hole door leading to the back closet was ajar. He had the monkey in his hands.

"That don't work," Hal said immediately. "It's busted."

He was apprehensive, although he barely remembered coming back from the bathroom that night, and the monkey suddenly beginning to clap its cymbals. A week or so after that, he had had a bad dream about the monkey and Beulah—he couldn't remember exactly what—and had awakened screaming, thinking for a moment that the soft weight on his chest was the monkey, that he would open his eyes and see it grinning down at him. But of course the soft weight had only been his pillow, clutched with panicky tightness. His mother came in to soothe him with a drink of water and two chalky-orange baby aspirins, those Valiums for childhood's troubled times. She thought it was the fact of Beulah's death that had caused the nightmare. So it was, but not in the way she thought.

He barely remembered any of this now, but the monkey still scared him, particularly its cymbals. And its teeth.

"I know that," Bill said, and tossed the monkey aside. "It's stupid." It landed on Bill's bed, staring up at the ceiling, cymbals poised. Hal did not like to see it there. "You want to go down to Teddy's and get Popsicles?"

"I spent my allowance already," Hal said. "Besides, Mom says you got to clean up your side of the room."

"I can do that later," Bill said. "And I'll loan you a nickel, if you want." Bill was not above giving Hal an Indian rope burn sometimes, and would occasionally trip him up or punch him for no particular reason, but mostly he was okay.

"Sure," Hal said gratefully. "I'll just put that busted monkey back in the closet first, okay?"

"Nah," Bill said, getting up. "Let's go-go-go."

Hal went. Bill's moods were changeable, and if he paused to put the monkey away, he might lose his Popsicle. They went down to Teddy's and got them, then down to the Rec where some kids were getting up a baseball game. Hal was too small to play but he sat far out in foul territory, sucking his root beer Popsicle and chasing what the big kids called "Chinese home runs." They didn't get home until almost dark, and their mother whacked Hal for getting the hand towel dirty and whacked Bill for not cleaning up his side of the room, and after supper there was TV, and by the time all of that had happened, Hal had forgotten all about the monkey. It somehow found its way up onto *Bill's* shelf, where it stood right next to Bill's autographed picture of Bill Boyd. And there it stayed for nearly two years.

By the time Hal was seven, baby sitters had become an extravagance, and Mrs. Shelburn's last word to the two of them each morning was, "Bill, look after your brother."

That day, however, Bill had to stay after school for a Safety Patrol Boy meeting and Hal came home alone, stopping at each corner until he could see absolutely no traffic coming in either direction and then skittering across, shoulders hunched, like a doughboy crossing no man's land. He let himself into the house with the key under the mat and went immediately to the refrigerator for a glass of milk. He got the bottle, and then it slipped through his fingers and crashed to smithereens on the floor, the pieces of glass flying everywhere, as the monkey suddenly began to beat its cymbals together upstairs.

Jang-jang-jang-jang, on and on.

He stood there immobile, looking down at the broken glass and the puddle of milk, full of terror he could not name or understand. It was simply there, seeming to ooze from his pores.

He turned and rushed upstairs to their room. The monkey stood on Bill's shelf, seeming to stare at him. It had knocked the autographed picture of Bill Boyd face down onto Bill's bed. The monkey rocked and grinned and beat its cymbals together. Hal approached it slowly, not wanting to, not able to stay away. Its cymbals jerked apart and crashed together and jerked apart again. As he got closer, he could hear the clockwork running in the monkey's guts.

Abruptly, uttering a cry of revulsion and terror, he swatted it from the shelf as one might swat a large, loathsome bug. It struck Bill's pillow and then fell on the floor, cymbals still beating together, *jang-jang-jang,* lips flexing and closing as it lay there on its back in a patch of late April sunshine.

Then, suddenly, he remembered Beulah. The monkey had clapped its cymbals that night, too.

Hal kicked it with one Buster Brown shoe, kicked it as hard as he could, and this time the cry that escaped him was one of fury. The clockwork monkey skittered across the floor, bounced off the wall, and lay still. Hal stood staring at it, fists bunched, heart pounding. It grinned saucily back at him, the sun a burning pinpoint in one glass eye. *Kick me all you want,* it seemed to tell him. *I'm nothing but cogs and clockwork and a worm gear or two, kick me all you feel like, I'm not real, just a funny clockwork monkey is all I am, and who's dead? There's been an explosion at the helicopter plant. What's that rising up into the sky like a big bloody bowling ball with eyes where the finger-holes should be? Is it your mother's head, Hal? Down at Brook Street Corner! The car was going too fast! The driver was drunk! There's one Patrol Boy less! Could you hear the crunching sound when the wheels ran over Bill's skull and his brains squirted out of his ears? Yes? No? Maybe? Don't ask me, I don't know,* I can't *know, all I know how to do is beat these cymbals together jang-jang-jang, and who's dead, Hal? Your mother? Your brother? Or is it you, Hal? Is it you?*

He rushed at it again, meaning to stomp on it, smash its

loathsome body, jump on it until cogs and gears flew and its horrible glass eyes rolled across the floor. But just as he reached it, its cymbals came together once more, very softly . . . *(jang)* . . . as a spring somewhere inside expanded one final, minute notch . . . and a sliver of ice seemed to whisper its way through the walls of his heart, impaling it, stilling its fury and leaving him sick with terror again. The monkey almost seemed to know—how gleeful its grin seemed!

He picked it up, tweezing one of its arms between the thumb and first finger of his right hand, mouth drawn down in a bow of loathing, as if it were a corpse he held. Its mangy fake fur seemed hot and fevered against his skin. He fumbled open the tiny door that led to the back closet and turned on the bulb. The monkey grinned at him as he crawled down the length of the storage area between boxes piled on top of boxes, past the set of navigation books and the photograph albums with their fume of old chemicals and the souvenirs and the old clothes, and Hal thought: *If it begins to clap its cymbals together now and move in my hand, I'll scream, and if I scream, it'll do more than grin, it'll start to* laugh, *to laugh at me, and then I'll go crazy and they'll find me in here, drooling and laughing, crazy. I'll be crazy, oh please dear God, please dear Jesus, don't let me go crazy—*

He reached the far end and clawed two boxes aside, spilling one of them, and jammed the monkey back into the Ralston-Purina box in the farthest corner. And it leaned in there, comfortably, as if home at last, cymbals poised, grinning its simian grin, as if the joke were still on Hal. Hal crawled backward, sweating, hot and cold, all fire and ice, waiting for the cymbals to begin, and when they began, the monkey would leap from its box and scurry beetlelike toward him, clockwork whirring, cymbals clashing madly, and—

—and none of that happened. He turned off the light and slammed the small down-the-rabbit-hole door and leaned on it, panting. At last he began to feel a little better. He went downstairs on rubbery legs, got an empty bag, and began carefully to pick up the jagged shards and splinters of the broken milk bottle, wondering if he was going to cut himself and bleed to death, if that was what the clapping cymbals had meant. But that didn't happen, either. He got a towel and wiped up the milk and then sat down to see if his mother and brother would come home.

His mother came first, asking, "Where's Bill?"

In a low, colorless voice, now sure that Bill must be dead, Hal started to explain about the Patrol Boy meeting, knowing that, even given a very long meeting, Bill should have been home half an hour ago.

His mother looked at him curiously, started to ask what was wrong, and then the door opened and Bill came in—only it was not Bill at all, not really. This was a ghost-Bill, pale and silent.

"What's wrong?" Mrs. Shelburn exclaimed. "Bill, what's wrong?"

Bill began to cry and they got the story through his tears. There had been a car, he said. He and his friend Charlie Silverman were walking home together after the meeting and the car came around Brook Street Corner too fast and Charlie had frozen, Bill had tugged Charlie's hand once but had lost his grip and the car—

Bill began to bray out loud, hysterical sobs, and his mother hugged him to her, rocking him, and Hal looked out on the porch and saw two policemen standing there. The squad car in which they had conveyed Bill home was at the curb. Then he began to cry himself . . . but his tears were tears of relief.

It was Bill's turn to have nightmares now—dreams in which Charlie Silverman died over and over again, knocked out of his Red Ryder cowboy boots, and flipped onto the hood of the old Hudson Hornet the drunk had been driving. Charlie Silverman's head and the Hudson's windshield had met with an explosive noise, and both had shattered. The drunk driver, who owned a candy store in Milford, suffered a heart attack shortly after being taken into custody (perhaps it was the sight of Charlie Silverman's brains drying on his pants), and his lawyer was quite successful at the trial with his "this man has been punished enough" theme. The drunk was given sixty days (suspended) and lost his privilege to operate a motor vehicle in the state of Connecticut for five years . . . which was about as long as Bill Shelburn's nightmares lasted. The monkey was hidden away again in the back closet. Bill never noticed it was gone from his shelf . . . or if he did, he never said.

Hal felt safe for a while. He even began to forget about the monkey again, or to believe it had only been a bad dream. But when he came home from school on the afternoon his mother died, it was back on his shelf, cymbals poised, grinning down at him.

He approached it slowly, as if from outside himself—as if his own body had been turned into a wind-up toy at the sight of the monkey. He saw his hand reach out and take it down. He felt the nappy fur crinkle under his hand, but the feeling was muffled, mere pressure, as if someone had shot him full of novocaine. He could hear his breathing, quick and dry, like the rattle of wind through straw.

He turned it over and grasped the key and years later he would think that his drugged fascination was like that of a man who puts a six-shooter with one loaded chamber against a closed and jittering eyelid and pulls the trigger.

No don't—let it alone throw it away don't touch it—

He turned the key and in the silence he heard a perfect tiny series of winding-up clicks. When he let the key go the monkey began to clap its cymbals together and he could feel its body jerking, bend-and-*jerk*, bend-and-*jerk*, as if it were alive, it *was* alive, writhing in his hand like some loathsome pygmy, and the vibration he felt through its balding brown fur was not that of turning cogs but the beating of its black and cindered heart.

With a groan, Hal dropped the monkey and backed away, fingernails digging into the flesh under his eyes, palms pressed to his mouth. He stumbled over something and nearly lost his balance (then he would have been right down on the floor with it, his bulging blue eyes looking into its glassy hazel ones). He scrambled toward the door, backed through it, slammed it, and leaned against it. Suddenly he bolted for the bathroom and vomited.

It was Mrs. Stukey from the helicopter plant who brought the news and stayed with them those first two endless nights, until Aunt Ida got down from Maine. Their mother had died of a brain embolism in the middle of the afternoon. She had been standing at the water cooler with a cup of water in one hand and had crumpled as if shot, still holding the paper cup in one hand. With the other she had clawed at the water cooler and had pulled the great glass bottle of Poland water down with her. It had shattered . . . but the plant doctor, who came on the run, said later that he believed Mrs. Shelburn was dead before the water had soaked through her dress and her underclothes to wet her skin. The boys were never told any of this, but Hal knew anyway. He dreamed it again and again on the long nights following his mother's death. *"You still have trouble gettin' to sleep, little brother?"* Bill had asked him, and Hal supposed Bill thought all the thrashing and bad dreams had to do with their mother dying so suddenly, and that was right . . . but only partly right. There was the guilt: the certain, deadly knowledge that he had killed his mother by winding the monkey up on that sunny after-school afternoon.

* * *

When Hal finally fell asleep, his sleep must have been deep. When he awoke, it was nearly noon. Petey was sitting cross-legged in a chair across the room, methodically eating an orange section by section and watching a game show on TV.

Hal swung his legs out of bed, feeling as if someone had punched him down into sleep . . . and then punched him back out of it. His head throbbed. "Where's your mom, Petey?"

Petey glanced around. "She and Dennis went shopping. I said I'd stay here with you. Do you always talk in your sleep, Dad?"

Hal looked at his son cautiously. "No, I don't think so. What did I say?"

"It was all muttering, I couldn't make it out. It scared me, a little."

"Well, here I am in my right mind again," Hal said, and managed a small grin. Petey grinned back, and Hal felt simple love for the boy again, an emotion that was bright and strong and uncomplicated. He wondered why he had always been able to feel so good about Petey, to feel he understood Petey and could help him, and why Dennis seemed a window too dark to look through, a mystery in his ways and habits, the sort of boy he could not understand because he had never been that sort of boy. It was too easy to say that the move from California had changed Dennis, or that—

His thoughts froze. The monkey. The monkey was sitting on the windowsill, cymbals poised. Hal felt his heart stop dead in his chest and then suddenly begin to gallop. His vision wavered, and his throbbing head began to ache ferociously.

It had escaped from the suitcase and now stood on the windowsill, grinning at him. *Thought you got rid of me, didn't you? But you've thought that before, haven't you?*

Yes, he thought sickly. Yes, I have.

"Pete, did you take that monkey out of my suitcase?" he asked, knowing the answer already. He had locked the suitcase and had put the key in his overcoat pocket.

Petey glanced at the monkey, and something—Hal thought it was unease—passed over his face. "No," he said. "Mom put it there."

"Mom did?"

"Yeah. She took it from you. She laughed."

"Took it from me? What are you talking about?"

"You had it in bed with you. I was brushing my teeth, but Dennis saw. He laughed, too. He said you looked like a baby with a teddy bear."

Hal looked at the monkey. His mouth was too dry to swallow. He'd had it in *bed* with him? In *bed?* That loathsome fur against his cheek, maybe against his *mouth,* those glass eyes staring into his sleeping face, those grinning teeth near his neck? Dear *God.*

He turned abruptly and went to the closet. The Samsonite was there, still locked. The key was still in his overcoat pocket.

Behind him, the TV snapped off. He came out of the closet slowly. Petey was looking at him soberly. "Daddy, I don't like that monkey," he said, his voice almost too low to hear.

"Nor do I," Hal said.

Petey looked at him closely, to see if he was joking, and saw that he was not. He came to his father and hugged him tight. Hal could feel him trembling.

Petey spoke into his ear, then, very rapidly, as if afraid he might not have courage enough to say it again . . . or that the monkey might overhear.

"It's like it looks at you. Like it looks at you no matter where you are in the room. And if you go into the other room, it's like it's looking through the wall at you. I kept feeling like it . . . like it wanted me for something."

Petey shuddered. Hal held him tight.

"Like it wanted you to wind it up," Hal said.

Pete nodded violently. "It isn't really broken, is it, Dad?"

"Sometimes it is," Hal said, looking over his son's shoulder at the monkey. "But sometimes it still works."

"I kept wanting to go over there and wind it up. It was so quiet, and I thought, I can't, it'll wake up Daddy, but I still wanted to, and I went over and I . . . I *touched* it and I hate the way it feels . . . but I liked it, too . . . and it was like it was saying, Wind me up, Petey, we'll play, your father isn't going to wake up, he's never going to wake up at all, wind me up, wind me up . . ."

The boy suddenly burst into tears.

"It's bad, I know it is. There's something wrong with it. Can't we throw it out, Daddy? Please?"

The monkey grinned its endless grin at Hal. He could feel Petey's tears between them. Late morning sun glinted off the monkey's brass cymbals—the light reflected upward and put sun streaks on the motel's plain white stucco ceiling.

"What time did your mother think she and Dennis would be back, Petey?"

"Around one." He swiped at his red eyes with his shirt sleeve, looking embarrassed by his tears. But he wouldn't look at the monkey. "I turned on the TV," he whispered. "And I turned it up loud."

"That was all right, Petey."

"I had a crazy idea," Petey said. "I had this idea that if I wound that monkey up, you . . . you would have just died there in bed. In your sleep. Wasn't that a crazy idea, Daddy?" His voice dropped again, and it trembled helplessly.

How would it have happened? Hal wondered. *Heart attack? An embolism, like my mother? What? It doesn't really matter, does it?*

And on the heels of that, another, colder thought: *Get rid of it, he says. Throw it out. But can it be gotten rid of? Ever?*

The monkey grinned mockingly at him, its cymbals held a foot apart. Did it suddenly come to life on the night Aunt Ida died? he wondered suddenly. Was that the last sound she heard, the muffled *jang-jang-jang* of the monkey beating its cymbals together up in the black attic while the wind whistled along the drainpipe?

"Maybe not so crazy," Hal said slowly to his son. "Go get your flight bag, Petey."

Petey looked at him uncertainly. "What are we going to do?"

*Maybe it can be got rid of. Maybe permanently, maybe just for a while . . . a long while or a short while. Maybe it's just going to come back and come back and that's what all this is about . . . but maybe I—*we*—can say good-bye to it for a long time. It took twenty years to come back this time. It took twenty years to get out of the well . . .*

"We're going to go for a ride," Hal said. He felt fairly calm, but somehow too heavy inside his skin. Even his eyeballs seemed to have gained weight. "But first I want you to take your flight bag out there by the edge of the parking lot and find three or four good-sized rocks. Put them inside the bag and bring it back to me. Got it?"

Understanding flickered in Petey's eyes. "All right, Daddy."

Hal glanced at his watch. It was nearly 12:15. "Hurry. I want to be gone before your mother gets back."

"Where are we going?"

"To Uncle Will's and Aunt Ida's," Hal said. "To the home place."

Hal went into the bathroom, looked behind the toilet, and got the bowl brush leaning there. He took it back to the window and stood there with it in his hand like a cut-rate magic wand. He looked out at Petey in his melton shirt-jacket, crossing the parking lot with his flight bag, "Delta" showing clearly in white letters against a blue field. A fly bumbled in an upper corner of the window, slow and stupid with the end of the warm season. Hal knew how it felt.

He watched Petey hunt up three good-sized rocks and then start back across the parking lot. A car came around the corner of the motel, a car that was moving too fast, much too fast, and without thinking, reaching with the kind of reflex a good shortstop shows going to his right, his hand flashed down, as if in a karate chop . . . and stopped.

The cymbals closed soundlessly on his intervening hand, and he felt something in the air. Something like rage.

The car's brakes screamed. Petey flinched back. The driver motioned to him impatiently, as if what had almost happened was Petey's fault, and Petey ran across the parking lot with his collar flapping and into the motel's rear entrance.

Sweat was running down Hal's chest; he felt it on his forehead like a drizzle of oily rain. The cymbals pressed coldly against his hand, numbing it.

Go on, he thought grimly. *Go on, I can wait all day. Until hell freezes over, if that's what it takes.*

The cymbals drew apart and came to rest. Hal heard one faint *click!* from inside the monkey. He withdrew his hand and looked at it. On both the back and the palm there were grayish semicircles printed into the skin, as if he had been frostbitten.

The fly bumbled and buzzed, trying to find the cold October sunshine that seemed so close.

Pete came bursting in, breathing quickly, cheeks rosy. "I got three good ones, Dad, I—" He broke off. "Are you all right, Daddy?"

"Fine," Hal said. "Bring the bag over."

Hal hooked the table by the sofa over to the window with his foot, so it stood below the sill, and put the flight bag on it. He spread its mouth open like lips. He could see the stones Petey had collected glimmering inside. He used the toilet-bowl brush to hook the monkey forward. It teetered for a moment and then fell into the bag. There was a faint *jing!* as one of its cymbals struck one of the rocks.

"Dad? Daddy?" Petey sounded frightened. Hal looked around at him. Something was different; something had changed. What was it?

Then he saw the direction of Petey's gaze and he knew. The buzzing of the fly had stopped. It lay dead on the windowsill.

"Did the monkey do that?" Petey whispered.

"Come on," Hal said, zipping the bag shut. "I'll tell you while we ride out to the home place."

"How can we go? Mom and Dennis took the car."

"I'll get us there," Hal said, and ruffled Petey's hair.

He showed the desk clerk his driver's license and a twenty-dollar bill. After taking Hal's Texas Instruments digital watch as further collateral, the clerk handed Hal thc keys to his own car—a battered AMC Gremlin. As they drove east on Route 302 toward Casco, Hal began to talk, haltingly at first, then a little faster. He began by telling Petey that his father had probably brought the monkey home with him from overseas, as a gift for his sons. It wasn't a particularly unique toy; there was nothing strange or valuable about it. There must have been hundreds of thousands of wind-up monkeys in the world, some made in Hong Kong, some in Taiwan, some in Korea. But somewhere along the line—perhaps even in the dark back closet of the house in Connecticut where the two boys had begun their growing up—something had happened to the monkey. Something bad, evil. It might be, Hal told Petey as he tried to coax the clerk's Gremlin up past forty (he was very aware of the zipped-up flight bag on the back seat, and Petey kept glancing around at it), that some evil—maybe even most evil—isn't even sentient and aware of what it is. It might be that most evil is very much like a monkey full of clockwork that you wind up; the clockwork turns, the cymbals begin to beat, the teeth grin, the stupid glass eyes laugh . . . or appear to laugh . . .

He told Petey about finding the monkey, but he found himself skipping over large chunks of the story, not wanting to terrify his already scared boy any more than he was already. The story thus became disjointed, not really clear, but Petey asked no questions; perhaps he was filling in the blanks for himself, Hal thought, in much the same way that Hal had dreamed his mother's death over and over, although he had not been there.

Uncle Will and Aunt Ida had both been there for the funeral. Afterward, Uncle Will had gone back to Maine—it was harvest-time—and Aunt Ida had stayed on for two weeks with the boys to neaten up her sister's affairs. But more than that, she spent the time making herself known to the boys, who were so stunned by their mother's sudden death that they were nearly sleepwalking. When they couldn't sleep, she was there with warm milk; when Hal woke at three in the morning with nightmares (nightmares in which his mother approached the water cooler without seeing the monkey that floated and bobbed in its cool sapphire depths, grinning and clapping its cymbals, each converging pair of sweeps leaving trails of bubbles behind); she was there when Bill came down with first a fever and then a rash of painful mouth sores and then hives three days after the funeral; she was there. She made herself known to the boys, and before they rode the New England Flyer from Hartford to Portland with her, both Bill and Hal had come to her separately and wept on her lap while she held them and rocked them, and the bonding began.

The day before they left Connecticut for good to go "down Maine" (as it was called in those days), the ragman came in his great old rattly truck and picked up the huge pile of useless stuff that Bill and Hal had carried out to the sidewalk from the back closet. When all the junk had been set out by the curb for pickup, Aunt Ida had asked them to go through the back closet again and pick out any souvenirs or remembrances they wanted specially to keep. "We just don't have room for it all, boys," she told them, and Hal supposed Bill had taken her at her word and had gone through all those fascinating boxes their father had left behind, one final time. Hal did not join his older brother. Hal had lost his taste for the back closet. A terrible idea had come to him during those first two weeks of mourning: perhaps his father hadn't just disappeared, or run away because he had an itchy foot and had discovered marriage wasn't for him.

Maybe the monkey had gotten him.

When he heard the ragman's truck roaring and farting and backfiring its way down the block, Hal nerved himself, snatched the scruffy windup monkey from his shelf where it had been since the day his mother died (he had not dared to touch it until then, not even to throw it back into the closet), and ran downstairs with it. Neither Bill nor Aunt Ida saw him. Sitting on top of a barrel filled with broken souvenirs and mouldy books was the Ralston-Purina carton, filled with similar junk. Hal had slammed the monkey back into the box it had originally come out of, hysterically daring it to begin clapping its cymbals *(Go on, go on, I dare you, dare you, DARE YOU)*, but the monkey only waited there, leaning back nonchalantly, as if expecting a bus, grinning its awful, knowing grin.

Hal stood by, a small boy in old corduroy pants and scuffed Buster Browns, as the ragman, an Italian gent who wore a crucifix and whistled through the space between his teeth, began loading boxes and barrels into his ancient truck with the high wooden sides. Hal watched as he lifted both the barrel and the Ralston-Purina box balanced atop it; he watched the monkey disappear into the maw of the truck; he watched as the ragman climbed back into the cab, blew his nose mightily into the palm of his hand, wiped his hand with a huge red handkerchief, and started the truck's engine with a mighty roar and a stinking blast of oily blue smoke; he watched the truck draw away. And a great weight had dropped away from his heart—he actually felt it go. He had jumped up and down twice, as high as he could jump, his arms spread, palms held out, and if any of the neighbors had seen him, they would have thought it odd almost to the point of blasphemy, perhaps—*Why is that boy jumping for joy* (for that was surely what it was; a jump for joy can hardly be disguised) *with his mother not even a month in her grave?*

He was jumping for joy because the monkey was gone, gone forever. Gone forever, but not three months later Aunt Ida had sent him up into the attic to get the boxes of Christmas decorations, and as he crawled around looking for them, getting the knees of his pants dusty, he had suddenly come face to face with it again, and his wonder and terror had been so great that he had to bite sharply into the side of his hand to keep from screaming . . . or fainting dead away. There it was, grinning its toothy grin, cymbals poised a foot apart and ready to clap, leaning nonchalantly back against one corner of a Ralston-Purina carton as if waiting for a bus, seeming to say: *Thought you got rid of me, didn't you? But I'm not that easy to get rid of, Hal. I* like *you, Hal. We were made for each other, just a boy and his pet monkey, a couple of good old buddies. And somewhere south of here there's a stupid old Italian ragman lying in a claw-foot tub with his eyeballs bulging and his dentures half-popped out of his mouth, his screaming mouth, a ragman who smells like a burned-out Exide battery. He was saving me for his grandson, Hal, he put me on the shelf with his soap and his razor and his Burma-Shave and the Philco radio he listened to the Brooklyn Dodgers on, and I started to clap, and one of my cymbals hit that old radio and into the tub it went, and then I came to you, Hal, I worked my away along country roads at night and the moonlight shone off my teeth at three in the morning and I left death in my wake, Hal, I came to you. I'm your Christmas present, Hal, wind me up, who's dead? Is it Bill? Is it Uncle Will? Is it you, Hal? Is it* you?

Hal had backed away, grimacing madly, eyes rolling, and he nearly fell going downstairs. He told Aunt Ida he hadn't been able to find the Christmas decorations—it was the first lie he had ever told her, and she had seen the lie on his face but had not asked him why he had told it, thank God—and later when Bill came in she asked him to look and he brought the Christmas decorations down. Later, when they were alone, Bill hissed at him that he was a dummy who couldn't find his own ass with both hands and a flashlight. Hal said nothing. Hal was pale and silent, only picking at his supper. And that night he dreamed of the monkey again, one of its cymbals striking the Philco radio as it babbled out Dean Martin singing "Whenna da moon hitta you eye like a big pizza pie *ats-a moray,*" the radio tumbling into the bathtub as the monkey grinned and beat its cymbals together with a *JANG* and a *JANG* and a *JANG;* only it wasn't the Italian ragman who was in the tub when the water turned electric.

It was him.

Hal and his son scrambled down the embankment behind the home place to the boat house that jutted out over the water on its old pilings. Hal had the flight bag in his right hand. His throat was dry, his ears were attuned to an unnaturally keen pitch. The bag seemed very heavy.

"What's down here, Daddy?" Petey asked.

Hal didn't answer. He set down the flight bag. "Don't touch that," he said, and Petey backed away from it. Hal felt in his pocket for the ring of keys Bill had given him and found one neatly labeled B'HOUSE on a scrap of adhesive tape.

The day was clear and cold, windy, the sky a brilliant blue. The leaves of the trees that crowded up to the verge of the lake had gone every bright fall shade from blood red to sneering yellow. They rattled and talked in the wind. Leaves swirled around Petey's sneakers as he stood anxiously by, and Hal could smell November on the wind, with winter crowding close behind it.

The key turned in the padlock and he pulled the swing doors open. Memory was strong; he didn't even have to look to kick down the wooden block that held the door open. The smell in here was all summer: canvas and bright wood, a lingering musty warmth.

Uncle Will's rowboat was still here, the oars neatly shipped as if he had last loaded it with his fishing tackle and two six-packs of Black Label on ice yesterday afternoon. Bill and Hal had both gone out fishing with Uncle Will many times, but never together; Uncle Will maintained the boat was too small for three. The red trim, which Uncle Will had touched up each spring, was now faded and peeling, though, and spiders had spun their silk in the boat's bow.

Hal laid hold of it and pulled it down the ramp to the little shingle of beach. The fishing trips had been one of the best parts of his childhood with Uncle Will and Aunt Ida. He had a feeling that Bill felt much the same. Uncle Will was ordinarily the most taciturn of men, but once he had the boat positioned to his liking, some sixty or seventy yards offshore, lines set and bobbers floating on the water, he would crack a beer for himself and one for Hal (who rarely drank more than half of the one can Uncle Will would allow, always with the ritual admonition from Uncle Will that Aunt Ida must never be told because "she'd shoot me for a stranger if she knew I was givin' you boys beer, don't you know"), and wax expansive. He would tell stories, answer questions, rebait Hal's hook when it needed rebaiting; and the boat would drift where the wind and the mild current wanted it to be.

"How come you never go right out to the middle, Uncle Will?" Hal had asked once.

"Look over the side there, Hal," Uncle Will had answered.

Hal did. He saw blue water and his fish line going down into black.

"You're looking into the deepest part of Crystal Lake," Uncle Will said, crunching his empty beer can in one hand and selecting a fresh one with the other. "A hundred feet if she's an inch. Amos Culligan's old Studebaker is down there somewhere. Damn fool took it out on the lake one early December, before the ice was made. Lucky to get out of it alive, he was. They'll never get that Studebaker out, nor see it until Judgment Trump blows. Lake's one deep son of a whore right here, it is. Big ones are right here, Hal. No need to go out no further. Let's see how your worm looks. Reel that son of a whore right in."

Hal did, and while Uncle Will put a fresh crawler from the old Crisco tin that served as his bait box on Hal's hook, he stared into the water, fascinated, trying to see Amos Culligan's old Studebaker, all rust and waterweed drifting out of the open driver's side window through which Amos had escaped at the absolute last moment, waterweed festooning the steering wheel like a rotting necklace, waterweed dangling from the rearview mirror and drifting back and forth in the currents like some strange rosary. But he could see only blue shading to black, and there was the shape of Uncle Will's nightcrawler, the hook hidden inside its knots, hung up there in the middle of things, its own sun-shafted version of reality. Hal had a brief, dizzying vision of being suspended over a mighty gulf, and he had closed his eyes for a moment until the vertigo passed. That day, he seemed to recollect, he had drunk his entire can of beer.

. . . the deepest part of Crystal Lake . . . a hundred feet if she's an inch.

He paused a moment, panting, and looking up at Petey, still watching anxiously. "You want some help, Daddy?"

"In a minute."

He had his breath again, and now he pulled the rowboat across the narrow strip of sand to the water, leaving a groove.

The paint had peeled, but the boat had been kept under cover and it looked sound.

When he and Uncle Will went out, Uncle Will would pull the boat down the ramp, and when the bow was afloat, he would clamber in, grab an oar to push with, and say: "Push me off, Hal . . . this is where you earn your truss!"

"Hand that bag in, Petey, and then give me a push," he said. And, smiling a little, he added: "This is where you earn your truss."

Petey didn't smile back. "Am I coming, Daddy?"

"Not this time. Another time I'll take you out fishing, but . . . not this time."

Petey hesitated. The wind tumbled his brown hair and a few yellow leaves, crisp and dry, wheeled past his shoulders and landed at the edge of the water, bobbing like boats themselves.

"You should have muffled them," he said, low.

"What?" But he thought he understood what Petey had meant.

"Put cotton over the cymbals. Taped it on. So it couldn't . . . make that noise."

Hal suddenly remembered Daisy coming toward him—not walking but lurching—and how, quite suddenly, blood had burst from both of Daisy's eyes in a flood that soaked her ruff and pattered down on the floor of the barn, how she had collapsed on her forepaws . . . and on the still, rainy spring air of that day he had heard the sound, not muffled but curiously clear, coming from the attic of the house fifty feet away: *Jang-jang-jang-jang!*

He began to scream hysterically, dropping the armload of wood he had been getting for the fire. He ran for the kitchen to get Uncle Will, who was eating scrambled eggs and toast, his suspenders not even up over his shoulders yet.

"She was an old dog, Hal," Uncle Will had said, his face haggard and unhappy—he looked old himself. "She was twelve, and that's old for a dog. You mustn't take on, now—old Daisy wouldn't like that."

Old, the vet had echoed, but he had looked troubled all the same, because dogs don't die of explosive brain hemorrhages, even at twelve ("Like as if someone had stuck a firecracker in her head," Hal overheard the vet saying to Uncle Will as Uncle Will dug a hole in the back of the barn not far from the place where he had buried Daisy's mother in 1950; "I never seen the beat of it, Will.")

And later, terrified almost out of his mind but unable to help himself, Hal had crept up to the attic.

Hello, Hal, how are you doing? the monkey grinned from its shadowy corner. Its cymbals were poised, a foot or so apart. The sofa cushion Hal had stood on end between them was now all the way across the attic. Something—some force—had thrown it hard enough to split its cover, and stuffing foamed out of it. *Don't worry about Daisy,* the monkey whispered inside his head, its glassy hazel eyes fixed on Hal Shelburn's wide blue ones. *Don't worry about Daisy, she was old, old, Hal, even the vet said so, and by the way, did you see the blood coming out of her eyes, Hal? Wind me up, Hal. Wind me up, let's play, and who's dead, Hal? Is it you?*

And when he came back to himself he had been crawling toward the monkey as if hypnotized. One hand had been outstretched to grasp the key. He scrambled backward then, and almost fell down the attic stairs in his haste—probably would have if the stairwell had not been so narrow. A little whining noise had been coming from his throat.

Now he sat in the boat, looking at Petey. "Muffling the cymbals doesn't work," he said. "I tried it once."

Petey cast a nervous glance at the flight bag. "What happened, Daddy?"

"Nothing I want to talk about now," Hal said, "and nothing you want to hear about. Come on and give me a push."

Petey bent to it, and the stern of the boat grated along the sand. Hal dug in with an oar, and suddenly that feeling of being tied to the earth was gone and the boat was moving lightly, its own thing again after years in the dark boathouse, rocking on the light waves. Hal unshipped the oars one at a time and clicked the oarlocks shut.

"Be careful, Daddy," Petey said. His face was pale.

"This won't take long," Hal promised, but he looked at the flight bag and wondered.

He began to row, bending to the work. The old familiar ache in the small of his back and between his shoulder blades began. The shore receded. Petey was magically eight again, six, a four-year-old standing at the edge of the water. He shaded his eyes with one infant hand.

Hal glanced casually at the shore but would not allow himself to actually study it. It had been nearly fifteen years, and if he studied the shoreline carefully, he would see the changes rather than the similarities and become lost. The sun beat on his neck, and he began to sweat. He looked at the flight bag, and for a moment he lost the bend-and-pull rhythm. The flight bag seemed . . . seemed to be bulging. He began to row faster.

The wind gusted, drying the sweat and cooling his skin. The boat rose and the bow slapped water to either side when it came down. Hadn't the wind freshened, just in the last minute or so? And was Petey calling something? Yes. Hal couldn't make out what it was over the wind. It didn't matter. Getting rid of the monkey for another twenty years—or maybe forever (please God, forever)—that was what mattered.

The boat reared and came down. He glanced left and saw baby whitecaps. He looked shoreward again and saw Hunter's Point and a collapsed wreck that must have been the Burdon's boathouse when he and Bill were kids. Almost there, then. Almost over the spot where Amos Culligan's Studebaker had plunged through the ice one long-ago December. Almost over the deepest part of the lake.

Petey was screaming something; screaming and pointing. Hal still couldn't hear. The rowboat rocked and bucked, flatting off clouds of thin spray to either side of its peeling bow. A tiny rainbow glowed in one, was pulled apart. Sunlight and shadow raced across the lake in shutters and the waves were not mild now; the whitecaps had grown up. His sweat had dried to gooseflesh, and spray had soaked the back of his jacket. He rowed grimly, eyes alternating between the shoreline and the flight bag. The boat rose again, this time so high that for a moment the left oar pawed at air instead of water.

Petey was pointing at the sky, his screams now only a faint, bright runner of sound.

Hal looked over his shoulder.

The lake was a frenzy of waves. It had gone a deadly dark shade of blue sewn with white seams. A shadow raced across the water toward the boat and something in its shape was familiar, so terribly familiar, that Hal looked up and then the scream was there, struggling in his tight throat.

The sun was behind the cloud, turning it into a hunched working shape with two gold-edged crescents held apart. Two holes were torn in one end of the cloud, and sunshine poured through in two shafts.

As the cloud crossed over the boat, the monkey's cymbals, barely muffled by the flight bag, began to beat. *Jang-jang-jang-jang, it's you, Hal, it's finally you, you're over the deepest part of the lake now and it's your turn, your turn, your turn—*

All the necessary shoreline elements had clicked into their places. The rotting bones of Amos Culligan's Studebaker lay somewhere below, this was where the big ones were, this was the place.

Hal shipped the oars to the locks in one quick jerk, leaned forward unmindful of the wildly rocking boat, and snatched the flight bag. The cymbals made their wild, pagan music; the bag's sides billowed as if with tenebrous respiration.

"Right here, you sonofabitch!" Hal screamed. *"RIGHT HERE!"*

He threw the bag over the side.

It sank fast. For a moment he could see it going down, sides moving, and for that endless moment *he could still hear the cymbals beating.* And for a moment the black waters seemed to clear and he could see down into that terrible gulf of waters to where the big ones lay; there was Amos Culligan's Studebaker, and Hal's mother was behind its slimy wheel, a grinning skeleton with a lake bass staring coldly from the skull's nasal cavity. Uncle Will and Aunt Ida lolled beside her, and Aunt Ida's gray hair trailed upward as the bag fell, turning over and over, a few silver bubbles trailing up: *jang-jang-jang-jang* . . .

Hal slammed the oars back into the water, scraping blood from his knuckles *(and ah God the back of Amos Culligan's Studebaker had been full of dead children! Charlie Silverman . . . Johnny McCabe . . .)*, and began to bring the boat about.

There was a dry pistol-shot crack between his feet, and suddenly clear water was welling up between two boards. The boat was old; the wood had shrunk a bit, no doubt; it was just a small leak. But it hadn't been there when he rowed out. He would have sworn to it.

The shore and lake changed places in his view. Petey was at his back now. Overhead, that awful, simian cloud was breaking up. Hal began to row. Twenty seconds was enough to convince him he was rowing for his life. He was only a so-so swimmer, and even a great one would have been put to the test in this suddenly angry water.

Two more boards suddenly shrank apart with that pistol-shot sound. More water poured into the boat, dousing his shoes. There were tiny metallic snapping sounds that he realized were nails breaking. One of the oarlocks snapped and flew off into the water—would the swivel itself go next?

The wind now came from his back, as if trying to slow him down or even to drive him into the middle of the lake. He was terrified, but he felt a crazy kind of exhilaration through the terror. The monkey was gone for good this time. He knew it somehow. Whatever happened to him, the monkey would not be back to draw a shadow over Dennis's life, or Petey's. The monkey was gone, perhaps resting on the roof or the hood of Amos Culligan's Studebaker at the bottom of Crystal Lake. Gone for good.

He rowed, bending forward and rocking back. That cracking, crimping sound came again, and now the rusty old bait can that had been lying in the bow of the boat was floating in three inches of water. Spray blew in Hal's face. There was a louder snapping sound, and the bow seat fell in two pieces and floated next to the bait box. A board tore off the left side of the boat, and then another, this one at the waterline, tore off at the right. Hal rowed. Breath rasped in his mouth, hot and dry, and his throat swelled with the coppery taste of exhaustion. His sweaty hair flew.

Now a crack ran directly up the bottom of the rowboat, zigzagged between his feet, and ran up to the bow. Water gushed in; he was in water up to his ankles, then to the swell of calf. He rowed, but the boat's shoreward movement was sludgy now. He didn't dare look behind him to see how close he was getting.

Another board tore loose: The crack running up the center of the boat grew branches, like a tree. Water flooded in.

Hal began to make the oars sprint, breathing in great, failing gasps. He pulled once . . . twice . . . and on the third pull both oar swivels snapped off. He lost one oar, held onto the other. He rose to his feet and began to flail at the water with it. The boat rocked, almost capsized, and spilled him back onto his seat with a thump.

Moments later more boards tore loose, the seat collapsed, and he was lying in the water which filled the bottom of the boat, astounded at its coldness. He tried to get on his knees, desperately thinking: *Petey must not see this, must not see his father drown right in front of his eyes, you're going to swim, dog-paddle if you have to, but do, do something—*

There was another splintering crack—almost a crash—and he was in the water, swimming for the shore as he never had swum in his life . . . and the shore was amazingly close. A minute later he was standing waist-deep in water, not five yards from the beach.

Petey splashed toward him, arms out, screaming and crying and laughing. Hal started toward him and floundered. Petey, chest-deep, floundered.

They caught each other.

Hal, breathing in great, winded gasps, nevertheless hoisted the boy into his arms and carried him up to the beach where both of them sprawled, panting.

"Daddy? Is it really gone? That monkey?"

"Yes. I think it's really gone."

"The boat fell apart. It just . . . fell apart all around you."

Disintegrated, Hal thought, and looked at the boards floating loose on the water forty feet out. They bore no resemblance to the tight, handmade rowboat he had pulled out of the boathouse.

"It's all right now," Hal said, leaning back on his elbows. He shut his eyes and let the sun warm his face.

"Did you see the cloud?" Petey whispered.

"Yes. But I don't see it now . . . do you?"

They looked at the sky. There were scattered white puffs here and there, but no large dark cloud. It was gone, as he had said.

Hal pulled Petey to his feet. "There'll be towels up at the house. Come on." But he paused, looking at his son. "You were crazy, running out there like that."

Petey looked at him solemnly. "You were brave, Daddy."

"Was I?" The thought of bravery had never crossed his mind. Only his fear. The fear had been too big to see anything else. If anything else had indeed been there. "Come on, Pete."

"What are we going to tell Mom?"

Hal smiled. "I dunno, big guy. We'll think of something."

He paused a moment longer, looking at the boards floating on the water. The lake was calm again, sparkling with small wavelets. Suddenly Hal thought of summer people he didn't even know—a man and his son, perhaps, fishing for the big one. *"I've got something, Dad!"* the boy screams, *"Well reel it up and let's see,"* the father says, and coming up from the depths, weeds draggling from its cymbals, grinning its terrible welcoming grin . . . the monkey.

He shuddered—but those were only things that might be.

"Come on," he said to Petey again, and they walked up the path through the flaming October woods toward the home place.

From the Bridgton News, *October 24, 1980:*

MYSTERY
OF THE DEAD FISH
By BETSY MORIARTY

HUNDREDS of dead fish were found floating belly-up on Crystal Lake in the neighboring township of Casco late last week. The largest numbers appeared to have died in the vicinity of Hunter's Point, although the lake's currents make this a bit difficult to determine. The dead fish included all types commonly found in these waters—bluegills, pickerel, sunnies, carp, brown and rainbow trout, even one landlocked salmon. Fish and Game authorities say they are mystified, and caution fishermen and -women not to eat any sort of fish from Crystal Lake until tests have determined . . .

WILLIAM HALLAHAN

The New Tenant

It started shortly after he got into bed.

He was just drifting off when he heard a rapping, the sound of someone prying a door. He sat up and listened. All he could hear was his wife's gentle breathing in sleep. Then he heard a little noise at the window and saw shadows floating down. He got up and looked out. It was snowing heavily. The flakes, brushed by the wind, tapped faintly on the pane.

Still uneasy, he got up and checked all the windows downstairs. Through them he could see the snow lit by distant street lights. There were no tracks in it. The front and back doors were secure. Still wondering what had made the noise that had disturbed him, he went back to bed.

As he began to drift off to sleep, he heard the noise once more. He sat up again and listened. He hadn't checked the cellar or the attic. He knew nothing about them; this was the first time he'd slept in this house. Since it was her home, maybe she knew what the noise was.

"What is it?" he heard her ask.

"A noise. Did you hear it?"

"No."

"There. Did you hear it then?"

"No."

"Listen."

She listened. "Bobby, this is an old house. It's full of noises and bumps and creaks." She turned away and went back to sleep.

The house was a stranger to him. And his wife was a stranger to him. He was three days married to his dead partner's wife, living in his dead partner's home and now the owner of his dead partner's half of the business—he'd gotten them all with a simple marriage ceremony.

He slipped under the covers again and watched the shadowy snowflakes tumble past the window. Then there was a rapping again; this time it was harder, more forceful. He sat up and listened as the rapping became a loud pounding. At first he was sure his ears were being tricked. What they reported was impossible: the pounding was inside his head. Someone was trying to break into his head in the dark in the bedroom in the middle of the night.

He located the sound at the center of his forehead, a booming noise echoing inside his head like that of a battering ram on the oaken door of a castle, reverberating down long stone corridors and throughout great courtrooms and draped chambers. Boom. Boom. *Boom.*

He found himself in a long hallway where the booms were shaking the very walls. He paused and saw a room, a bedroom, his own childhood bedroom. He fled, driven by the terrifying pounding. He came upon another room, the walls covered with hooks upon which hung old costumes—his cowboy suit from first grade and his cap and gown from college, his navy blues and his first business suit—all the costumes and disguises of his life. It was a garret-like room with a dormer window; when he glanced through it, he saw the bedroom where his wife slept beside him, stirring slightly; beyond, he saw the bedroom window and the snow falling thickly past it.

There was a shattering, tearing sound now, boards being sundered and torn away by some great furious power.

He was absolutely terrified and stood in a musty attic corridor wringing his hands, immobilized by a fright greater than any he'd ever felt before. He knew he was about to die.

Panic impelled flight, and he ran from room to room inside his head in a vague twilight, past forgotten schoolrooms, past his office, his parents' living room, up a cellar stairway to a large entryway with films projected multitudinously on the walls, all the shameful, embarrassing things he'd ever done, being projected over and over without end.

The pounding noise reminded him that someone would now have access to his most intimate secrets, that he would be exposed to public scrutiny and ridicule.

He tried to formulate a plan of defense. He thought of weapons and instantly was confronted with an arsenal, a stone-walled room containing military howitzers, even, but the formidable power behind the pounding made them all seem puny. He was being pursued by the greatest power that had ever come into his life. Defense, he knew, was useless. He fled down the corridors that appeared before him.

There was a terrible shattering of wood, a ripping asunder—then silence. The thing, whatever it was, had made an entry hole in his forehead and was now inside. It would come after him.

Whimpering unashamedly, eager to surrender, to kneel or to lie supine in abject obeisance, he walked in circles unable to select the corridor that might lead to safety. He chose a flight of old dished wooden attic steps. At the top, he passed through a doorway and shut the door.

He was in an old attic, his grandfather's. Quickly he moved trunks, heavy ancient library tables, an old monitor refrigerator, a filing cabinet and other impediments against the door, then retreated to a corner and slumped down, spent, whimpering like a small animal. The attic was filled with moonlight and the movement of the furniture had raised dust that sailed, merrily free, in and out of the moonbeams.

There was silence. Just silence. He felt the thing was

searching for him, going from room to room, opening doors, peering around corners, poking into old closets. Moments passed. He prayed for a noise, a sound, anything.

Then he heard it. A tread on the lowest step: boot sole on wooden step. Then another. And another, slowly, loudly, purposefully. They mounted to the doorway and his barrier of old furniture. Then they stopped. The old white ceramic doorknob turned one way, then the other in the moonlight.

He waited, panting, wondering if the thing could get through all that furniture piled against that door, which seemed so flimsy, so frail; the furniture seemed to have shrunk.

The door gave a little, seeming to bow slightly as if under great pressure. Then it rested. Silence roared in his ears. He prayed for a quick, painless death.

He was alone. He felt that the presence was no longer outside the attic door. Where could it have gone? He glanced out the attic window and saw his wife, moving softly under the blankets. He knocked on the window to her. Tapped with a knuckle. Loudly. But she didn't hear him.

He sat down in a crouch and wrapped his arms around his knees like a forlorn child. What must he do? Where was the presence?

"Peekaboo," said a voice beside him, and he stood and screamed in terror at it.

It was an amorphous shadow, a twilight gray; it moved toward him, then over him and around him, enwrapping him. He was trapped in total darkness, unable to move even a finger. He screamed and screamed but no noise came from his throat. He heard the sound of solitary footsteps on old wooden flooring, felt himself being carried, and he knew he was to be executed. Without explanation, without appeal, without mercy, he was to be executed.

The movement stopped. There was a pause. Then he was dropped. He fell. Rocketed straight down, a twilight gray mass attached to a long black cord like an umbilicus. As he fell, the cord payed out behind him. He fell a great distance until he reached the end, where he was almost arrested by the cord. But then it snapped. He was disconnected from his body.

He was drifting, stunned and disoriented. Am I dead? he asked himself. He felt grief stricken, inconsolable. The solitude and loneliness were almost unendurable. This, he knew, was hell: not a Dantesque chamber crowded and filled with cries of pain, but a vast empty space with no companionship. The greatest pain possible is solitude and the greatest solitude is the knowledge that the pain has no end. Tormented forever by the worst torture of all: memory.

He found himself traveling through the streets of the city. The snow was falling heavily, covering the ways and drifting in the doorways, a heavy fall, a scene in the middle of the night totally devoid of people and vehicles. The street lamps strung off into the distance like a parade of stars beckoning him to eternity.

He came upon a tavern. Inside in convivial warmth, three men stood at the bar talking with the bartender, rubbing shoulders, laughing. The sense of grief and dispossession tormented him even more.

A terrible thought crossed his mind: dispossess one of them.

He studied the four men, looking carefully at each face like a man shopping for a new suit. He found he could see inside each man, see the fontanelle in the middle of each forehead where entry would be gained. It should be easy. The surprise of attack and the numbing terror it would bring were sufficient to conquer any one of them.

But the terrible, lonely grief he felt was something he didn't want to visit on any man. Were he to spend the rest of his days in a borrowed body, glowing in the warmth of life and friendship, he would be haunted by the terrible fate to which he'd condemned another. He looked at the faces of the four men; in minutes one of them could be cast adrift in space.

He moved away from the tavern to seek someone else, an

enemy, one deserving such a fate—an Al Capone or a Hitler now living. He considered his own personal enemies. Who was the most deserving among them?

Then a memory went off like an alarm bell. "Peekaboo," the voice had said and now he recognized it: his dead partner, Leo Hemmings.

And from that simple recognition, he surmised the whole story. Hemmings had died ten months before from heart disease. Soon after, he found himself negotiating with Hemmings' widow Louise for the purchase of Hemmings' share of the business. A divorcé himself, he saw the merit in what she was leading him to: he was unattached, she was now a widow; they had known each other for many years; she was a very pretty woman, still under forty, a good cook, a good homemaker and a devoted wife to Leo—in fact, the Hemmings' continuing love affair was a fond joke among their friends. She was a woman of deep, lifelong attachments.

The logic was unassailable: form two partnerships with her, in marriage and in business. The financial and tax advantages would be significant. He proposed. Or did she?

Now he was married to her for little more than seventy-two hours. This was the first night he'd spent in Leo's house. And Leo had lain in wait for him, waiting to recapture his life, his wife and his business—in his partner's body.

The biggest enemy he had was Leo Hemmings, the dead man who refused to stay dead.

He turned and went slowly back to Leo Hemmings' house.

* * *

Leo Hemmings lay in his bed in his partner's body.

He stroked his wife's hair and felt exultant joy. He was able to touch her again, to kiss her, to be with her, to share his days with her. He touched her wet cheek, then kissed it.

He'd had great good fortune in his life. Victory after victory in high school and college football, business success, good income, lots of travel, golf, friends, laughter, children who were loving and successful. But the greatest joy of his life was this woman beside him. Their marriage had been one long and joyful honeymoon. Parting from her was the worst part of dying. He would have come back to her through ten deaths. And only as he was dying had he taken her into his confidence. He told her of his studies in Eastern religious rites, spiritual exercises. If he could, he promised, he would return in another's body. He told her simply to marry his partner and Leo would do the rest. Then, for months, he lay in wait.

The pain had been terrible. The fear that he might not be able to bring it off terrified him. The thought of an endless future without his wife was a searing agony. He saw that a perfect love on earth was not a gift; it was a calculated punishment to intensify the suffering in eternity.

But he'd cheated the system. He was back, alive in his partner's body, with ample time to plan for the two of them when it came time to die again.

Now he was intoxicated with the great joy of being. Sensually he moved his body—his partner's body. He felt comfortable and safe under the blankets next to her. His eyes feasted on her figure, darted after the falling shadows of snowflakes on the windowpane. His ears listened attentively to their gentle tapping on the glass. He smelled the perfume of her hair and body, felt the softness of her hair and flesh. He could taste his love for her. This was the greatest moment of his life. *Lives.*

He lay wide awake and renewed his plans for revamping the business—things he was never able to do while he had a partner. It was such a great stroke—pure genius: by willing himself to die, he'd acquired his partner's body and his share of the business. By dying, he'd improved his life immeasurably.

She stirred in his arms. "Are you sure he can't come back?"

"Yeah. He doesn't have the element of surprise. It's hopeless for him."

"I feel . . . nervous. All those months I slept alone, I couldn't sleep for fear that someone would break in."

"I know. I was right here watching you."

"I hear someone."

"Did you know he secretly loved you all these years?"

She looked fearfully at him. "No."

"He had pictures of you all over the inside of his head—all of you. Very chaste. Very idealized. He had a second-rate imagination."

"Don't, Leo. I feel terrible about him."

Leo luxuriated in the bed.

"I hear a noise," she said.

"This is an old house. Full of creaks."

"I hear someone trying to open a window."

"No. It's just old creaks. The snow on the roof is heavy. The house feels it."

"I'll go see."

He smiled at her. "If it makes you feel any better."

"Don't you hear it?"

"Hear what? I don't hear anything."

"I'll go see."

"Hurry back," he said.

He lay back and listened to her slippered footsteps go down the stairs. He heard the wall switches as she went from room to room. Then he heard a bump. Another bump. A sigh of anguish. She called him: *"Leo!"* Then there was a crash: a table tumbling, a lamp smashing.

He jumped up and ran to the stair head. There was darkness at the foot of the stairs. "Louise!" he cried, "are you all right?" He ran down.

"Yes. Yes. I knocked over the lamp. Such a shame. A wedding present."

He looked at it. Crystal . . . leaded crystal, one of a pair, very expensive, a wedding present from his partner. The memory irritated him.

He put his arm around her and led her back up the stairs. He asked himself again if he was perfectly sure that his partner could not return and battle his way back into his own body. And he assured himself again that he was more than a match.

He led his wife back to their bed and put her under the covers.

"You're smiling," he said to her. "What does that mean?

She smiled more broadly, a beaming smile of mirth and victory. "Peekaboo, Leo."

ROBERT BLOCH

In the Cards

"Saturday night?" Danny said. "What do you mean, I'll die on Saturday night?"

Danny tried to focus his eyes on the old woman but he couldn't make it—too smashed. She was just a big fat blur, like the cards spread on the table between them.

"I am truly sorry," the old woman murmured. "I can only read what I see. It is in the cards."

Danny grabbed for the edge of the table and stood up. The smell of incense in the darkened room was making him sick. It wasn't easy to stand and it wasn't easy to laugh, either, but he managed.

"Hell with you, sister. You and the cards too."

The old woman stared at him but there was no anger in her eyes, only compassion, and somehow that was even worse.

"I'm not gonna die on Saturday night," Danny told her. "Not me. You're talking to Danny Jackson, remember? I'm a star. A big star. And you, you're just a—"

Standing there, lurching there in the darkness, he told her what she was, using a vocabulary ripened and enriched by thirty years in show biz.

Her eyes never flickered, her glance never wavered, and

there was still nothing in her gaze but pity when he finally ran out of breath.

And ran out of the reeking room, her pity pursuing him.

"You will die on Saturday night."

Damned echo in his ears, even when he gunned the Ferrari and roared away from the curb. The car swayed, playing tag with the yellow line; good thing it was so late and the street was clear of traffic.

It was late and he was bombed, bombed clean out of his silly skull. Had to be, or he'd never have driven all the hell down to South Alvarado just to roust a phony, faking old fortune-teller out of bed and lay a fifty-dollar bill on her for a phony, faking fortune, the old witch, the old bitch—

But they were all bitches, all of them, and Lola was the worst.

Danny made it out to Bel Air, avoiding Sunset and coming up Pico until he could cut over on a side street through Westwood. When you're on the sauce you learn the right routes to take, the routes that get you safely through the streets, safely through the minutes and the hours and the days and the nights, even when your nerves are screaming and Lola is screaming too.

And of course Lola *was* screaming, she'd been waiting up for him and she cut loose the minute he opened the front door.

"Goddam it, where were you, don't you realize you've got a six o'clock call tomorrow morning—?"

There was a lot more, too, but Danny slammed the door on it, the door of the guest room. He hadn't slept in the same bed with Lola for three months, and it wasn't just because of what Dr. Carlsen had told him about his ticker, either.

It was better here in the bedroom, dropping his clothes and flopping down on the old king-size, away from the bitch, away from the witch.

Only the witch didn't go away. Here in the dark, Danny could see her eyes again, staring at him as if she understood, as if she *knew*. But nobody knew what the doc had told him, not

Lola, not the studio, not even his own agent. So how could some old bag take one look at him and figure it out?

In the cards. It's in the cards.

Her eyes, he remembered her eyes when she'd said it. They were so deep and black. Black as the Ace of Spades lying there on the table. The Queen of Spades had turned up, too, and that's when she made that crack about him dying on Saturday night.

Tomorrow was Wednesday. Wednesday, Thursday, Friday, Saturday—

To hell with it. That's what he'd told the old klooch and that's what he told himself. Tomorrow was Wednesday and he'd better think about that; Lola was right, he did have a six o'clock call, the test was shooting, and this is what counted. Not counting the days until Saturday, just the few short hours until that test.

Wednesday. Named after Woden, the god of war and battles. Danny's name had been Kuhlsberg once, not Jackson, and he knew, he remembered. Wednesday was war, all right, and it was a battle just getting out of bed with that head of his pounding away. Thank God he could sneak out before Lola woke up, and get through the foggy streets before the traffic began to build up on the San Diego Freeway.

But the fight was just beginning, the fight to smile there under the lights while Benny plastered on the old pancake makeup and fitted the little wings to the perspiring temples where the hairline had eroded. The perspiration was just the alcohol oozing out of him, it wasn't flop-sweat, because Danny knew he had nothing to worry about. The test was just a formality, all they wanted was six minutes of film to show the network brass and the agency people in New York. The series was all set, Fischer had told him that last week, and Fischer never conned him. Best damned agent in the business. So no panic, he knew his lines, all he had to do was step out onto the set and walk through the scene. If there were any fluffs, Joe

Collins would cover for him. Joe was a good man, he'd never carry a lead himself but he was a real pro. And Rudy Moss was a hell of a director and an old buddy of his. They were all friends here, and they all knew how much was riding for them on this series.

"Ready for you, Mr. Jackson."

Danny smiled, stood up, strolled out to where Joe Collins was waiting on the set. He found his chalk marks, somebody from the camera unit dragged out his tape, the mike-boom came down and he tested his voice for gain. Then they hit the lights and Rudy Moss gave him his cue for action and they rolled.

They rolled, and he blew it.

The first take he forgot the business with the cigarette. They cut and started from the top, and he got fouled up in his crossover to Joe, stepped right out of camera before he realized it. So they rolled again, and by this time he was uptight and Moss didn't like what he was getting, so it was back and take it from the top once more. Then Danny started losing lines—but those things happen. The only trouble was, he had to stand there under those lights and there were interruptions when a plane went over and ruined the sound and somebody came barging in right in the middle of his long speech and then Joe jumped one of his cues and the idiot script girl threw him the wrong prompt and he was sweating, wringing wet, and his hands started to twitch and Moss was very patient and it was Take Sixteen and no break for lunch and he could see the looks the crew was giving him and finally they wrapped it up at three-thirty, eight and a half solid hours for a lousy dialogue bit, nothing but two-shots and close-ups, and it was a bomb.

Everybody was very polite and they said, "Nice work, Mr. Jackson," and "Great," and "You did it, boy," but Danny knew what he'd done.

The fight was over and he'd lost.

No sense going home because Lola would ask him how did it go and Fischer would be calling and to hell with it. There was a little joint out on the ocean, below Malibu, where the lights were nice and dim and you could get a good steak to anchor the martinis.

That was the right answer, and though he scraped a fender getting out of the parking lot after they closed up the place, he made it without pain. Lola wasn't waiting up for him tonight—tonight, hell, it was morning already, Thursday morning—but the bed in the guest room felt better than ever.

Until he closed his eyes and saw what was in the cards. Thursday morning, *Thursday. And two days from now—*

If the old bitch was so good at telling fortunes, if she could see everything in the cards, why hadn't she tipped him off about the test? There was a *real* life-and-death matter for you, and she never even mentioned it. Of course she didn't, what could she or anybody else see in a lousy pack of playing cards? That's all they were, ordinary playing cards, and she was just a cheap grifter and Saturday was just another day of the week.

And this was Thursday. Thursday noon, now, with Danny getting up and groping his way into the john and shivering in the shower and shaving and stumbling downstairs and finding the note and reading it twice, three times, before it finally sank in.

Lola gone. Left him. "*Sorry . . . tried to get through to you . . . can't stand watching you destroy yourself . . . please . . . need help . . . try to understand.*" God, the phrases in that note, like daytime soaper dialogue. But it all added up. Lola was gone.

Danny called her mother's place in Laguna. No answer. Then he tried her sister up at Arrowhead. Nothing. By this time he'd cased the joint, seen that she'd cleared out the works, everything; must have taken her all day to pack the station wagon. She meant it; probably been planning the caper for weeks. Next thing he'd be getting a call from some hotshot lawyer, one of those Lear-jet boys. Christ, the least she could have done was waited to find out if he was going to get the series.

The series! Danny remembered now, he was due in Projection Room Nine at two o'clock; they were screening the test.

But it was after one now, and besides, he didn't need to see the running. He knew what they had in the can—six minutes of worms.

So he climbed in the car and went to Scandia for lunch instead; at least he intended to have lunch, but by late afternoon he hadn't gotten any further than the bar.

That's where his agent caught up with him, somewhere between the fifth and the sixth Bloody Mary.

"Thought I'd find you here," Fischer told him. "Get moving."

"Where we going?"

"Up to the office. I'd hate to have all these nice people here see me hit you right in the mouth."

"Get off my back, Fischer."

"Get off your butt." He hauled Danny from the stool. "Come on, let's go."

Fischer's office was on the Strip, only a few blocks away. But by the time they got there, Danny was up the wall; he knew what Fischer was going to say.

"No calls," Fischer told the girl on the board. Then he took Danny into the private office *behind* his private office and closed the door.

"All right," Fischer said. "Tell me."

"You saw the test?"

Fischer nodded, waiting. His mouth was grim, but the hard face and the hard talk never fooled Danny; he knew it was just an act. Fischer was a sweet guy inside, always bleeding for his clients. You could see the compassion in his eyes, it was there now, the same look of pity that the fortune-teller had—

Danny wanted to explain about the fortune-teller but he knew how it would sound and besides it wouldn't do any good. All he could do was say, "I wasn't loaded. I swear to God I wasn't loaded."

"I know that. And nobody said you were. I wish you *had* been—I've seen you play a scene with a couple of drinks under your belt and come off great." Fischer shook his head.

"Everybody on the set knew what was wrong with you yesterday, but even that wouldn't matter. The trouble is, everybody in the projection room could see it today, up there on the screen. You were hung over."

"It was that bad, huh?"

"That bad?" Fischer sighed, swiveled his chair around to face Danny. "Do I have to spell it out for you, Danny? A guy makes three pictures in a row, all bombs, and he's had it. Sure, I know that Metro thing wasn't your fault, but the word is out and I haven't had an offer for six months. When it comes to films, you're scrubbed. Moynihan tells me—"

"Never mind about Moynihan," Danny said. "He's my business manager. He shouldn't even be talking to you."

"Who else can he talk to when you won't listen?" Fischer opened a folder on his desk, glanced at a type-sheet. "You owe eighty-three on the house and nine on the cars. You're in hock on the furniture, that's another twenty including the redecorating. Your checking account is minus zero. And if they yank your credit cards, you won't have enough left to buy a bagel at Linny's."

Cards? Why did he have to mention cards? Danny felt a rush of heat and loosened his collar.

"Knock it off," he said. "All I need is a break."

"I *got* you a break." Fischer was staring at him across the desk, just like the old lady had stared at him across the card table. "For three months I've been rupturing myself to line up this TV deal for you. Salary, residuals, participation—I don't have to tell you what you got riding. If it hit, you'd be set for life."

Life? Suppose I have only two more days? Danny's chest was pounding, he couldn't take any more of this, but he had to listen. Through the blur he could see Fischer's finger jabbing out at him.

"So you make the test. And what do I see? You, walking around up there like a goddam zombie—"

Zombie. Danny knew what a zombie was. *The living dead.*

Something was throbbing inside, throbbing so loud that he could just barely hear Fischer saying, "Why, Danny?—that's all I want to know. Tell me why."

But Danny couldn't tell him why because he had to take off his jacket, had to take off his shirt, had to tear off his skin and dig out whatever it was that was throbbing and pounding, throbbing and pounding underneath. He brought his hand up, feeling the pain shoot through his arm and then—

Nowhere.

Danny opened his eyes and saw the white ceiling. White as in Cedars or Sinai, a hospital ceiling.

So that's where I am. I'm not dead. And what day is this?

"Friday," said the fat nurse. "No, mustn't sit up. Doctor wants us to be careful."

Fat nurses and baby talk, that's all he needed. But Doc Carlsen was a little more helpful when he showed up in the evening.

"No, it's not a stroke, nothing like that. From where I stand it may not even have been a cardiac. Dehydration, malnutrition, general exhaustion—you've been drinking again, haven't you?"

"Yeah."

"I've prescribed some sedation for tonight. You'll have some lab tests tomorrow, just to play safe."

"When can I go home?"

"After we check out the tests. Meanwhile, a little rest won't hurt you."

"But tomorrow—"

Danny broke it off right there. What could he say, that tomorrow was Saturday, tomorrow he was going to die, it was in the cards?

Dr. Carlsen didn't believe in cards; he believed in tests and charts and specimens. And why not? Those things made a hell of a lot more sense than the Ace of Spades on a dusty table in some creep joint down on South Alvarado.

Being here in the hospital made sense, too. At least he had

somebody looking after him and if there *was* trouble tomorrow—

But there wouldn't be. All he had to do was swallow the Nembies and go to sleep.

Danny stared up at the white ceiling until it turned black and then there was nothing again, nothing but sleep, sweet sleep and the Queen of Spades sat across the table from him and watched while he reached for a drink only the drink wasn't there because Lola had taken it away with her when she left and he knew it didn't matter, it was only a lousy test and he could walk through it in his sleep, sweet sleep—

Danny was very much alive on Saturday morning and hungry as hell. But they wouldn't give him breakfast, not even a cup of coffee, until after they wheeled him down to the lab for the tests.

For a moment, when they were taking blood, he panicked, but like the nurse said, it wasn't going to kill him, and it didn't.

And afterward he had lunch, a big lunch, and they let him get up to go to the john and a nice fag orderly came in and gave him a shave and he dozed off again until dinnertime.

So Saturday was almost over and he was still with it. Hell, he was even beginning to feel good, and if he could just have a drink and a cigarette—

"Sorry. Doctor wants us to take our sedative again tonight." The fat nurse was back, a real sweetheart. But Danny took the pills and the water and settled back, because it was nine o'clock, only three hours to go, and if he made the stretch everything would be copacetic.

If he made it? Hell, he was going to make it, he knew it now, he could feel it in his bones, in his ticker. No throbbing, no pounding; all is calm, all is bright. Bright as the white ceiling which was turning gray now, turning black again, black as the Ace of Spades.

Something started to thump in Danny's chest, but he tensed up, forcing himself to relax—that was funny, tensing up to relax, but it seemed to work, it was working—and now everything was calm again, calm and peaceful, he could sleep because it was quiet. *Quiet as the tomb*—

Danny screamed.

Then the lights went on and the fat nurse came running into the room. "Mr. Jackson, what's the matter, don't you know it's one in the morning—"

"One in the morning?"

She nodded.

"*Sunday* morning?"

When she nodded again, Danny could have kissed her. In fact he *tried* to kiss her because he'd made it now, he was home free.

It was easy to go back to sleep then. Everything was easy now that it was Sunday.

Sunday, with the big breakfast and the big paper. Sunday, with the fresh shave and the fag orderly bringing in the flowers from the studio—wait a minute, what the hell was this, there was nothing in the papers, how did the studio know?

Danny found out when they plugged the phone in and he got his first call. Fischer.

"Look," Danny said. "I'm sorry about the other day—"

"I'm not," said Fischer. "Shut up and listen."

So Danny listened.

"Maybe it was the best thing that could have happened. Anyway, it gave me a notion. I called the studio and tipped them."

"*You* called the studio?"

"Right. Told them about Lola, too."

"Where'd you pick that up?"

"She phoned me Thursday night. Don't worry. I made her promise not to break the story to the papers until we were ready."

"Ready for what?"

"Stop interrupting and listen," Fischer said. "I told the

studio the truth only I juggled the dates a little. Said that Lola split with you on Tuesday instead of Wednesday and you knew it when you came in to do the test. The Pagliacci bit, your heart was breaking but the show must go on—you didn't look so good in there but you were giving it the old college try and how could they fault you when you were so shook up you actually collapsed the following day?"

"Do you have to sound so happy about it?" Danny asked.

"I *am* happy, and you're gonna be happy too. Because they went for the bundle. Considering the circumstances they're going to scrap the test, they've already gotten on the horn to New York and everything's set. You'll do another shot next week, as soon as the doc says it's okay. How's that for openers, buddy-boy?"

It was very good for openers, and it kept getting better. Because the next one who called was Lola. Crying up a storm.

"Sorry . . . all my fault . . . should have stood by when you needed me . . . told the lawyer to forget it . . . doctor said I could come to see you tomorrow . . . oh my poor baby . . ."

Oh my aching—

But it was fine, it was A-OK, because a divorce right now, even a separation, would have clobbered him for life. And he *had* a life, a whole new life, starting today.

Dr. Carlsen laid the topper on it that afternoon. "Preliminary lab reports are in. Too early to nail it down, but it looks as if I made a pretty good educated guess. Little murmur, slight irregularity there, but nothing we can't control with medication. And a dose of common sense."

"When do I cut out of here?"

"Perhaps tomorrow."

"I was thinking of right now."

Dr. Carlsen shrugged. "You're always thinking about right now. That's your problem." He sat down on the edge of the bed. "I was talking about common sense, Danny. Want me to spell it out for you? Two, maybe three drinks a day—one before dinner, one after, perhaps a nightcap if you're out for the evening. Regular hours. We can talk about the diet and exercise later. But the main thing is for you to stop running scared."

"Me?"

Danny gave him the big smile, but it didn't register. "You're not on now," the doc told him. "I know what knocked you down. It was fear. Fear of what was happening to your career, fear because your marriage was coming unglued, fear of a heart attack—"

Okay, smart-ass.

"Don't you understand, Danny? Sometimes the dread is worse than the disease itself. If you can learn to face up to things you're afraid of—"

Danny smiled, Danny nodded, Danny thanked him, Danny hustled him the hell out of there.

Maybe the doc was right at that, the part about fear made sense. The only trouble was, he didn't know what Danny had really been afraid of. And if he told him, he'd get on the horn and call in a shrinker. You just don't go around spilling about phony fortune-tellers who predict you'll die on Saturday night.

But that was over and out now. This was Sunday and he felt great and he wasn't afraid of anything anymore.

He wasn't afraid to climb out of bed and take his clothes out of the closet and get dressed and march down the hall to the desk. He wasn't afraid of the fat nurse or the head nurse either, when he told her he was checking out of there.

Sure there was a lot of static and threats about calling Doctor and this is all highly irregular, Mr. Jackson, but if you insist, sign here.

Danny signed.

The night air felt good as he waited for a taxi out front, and everything was quiet—there was that Sunday feeling in the streets. That *Sunday* feeling.

Danny gave the cab driver his address and settled back for the long haul out to Bel Air. The driver was smart, he ducked the traffic on Wilshire and swung down over Olympic. Crummy neighborhood, lots of neon fronting the cheap bars—

"Hold it, changed my mind. Let me out here."

What the hell, why not? Didn't the doc say he could have a drink before dinner? Besides, it wasn't the drinks, it was the fear. And that was long gone now. It had died last night.

That called for a celebration. Even in a Mickey Mouse joint like this, topless waitresses and faceless customers; that little bird down at the end of the bar wasn't too bad, though.

"Scotch rocks." Danny glanced along the bar. "See what my friend wants."

She wasn't his friend, not yet, but the drink did it. And by the time they had a second one he and Gloria switched over into a back booth.

That was her name, Gloria, one of the strippers in the floor show here, but she didn't work Sundays, sort of a busman's holiday if you get what I mean.

Danny got what she meant and he got a lot more, too; good figure, nice legs, the right kind of mouth. Hell, this was a celebration, it had been a long, long time. So Lola was coming back tomorrow, big deal. This was tonight. *Sunday* night. The first night, the grand opening of a smash hit, a long run. *The New Life of Danny Jackson.*

"Danny Jackson? *You?*" Gloria's mouth hung open. Nice, sensual lower lip. He could always tell, it was like radar, or flying by the seat of your pants. Not the seat exactly, but close. Funny, very funny, and that calls for another drink—

"Of *course* I know who you are." Gloria chug-a-lugged pretty good herself, and now they were wedged into the same side of the booth together, all comfy-cozy.

And he was telling her how it was that he just happened to fall in here, everything that happened, no names of course, but it was easy to talk and maybe if he had just one more for the road—

The road led next door, of course; he'd noticed the motel when he got out of the cab. All very convenient.

George Spelvin and wife is what he signed, and the clerk gave him a funny take but Danny wasn't afraid, he wasn't running scared any more.

The Ace of Spades was just another card in the deck and this was a brand new deal; the Queen of Spades was gone and Gloria was here instead. Cute little Gloria, red hair against a white pillow, and the bed lamp throwing shadows on the wall. Big black shadows like big black eyes, staring and watching and waiting—

But no, the fear was gone, he was forgetting. *Sunday* night, remember? And he wasn't destroying himself, that was over and out, it had all been a mistake. A mistake to get drunk, a mistake to surrender to a sudden impulse and have his fortune told, a mistake to believe a kooky old klooch and her line about the cards. Cards don't control your life, *you* control your life, and he'd proved it. Well, hadn't he?

"Sure, Danny. Sure you have."

He must have been thinking out loud then, telling Gloria the whole story. Because she was unbuttoning his shirt and helping him and murmuring, "Sunday, that's what it is, remember? Nothing to be afraid of, I won't hurt you—"

Damned right she wouldn't. She was just what the doctor ordered. Only he hadn't ordered *this*, just one drink before dinner and regular hours and don't be scared. That was the important thing to remember, don't be scared. Okay, so he wasn't scared. And to hell with the doctors and the fortune-tellers too.

Danny was ready and he grabbed Gloria and yes, this was it, this was what he'd been waiting for. He stared down into eyes, her dark eyes, like the eyes of the old woman. And now they were widening with pleasure and he could see the pupils, black aces on a dusty table. And there was no pleasure, only this tearing pain, as the Ace of Spades kept coming up, up, *up*—

Danny didn't know it when he died, and he didn't know why

he died, either. Gloria had told him nothing, not even the name she used when she did her strip act. It was just one of those phony names strippers always use. Saturday is what she called herself—Saturday Knight.

GEORGE A. ROMERO

Clay

Nobody knew who he was. People knew him to see him. He'd been around the neighborhood for as long as it could be called a neighborhood, but nobody knew exactly who he was. The few who came in contact with him, store owners and clerks, people at the church, the old Monsignor himself, recognized him as Tippy. That was it. He wasn't known, he was simply recognized, and only by the ones who had been around Castle Hill Avenue long enough. Recognized, like an old piece of furniture one periodically rediscovers in an attic.

For that matter the old Monsignor was merely recognized, not really known anymore. He, too, was a remnant from the past, soon to be swallowed and lost forever in the huge digestive tract of the city. He was all but forgotten already, even though he still rattled about in the massive stone church he'd caused to exist. When only the stone was left would he be remembered at all? When he was a boy his father had walked him through a cemetery, pointing out, "The bigger the tombstone, the harder to find the name of the deceased." It was meant to be a lesson in humility.

The Monsignor was closer to Tippy than anyone in the world, although it was unknown to either man. He was the closest because he was the only person whose life was touched by the tattered Irishman. The priest felt guilt whenever he saw Tippy. It was a feeling he'd carried privately since 1942. It would bite at him like an angina and drive him to penance in the middle of a stormy night, usually a night after he'd run into Tippy on the street, or seen him at Mass, or heard one of his strange confessions. The penance would make things worse: He'd say the words by rote, and feel guiltier for saying them, hypocritical. "I detest all my sins because of Thy just punishment, but most of all because they offend Thee, my God, Who art all good and deserving of all my love." The priest knew there could no longer be a true Act of Contrition when there was no longer faith.

What that old man felt inside him was not repentance, but self-pity and fear. Not fear of eternal reprisal, but of there being no eternity at all. Fear that his body was clay and clay alone, not containing the soul he'd been promised. The soul he'd promised in turn to Tippy when Tippy was a boy in 1942.

The old Monsignor was a shepherd who'd come to loathe the sheep. He hated their smell and their complaining sound. He hated everything about them that made them animal. Growing up in farm country upstate, he'd seen a wild look in the eyes of sheep as they let themselves be led from mud pit to shearing to slaughter. In the city he'd seen that same wild stare just above a toothless grin or an outstretched hand reaching up from the gutter. "Father, can ya do me any good?" Too often he'd thought as he stared back at the writhing beast, "No, but you can do me evil."

He'd retreated from any association with the creatures around him. How could he hold himself up as holy, hold himself up as one of God's chosen, if he admitted to being one of *them?* To survive, he'd convinced himself that he was separate from the rest; he'd come to view that separateness not as sin, but somehow as making him less of a sinner. He'd buried his abandonment of the flock behind the books and ledgers of the orderly parish he'd managed. He'd built the church, then the school. He'd stayed. He'd kept St. Matthew's alive and flourishing just eight miles from the cesspool that was Manhattan: a feat, in his mind, not unlike keeping a sand castle intact in a pounding surf.

But despite his diocesan accomplishments, he'd come to old age and arthritic exhaustion in mortal fear. He'd stare at his body, wrinkled and pale blue in a night's lightning flash, and think of the clay, of the wounded eyes of Tippy as a boy. He'd held those eyes in attention for a moment, then let them go. Disembodied, they stared at him, out of dreams, out of shadowy corners of his room. There was faith in those eyes, and on their surface, wet with tears, the priest saw a reflection of his old self, a reflection growing dimmer with the years, as it might on a tarnishing piece of silver.

Now those eyes stared up from the pews each Sunday, out of the face of a poor, retarded nonentity beasts of the city had puked into life. Damn those eyes! They had faith in them still. Was it too late to reach out, to break the silence? Yes. What about all the others he'd ignored since he started ignoring Tippy? The priest could never open that floodgate for fear of the thousand lost beings that might enter to haunt him. One pair of eyes was enough. And, after all, Tippy was at Mass every week. He made his confession regularly. If there were such things as souls then his was clean enough. His sins were grotesque but childish. The tragic aberrations of a lonely damaged mind, of no apparent harm to anyone but the sinner himself. Tippy was mad, and nothing the priest could have done would ever have prevented that. Perhaps it was the madness that enabled him to keep the faith.

God, what was the last name? O'Malley? O'Meara? O'Something.

Tippy O'Something's father had been one of New York's finest when New York was at its finest, if there ever was a fine New York. He had walked the beat before Metropolitan Life had created Parkchester, before the parish had a church, before the old Monsignor had even become a novice.

Tippy's life was all emotion without intellect, sensation without reason. The good taste of a stew, the pain of a paddle, a strap, a fist or a boot heel, the cold of a winter without heat: all were things that simply were. There was no affection, but there was no hatred either, just reaction in kind to the cruelties of the world.

In the first ten years of his life, before 1942, a number of things made impressions on Tippy that he would carry in memory as the priest carried a memory of him. He remembered his dad's police jacket and his mother's breasts, which he once saw when she came chasing after one of her men friends who was chasing after Tippy. His mother never brought men friends around when Tippy's brothers were home, but Tippy promised not to tell dad, so she brought them when he was home.

He knew what they did in her bedroom because he'd asked once and she'd shown him with a banana. That time he'd seen her bottom part. It hadn't seemed nearly as impressive as her breasts. He thought his own bottom part was much more important looking. His mother had said she needed her men friends because, while dad was good enough, she had to have an Italian or a Jew once in a while to remind her she was a woman. Tippy had supposed that meant dad never did the banana trick with his thing in mom's bottom part.

He didn't remember any of the men friends, just that he didn't like most of them. He didn't even remember the one who chased him, just that the man came into his room with no clothes on. He smelled of whiskey and he wanted to put his thing in Tippy's mouth.

Tippy ran through the house. The naked man chased him and his mother came screaming from the bedroom, her breasts bouncing. She was bruised on her face and a cut over her eye ran red. She broke a lamp over the man's head. It was the last thing Tippy saw before he fell out the window.

The blackness outside came with a rush of cold air. Tippy

couldn't tell if he was right side up or upside down. Then he hit. He knew he hit because he heard the sound and his breath stopped and he felt even colder. But there wasn't pain, not right away. He just felt like he was made of clay, and it seemed as though part of him was breaking off. He couldn't tell which part—his chest, his neck, the top of his head—but something on him or in him was breaking away and leaving the rest of his body behind. Could it be stuck back and molded in the way he molded the clay he played with?

Then came the pain.

Then came . . . nothing.

"You damn near died." He remembered his dad saying that. But was that about the time he fell or the time he was so sick? The time he had a hundred and six. "A hundred and six? Why, ya should be proud of that. The hottest New York gets is only a hundred." He remembered his dad saying that, too, and he remembered his dad laughing. He didn't feel like he was breaking apart that time, but he did feel like he was made of clay again. When his mom pushed the big glass onto his chest he expected it to squish in deeper than it did. Under the glass, candle wax dripped. He expected it to burn but it wasn't much hotter than his feverish skin.

That night his father took the candle and glass away and put leeches on Tippy's chest and his mother argued and his father screamed. Then his father started to drink and he screamed louder. "Don't you tell me you know what's good for 'im, woman, you that don't care but ta let 'im see ya runnin' naked with a man ain't 'is father. You're a slut, and if I didn't need ya in this house I'd not even let ya near my children. Ya need ta feel like a woman, is it? Well don't I need ta feel like a man? And all the while I'm payin' the mortgage on this mausoleum you're here takin' pleasure up yer nasty little twat! Ain't it enough I'm in the streets dealin' with hoodlums and whores? Do I hafta have them in ma home?"

After that Tippy just heard a lot of punching and crashing and screaming and crying. Then one of his brothers came in and asked if Tippy died could he have his toys.

After his brother left his dad came in with his bottle of whiskey and sat in a chair. His mom tried to come in as well, but dad jumped up and slammed the door in her face. She went off crying and Dad flopped back into his chair. Tippy closed his eyes. The feeling that he was made of clay came over him again. Once in a while a leech would move and it felt like a thumb in the clay's surface. Once in a while he could hear his dad swallowing.

When he was well his brothers just took his toys, what few there were, without asking. They never took his clay, though. They didn't like it the way he did. He had five boxes of it, three from three Christmases and two from birthdays in between, only he didn't keep the boxes, just the clay, in a lump in a drawer. He'd worked it so much the individual colors were almost gone: The greens, reds and yellows had turned to a kind of gray. It still felt the same, though. He'd take it out at night and try to make things. He tried to make breasts once, and to stick them onto his chest which still had marks from the leeches. He was so glad he had his own room. Other poor people had to live in rooms together. He was glad his dad was paying for the . . . mor . . . morgasoleum.

"It ain't right a cop should be a poor man." His father only talked to Tippy when he was drunk. He screamed at him and beat him up other times, but he only talked properly when he was drunk. Not that he wouldn't ever rage with the whiskey—he would sometimes, and he'd scream louder and hit harder than normal—but sometimes the whiskey would seem to make him sad and those were the times he talked.

"But I've got the four of yas and the liquor ta pay for and the place here. But I will not go to a desk job, never. Not that they'd have me, wi' me not knowin' me r's as good as some. Oh, Tip. This old New York's no place fer the children of

God." Then he blessed himself and kissed the little crucifix he wore on his neck chain.

"Caught a man robbin' a Chinese laundry today. He run and I chased 'im and I got 'im in the gutter and beat 'im 'til he was a lump looked like yer famous clay there. Then I found I knew the man. Feller I used ta drink with over at Pelham Bay. He didn't know me. He'd gone from drink ta morphine and he didn't know me at all."

Tippy picked his dad's police jacket off the back of a chair and put it on as he listened. It was a wonderful jacket, with gold stripes on the sleeves and brass buttons up the front. The sleeves were way too long on the boy and the bottom hung at his shins. If he were made of clay, he thought, he could stretch himself out and make the jacket fit.

"They say that in less than ten years, Tip, there'll be eight million people in New York. How many of 'em'll know me then? Know me name. Me own old dad told me when he put me on the boat, he said, 'Just don't let 'em forget yer name. When they know who ya are it's harder for them ta do ya harm.' Well, they know me name around here all right. Just let 'em try ta forget it. I'll kick it down their throats if I have to. They'll hate me, and many of 'em already do, 'cause I won't let 'em do their dirt. They'll hate me but they'll damn well know who I am."

Tippy wasn't allowed to go far on his own. He had to stay in sight of the front window, under the shadow of the elevated trains. He had a few pals. They beat him up, mostly, and made fun of him, but they used him when they needed another player for potsy or stickball, and that was often enough so that he got some recreation. He was never sent to school. His mother and dad argued about that, too, and wound up throwing things at each other again. If he went to school he couldn't go to work and they needed the money. His brothers already worked. His father said, "A man has a right ta work his children if he needs. I'm not a truant officer, I'm a cop on the street."

Tippy knew he'd have to go to work soon and that would mean less time to play, so when his mother fell bed-sick he took advantage of it and stayed outside longer. He even walked out of sight of the front window three different times. That's how he met his friend Lucille. They would sit and talk and she would tell him what was uptown and downtown in places she was allowed to go. She was even allowed to ride the train by herself. And she was allowed to go to movies. Tippy imagined that was how it was if you had money. She told him about a giant ape she'd seen in a movie, and about how the ape had destroyed an elevated train just like the one over their heads as they spoke. She told him things that were going on around the neighborhood, some of them having to do with Tip's dad. How he'd arrested one of his best friends and informed on another. How he would take a bit of money from stores while promising to keep them protected, and how he beat up a man in a candy store when he wouldn't pay the bit of money. Tippy didn't care about those things. He felt it all had to do with his dad being more important than the others on Castle Hill. Because his dad had a name, and a uniform. Tippy loved uniforms. Uniforms made anyone important: a copper, a solider, a priest. He wasn't sure you even needed a name if you had a uniform because the uniform said who you were.

Lucille always wanted to play house. She said Tippy was the only boy who'd ever play it with her. She'd be the mum, him the dad. They'd eat supper on her toy plates with Tippy's clay as the food. Then they'd scream at each other in some invented argument, and sometimes they'd even hit each other. Once Tippy tried to tell Lucille about the banana trick and about how their bottom parts were different. Lucille said she knew that already and that she'd like to try and play it with Tip. They were afraid to go to either's house, though, and they couldn't do it in the street, so they just sat there where the sun couldn't reach them for the great tracks overhead.

The night his mother died she wanted to give Tippy the funny-shaped star she wore on her neck chain. His father snatched it away before she could unclip it with her shaking fingers.

"That'll be the day," his father said. Those were the last words ever spoken between Tippy's mom and dad and it was the last time they ever touched. The woman turned to Tippy, who was sitting closer than his brothers. She cried for a while. Then that stopped. Then she just said good-bye and closed her eyes.

Later his father came into Tippy's room smelling of whiskey. "There's only one God anyway, for all of us. For the nigger, the Jew or me or you. And He'll always forgive ya yer trespasses. He's forgiven her, yer mum. He's forgiven me. I beat her about. I beat you about. I beat about a hundred others on the street. I've killed four men so far and still I'm forgiven. And so is she, yer mum. Ya get angry, that's all. Ya get angry and ya hafta beat things about now and again. Ya hafta beat things about a bit just ta show yer here. Just ta show yer here! Anyway, don't ever forget there's a God. She's gone. Someday I'll be gone. Yer brothers'll not look after ya. Yer God will."

The priest, too, had been raised without much affection, but with intelligence and gentility, with books to read and hymns to sing and lessons after supper. His father was an accountant and his mother volunteered at the library. He was the only child, and the three lived together with privacy and propriety, the way people should. Issues were discussed, not argued.

He had plenty of sky, and the fresh green hills around him, and a bicycle, bat and glove. The only violence in his life was at sport and the only hard labor was pedaling uphill to home; they lived halfway up a small mountain. Below them, in the valley, grew the wine grapes, and above them, at the summit, stood the seminary. Both were in view from the front window.

He had an unemotional youth, which made it easy for him to accept a simplistic preordination for mankind, and therefore for himself. Without passions, one can resist temptations easily, but one can mistake order for goodness. He wasn't prepared at all for the disorder of the city. A disorder that seemed to make lies of his beliefs.

He came to the neighborhood when the diocese was funding new construction to keep up with the population. While St. Matthew's was being built he served Mass every Sunday at Roone's, an old tavern under the el. The regulars at the bar didn't mind the weekly intrusions. They would set aside their schnapps and even genuflect at the Offertory. There was a pride in the parish come to Castle Hill. The importance of it cut through the smoke and the smell of beer on varnish, cut through the malarkey about Roosevelt, the unions and the new Irish fighter. The boys at Roone's allowed the parish as a good thing, progress for the neighborhood. And it was only a wee sacrifice to shut off the taps for an hour or two on Sunday. Many of the men hadn't been to Mass since before the boats that brought them to New York.

During the week an occasional wedding, or a funeral—and the bar just a few yards from the casket—would be just another reason to drink. In the autumn of 1942, it was Mrs. O'Something's casket. The priest spoke the service and old man O'Something had to recruit from among the boys at the bar to carry his dead woman's coffin out to its hearse. No other family attended. Just Officer O'Something and his three young children, him in his dress uniform, digging in a torn and stitched cloth change purse for silver to buy rounds for volunteers.

"I know yas hate me, boys," he said. He'd been drinking before, at home. His stern face was red and resolute as if he were making a pinch in an alley. "And I hate yas back. But I ask yas ta tip one wi' me and then help me carry me . . ." Margaret? Mary? Mathilda? ". . . out ta the only car she's ever rid in."

"That's me name." A child's voice spoke softly up at the priest who'd been carefully folding his vestments on top of the coffin. The youngest of the policeman's children plopped something down on the lid of the great box near the priest's linens. It was a lump of modeling clay, half molded into some indiscernible shape, soft and drooping from the warmth of the boy's hands.

"Me dad said, 'Tip one wi' me.' That's me name. Tip."

"Is it now," the priest said.

"Will ya not even do me this favor in me hour o' grief?" Tip's father was staring them down and the boys at the bar looked at each other, then they looked at Roone, the proprietor. They all knew the dead woman's reputation; stories got around in bars. Fact is, one of them there had actually slept with her, but that was known only to himself and to young Tip.

Roone looked over at the policeman's children. Then he said, "Sure we'll drink with ya if that's what ya want." And the whiskey started to flow. The priest declined, forgiven only because of his collar. Tip wasn't allowed a drink but his brothers, only two and four years older than he, were actually forced to swallow glassfuls of the burning stuff. After the change purse was empty, but for carfare home from the cemetery, Roone kept pouring on the house, with Officer O'Something careful to point out that there were no favors to be expected in return for the gesture. [Favors of the semiofficial kind.]

During that October drunk young Tip sat waiting near his dead mother, and he and the priest talked. "Is me mum really in the box, then?"

"No. She's long gone, Tip."

"Gone where, is it?"

"If she was good, to Heaven. Pray to the Lord that's so. If she was bad, to the other place."

"There's nothin' in the box then?"

"Oh yes. The poor stuff she was made of. The stuff you saw walkin' about. Her body, which means nothin' at all to you, me or the Lord."

She was long gone from her body. The part of her that was really her had broken away and left. That made sense to Tip. It had almost happened to him. He knew what it felt like. And here was a man in a priest's uniform tellin' it after all.

Then the priest picked up the lump of clay from the inexpensive coffin. Little fragments of green, yellow and red stuck to the crevices of the simple carving on the lid. The boy picked them off with his fingernails, rolling them into a colorless ball as he listened.

"We're made of clay like this, Tip, while we're here on Earth, that is. It's a mystery, Tip. So don't worry if you don't understand it. Just believe it as the truth. What's this you've made here with this clay?"

"It's King Kong."

"And what on Earth is King Kong?"

"It's a giant great ape what destroyed New York, and even the el, when they brought him here from the jungle. It's in a movie. I didn't see it, but me pal told me the story."

"Oh, it's a monkey then."

"An ape."

"Well. You or I or anyone can take this clay and make it into the body of an ape—a donkey, a flower, a person—and it still wouldn't be alive, would it? Only God can take this clay and shape it and then make it alive. Because only God knows how to put a soul inside the thing he's made. Not that apes or donkeys have souls, mind you."

"Do Italians and Jews have souls?"

"Hah . . . some say not." Oh, why did he let himself say that? Why did he let himself sink to that nasty little joke? A city joke, it was. A good laugh for a city brute. Not for him.

"Me mother was a Jew," Tippy said, and before the priest could speak again the boy's father came snorting out of the smoke at the bar.

"Turned Catholic and gone to her salvation!" The red-faced policeman bellowed. Contorted with rage, he looked vengeful, *"Gone to Heaven is me . . ."* Mary? Margaret? Or was it Ethel? Or Ruth?

"If she was good," the boy said. "If not, she's gone to the other place."

And the great drunken oaf of a "man in blue" lifted young

Tip clean off the floor, bringing fist after fist into the boy's face, knocking loose some teeth in a sea of blood. It was then that Tip's eyes found the priest where he sat dumbstruck: sad, pleading eyes that flashed forgiveness; understanding, even as they were being puffed shut by the brutal pounding.

Some of the barflies rushed to stop him, but old O'Something held young Tip's lapels with his left hand while his right fell like a sledge again and again. The vengeance the priest had read on his face had erupted over the limp boy like pus from a seething boil. The priest jumped up but was ineffectual; he didn't know how to face such violence. Like cattle the group stampeded into him, over him. He could smell the whiskey in their expelled gasses, he could feel the sweat in their gritty clothing, he could see the filth in the pores of their skin. It all made him want to vomit.

In the struggle the coffin was knocked from the bar tables holding it and the priest's vestments were ground into the dust and sawdust on the floor as the drunks at Roone's lapsed into Gaelic with their reproaches. The raging old O'Something had to be knocked unconscious before he let go of his unconscious son, who fell into a corner still clutching his lump of clay.

The priest saw the boy on the street the following week. His face was still puffed, with running sores in two places. There were no bandages. The boy said, "Hello, Father," and the priest said "hello" back at him. The boy stood a moment, looking up, and at that moment the priest might have saved himself years of agony by simply saying a few words. But the words never came and the boy walked away.

And that's how it was week after week, under the el, at the grocer's and at Mass, with nothing but hello and good-bye. Oh, what cruel punishment for the priest to have to face it so often, what bitter fate that the two should have stayed so long in the neighborhood together. What damning things were those hellos and good-byes with no conversation in between, while St.

Matthew's became a magnificent stone work, half a block long and with spires taller than the neighboring tracks.

In 1947 one of Tippy's brothers was crushed by a truck carrying steel girders. Three years later his other brother died in a street fight with several other union organizers. His father, the old policeman, died in '54 of liver cancer. The priest was at all three funerals and so was Tippy.

Someone from the Police Department made all the arrangements for O'Something's burial so conversation with the son wasn't necessary even in an official sense. Tip just stood about, half smiling, his nose running a bit. He had a lump of clay in his pocket but nobody could see it. The sun rays fell on him through the stained glass of the window that showed Jesus resurrecting; the light made Tip's face go all green and yellow and red. "Hello," he said to the priest. It was the singsong, overzealous hello of a retard. The priest had never noticed before. Cities conceal such characteristics—the mob makes madmen less visible, along with good men—but there, in the nave of the church, standing close to his old dad's coffin, Tippy, at twenty-two years, was clearly feebleminded. The realization washed over the priest even as the sound of Tip's enthusiastic hello echoed off the great stone walls of the basilica—and still the priest kept silent. The silence seemed to echo as well.

In the days that followed, the priest drummed up the resolve to go visit Tip. But before it happened someone brought the news that old man O'Something had left an old brownstone and a bit of money he'd been misering away, and that Tip'd actually gotten a job hefting crates at the new Parkchester Gristede's. The priest never made his visit.

So time marched, and the priest was forced, by the walls of the city that locked them together, to watch Tip progress, or regress, until eventually the two became the old Monsignor and the withered derelict people ignored. Old things that waddled through the neighborhood, bearing no resemblance to their former selves, except to one another's eyes.

The old Monsignor reasoned that it was the fate of people in cities to go about banging off the walls until their brains were pulp, with no air to breathe, no earth to touch, no feeling of contact, no matter that they lived above, below, beside, within inches of one another. He used to think cities were the Devil's swamps, with the Demon himself in residence. Now that he'd seen the brutes of New York at work he knew they'd be sinners even if the Devil didn't prompt them. Did the Devil even exist? And if not, did the Other exist? Were we here alone? Beasts prowling on a spinning rock in the nothingness of space. We no longer even knew each other's names.

Damn! Was it O'Malley? O'Meara? He'd have to check the funeral records.

Over the years four dying men had staggered bleeding into the church to make their last confessions. Burglers had seven times stolen ornaments from the altar. There'd been countless desecrations; the graffiti on the stone walls outdid the elaborate paintings on the trains that rumbled overhead. The priest had found marijuana in the poor box, and bags of shit and, in one case, a bloody fetus on the rectory doorstep. It all went to justify his fear.

So he carried out what he felt more and more to be a charade. He'd baptize them, marry them and extreme unct them, but he'd never get closer than that for fear of being contaminated.

Once in a sermon he spoke of an ape that came from the jungle and destroyed New York. The ape, in the sermon, was man. That night he felt the guilt. It came with the undulating shadows of an electrical storm. He'd lived quite properly. He'd never known, had even shunned, animal passion, and that had brought him to lie alone in the dark with his intellect. His faith had disintegrated; his guilt could never be absolved.

Old Tippy loved to do penance, to feel forgiven as he knelt at the altar rail among a hundred glowing candles, bathed in the smell of incense, surrounded by the figures of saints and angels, and looking up at the body of God Himself, arms outstretched, bleeding wounds gaping in hands and feet and side. God was long gone from His body just as Tippy's mother was long gone from hers. Just as Tippy and all other people would be long gone after they died. He was so glad the priest had told him how it worked. He couldn't wait until it was his turn to go to Heaven. He knew he'd go there and not to the other place because he knew he was basically good. And even when he was bad he told it in confession and the penance made him good again.

Tippy always went to the old Monsignor to confess his sins. He didn't like the new young priest who smelled of cologne and used modern talk. He didn't need talk. Only forgiveness. The musty little confessional, the one closest to the altar, was a dark wood and purple velvet womb that Tippy'd been returning to for some thirty-five years. The even tone of the old Monsignor's voice, never shocked, never angry, was like a warm blanket used by the hand of God to tuck the absolved Tippy back into his proper place in a frightening world while he waited for the world after. Tippy loved to go to confession. He loved and believed fully in God.

The Monsignor had only recently associated the hesitant voice with old Tip. One day, hearing the middle-aged whisper tell of the sins of a child, he peeked out the door as the sinner waddled away toward his penance at the altar rail. Tippy was wearing his old dad's police jacket, and there were holes in his soles, visible as he knelt in the smoke from the candles.

They'd stopped selling the clay a while back. At least Tippy could never find it anymore. Not the good kind. He'd tried the new kinds and they were no good at all. The colors weren't right. He couldn't smooth them and blend them together. They didn't feel good against his skin. The old kind was the best. Green, yellow and red. Hard in the cold air, soft in the hand. Over time Tippy'd bought hundreds and hundreds of boxes of the stuff. It stayed good forever.

If the priest had ever visited Tippy's brownstone under the el, if he'd ever gone up to the third floor, he would have seen the beast of the city at its most dissolute. The priest, in his most frenzied conjurations of the depths man plumbed, could never have imagined the profound horror of those dimly lit rooms where sat the life-sized lumps of putty that were Tippy's friends. Tippy's lovers. Some were in chairs, some on the floor. Two were propped at the dinner table. In a back room one lay on the bed, and in the bathroom one was twisted into the tub. They were crudely shaped to resemble human figures; their features were grotesque and clumsily crafted. They bore lumpy noses and had great gaping holes for mouths, their arms and legs were too long or too short and their torsos were bent and sagging from their own weight. They had all the proper sexual parts under their clothing. They were dressed in things that had belonged to Tippy's brothers, his dad and his mom.

The rooms on that floor had been the brothers', so Tippy had had to do a little converting. He'd brought up his own bed, because he liked it better than either of the ones up there. And he'd brought up the dining table and chairs to use both as work space and as a place for family supper. Everything else was as it had always been as long as the O'Somethings lived there. Oh, except for the two good stuffed chairs with embroidered cushions—these Tippy had covered with bed sheets so the clay wouldn't rub into the fabric. The clay rubbed into everything. The cracks in the floor, the pattern on the silverware, the carving on the headboard of Tippy's bed.

Tippy was quite content upstairs with his pals. He'd play with them and mold them differently to suit his moods and purposes. He'd sit them at table and push food into the openings that were their mouths. At night he'd sit with them and hold them and comfort them and tell them stories of the things he'd done when he'd gone beyond where the front window could see. Other times, he'd pretend to be drunk and angry, and he'd throw things about the room and scream and pull the figures apart brutally.

He hated to go to work because he needed the days for repair and for thinking up new tricks. He kept his job, though, at Gristede's, because he needed money to support his family. Saturdays and Sundays he spent at home, except for going to Mass. He was constantly making improvements on his brood. He'd saved enough money so that they all had wigs now, and recently he'd given them all steelie kabolas for eyes: He'd found them in his brother's marble box, painted on irises, and shoved them into the clay heads. Then he gave the females eyebrows that he clipped from his own pubic hair, which was just growing back in so it was the right length for eyebrows. He'd cut it off a few months ago for another purpose.

He made little clay leeches for when his family was sick. He put tubes of toothpaste inside the male penises. It made them permanently erect but it made them able to squirt something that looked like what Tippy squirted, and it tasted good. Tippy'd tried other things—shampoo, hair conditioner, mayonnaise—but none of them tasted as good as toothpaste. He wanted to make a tongue for a female out of a piece of liver from Gristede's, but the mouth broke apart at the jaw as he tried to secure the piece of raw meat. So he molded the clay back together and put lipstick on the mouth inside. He found that the liver worked well in the vaginal orifice, though. It felt even warmer and smoother than the clay.

He would fish his own stools out of the toilet and mold them into the figures' buttocks. He would shove his fingernail clippings into the ends of their fingers. He would shove his snot into their nostrils. He would open cavities in their clay chests and fill them with chicken innards, or with tomato juice, so they would seem to bleed when he stabbed them.

He used baby bottles and milk in the breasts of the female he liked best. Lucille. She was his favorite. He slept only with her at night. He constantly worked on her with loving hands, trying to refine her features. He even gave her eyelashes and toes. None of the others had toes. He gave her teeth, which he broke, one at a time, off one of those chatter-mouth toys, and inserted individually in her clay mouth. Between her legs was the pubic hair shaved from Tippy's own groin. In the clay beneath the hair was a hole made by a banana.

The problem was moving her. Lucille was very heavy, and she broke apart easily. He had run a strip of wood from her torso through her neck and up into her head. That kept the neck joint from breaking, though it added to the weight, but Tippy didn't like the idea of that hard piece of wood inside Lucille. He thought her inside should be just as soft as her outside, and anyway the wood strip didn't solve the problem of the arms and legs. They were impossible. Whenever he moved her they would break, and he would have to reattach them and mold them back in. One morning he awoke in only one of Lucille's arms; the other was on the floor where it had fallen in the night. The fingers were damaged and the wrist was bent. Somehow that was the last straw. That morning Tippy knew he had to do something about the problem.

Maria Esposito walked hurriedly home through the shadows under the el. The train she had just ridden from her job downtown was rolling off into the dark, and the loud roar scared her as it did every night. She tried to think of bright things: of breakfast, of birthday presents, of store windows with dancing mannequins wearing the jeans she was saving to buy. Every night the same thoughts fought against the dark and every night she survived the imagined perils lurking in the shadows. She was becoming experienced at the ritual. She was becoming a seasoned city dweller.

Tippy didn't know Maria Esposito's name, but he knew she was exactly the right size. He'd been watching her recently. She was exactly the right size to put inside Lucille.

The train's wheels screamed a piercing metallic scream as it rounded a curve in the elevated rails. Beneath that noise nobody heard Maria Esposito's last words, even though she shouted them as loudly as she could, and in the darkness of the alley, on the other side of the building from the el, nobody saw old Tippy carry her unconscious body in through the back entrance of the old O'Something brownstone.

Tippy stabbed Maria Esposito on his dining room table, carefully and slowly through the heart, with a wire coat hanger he'd straightened. He caught as much of the blood as he could, in pots, for later use. The girl came around to semiconsciousness before she died. She felt the burning pain in her chest. She tried to speak, to scream, but she was too weak. She saw Tippy smiling down at her. At first she thought she was in a hospital, that Tippy was some sort of orderly who would tell her she was all right. There'd been an accident, but she was all right. Then she realized she was in somebody's house. An old house with little-flower-patterned wallpaper, and sheets over the furniture. Even through her excruciating pain she could smell the foul stench of the place, the stench of rotting food and month-old milk and human waste that hadn't been flushed away. Then she knew she was dying. She was in the clutches of a madman and he had stabbed her and she was dying. Her only hope was that it was all a dream. It was fuzzy like a dream, somehow unreal around the edges, out of focus, impossible. Those shapes. What were they? There, in the corners, at the edges of sight, just that much darker than the shadows that they could be seen at all. Her head turned toward one of them. Her eyes brought it into sharpness. It was a thing that looked like a woman. It had a hairdo and was dressed like a woman, but where its face should be there was just a grayish grotesque lump, a distorted mass of what looked like clay.

Then she felt something and she looked toward the sensation. She saw what seemed to be a policeman. He was using his billy club to mold some substance onto her legs. The substance was green and yellow and red.

"Bless me, Father, for I have sinned. It's a week since me last confession."

"Yes, my son."

"Well . . . I was bad to George."

"George this time."

"Yes, Father. I pulled his fingers off 'cause I was angry with him."

"Mmmmm hmmmm. Anything else?"

"I didn't feed Henry this whole week. I was angry with him, too."

"What else?"

"Well," Tippy hesitated in the dark before the deep smell of incense made him secure enough to go on. "I put my thing into Lucille again."

"Once?"

"No."

"How many times?"

"Nine."

"Mmmmm hmmmm. Anything else?"

Another hesitation. Then, "No, Father."

"Well. You know your sins with . . . Lucille . . . are your worst sins. You mustn't think impurely anymore or next you'll go from toy people to real ones. You've never done anything impure with a real woman, have you?"

Yet another hesitation. "No, Father."

"No. No, I'm sure you haven't. How could you? How could you get close enough, you poor . . ." The old Monsignor caught himself. He made the sign of the cross with a shivering hand. "Three Our Fathers and three Hail Marys for your penance."

Then the priest shut the sliding screen that separated him from his nemesis. After a moment he heard Tippy shuffle out of the confessional. He saw a shadow pass by the little crucifix-shaped hole carved in his door as the derelict moved off toward the altar. He imagined the unshaven wretch huddled in a dark bedroom with a little grouping of clay figures. George. Henry. Lucille. In his mind the figures were small and impossibly misshapen, like the ape on the coffin lid at Roone's. He imagined the poor madman poking a hole in one of the vile things and sliding it up and down on his penis in the shadows. The vision made him gag. He didn't even hear the voice of the old woman who'd taken Tippy's place and who'd already begun to pour her sorrows at him through the screen. He only hoped he could sleep that night.

Tippy lit a candle at the altar rail. He hadn't told the old Monsignor about the girl. His dad had killed four, he said, and he was still forgiven. The girl was Tip's first. And besides, he hadn't done anything impure with the girl. He hadn't. She was long gone when he'd done the impure things. Long gone like his mum. He'd even waited to make sure. He'd given her plenty of time to get gone, and now, if she was good, she was in heaven. The part of her that was left was clay, clay he was using just to keep the other clay that was Lucille together.

He said his Our Fathers and his Hail Marys and then he knelt a while before leaving the church. He couldn't wait 'til next week when he could come back again. The place made him feel so safe.

JOHN COYNE

A Cabin in the Woods

Michael remembered clearly the first piece of fungus: a thin, irregular patch twelve inches wide, grayish, like the color of candle grease, growing on the new pine wall of the bathroom. He reached up gingerly to touch it. The crust was lumpy and the edges serrated. He pulled the resinous flesh from the wood, like removing a scab, tossed the fungus into the waste can and finished shaving.

He had come up from the city late the night before, driving the last few hours through the mountain roads in heavy fog and rain and arriving at his new cabin in the woods after midnight. It was his first trip to the lake that spring.

Michael had come early in the week to work, bringing with him the galleys of his latest novel. He needed to spend several more days making corrections. It was the only task of writing that he really enjoyed, the final step when the book was still part of him. Once it appeared between covers, it belonged to others.

He was in no hurry to read the galleys. That could be done at leisure over the next few days. Barbara wasn't arriving until Friday and their guests weren't due until Saturday morning. It was a weekend they had planned for several months to celebrate the completion of the new house.

So while shaving that first morning at the cabin, Michael found himself relaxed and smiling. He was pleased about the house. It was bigger and more attractive than even the blueprints had suggested.

It had been designed by a young architect from the nearby village. Local carpenters had built it, using lumber cut from the pine and oak and walnut woods behind the lake. They had left the lumber rough hewed and unfinished.

The cabin was built into the side of the mountain, with a spectacular view of the lake. Only a few trees had been cut to accommodate the construction; so from a distance, and through the trees, the building looked like a large boulder that had been unearthed and tumbled into the sun to dry.

"I want the ambience *rustic,*" Barbara explained to the architect. "A sense of the *wilderness.*" She whispered the words, as if to suggest the mysterious.

"Don't make it too austere," Michael instructed. "I don't want the feeling we're camping out. This is a cabin we want to escape to from the city; we want some conveniences. I want a place that can sleep eight or ten if need be." He paced the small office of the architect as he listed his requirements, banging his new boots on the wooden floor. Michael liked the authoritative sound, the suggestion to this kid that here was someone who knew what he wanted out of life.

"And cozy!" Barbara leaned forward to catch the architect's attention. She had a round pretty face with saucer-sized blue eyes. She flirted with the young man to make her point. "And a stone fireplace the length of one wall. We may want to come up here with our friends during skiing season." She beamed.

The architect looked from one to the other and said nothing.

"He's not one of your great talkers, is he?" Barbara remarked as they left the village.

"That's the way of these mountain people. They come cheap and they give you a full day's work. It's okay with me. I'd rather deal with locals than someone from the city."

Still, the cabin cost $10,000 more than Michael had expected. The price of supplies, he was told, had tripled. However, they had landscaped the lawn to the lake and put in a gravel drive to the county road. Michael said he wanted only to turn the key and find the place livable. "I'm no handyman," he had told the architect.

While the second home in the mountains was costly, Michael was no longer worried about money. When he had finished the new novel and submitted it to the publisher it was picked up immediately with an advance of $50,000, more than he had made on any of his other books. The next week it had sold to the movies for $200,000, and a percentage of the gross. Then just before driving to the mountains, his agent telephoned with the news that the paperback rights had gone for half a million.

"Everything I touch is turning to gold," Michael bragged to Barbara. "I told you I'd make it big."

What he did not tell Barbara was that this was his worst book, written only to make money. He had used all the clichés of plot and situation and it had paid off.

He finished dressing and made plans for the day. The station wagon was still packed with bags of groceries. The night before he had been too tired after the drive to do more than build a fire and pour himself a drink. Then carrying his drink, he had toured through the empty rooms—his boots echoing on the oak floors—and admired the craftsmanship of the mountain carpenters. The cabin was sturdy and well built; the joints fit together like giant Lincoln Logs.

The three bedrooms of the house were upstairs in the back and they were connected by an open walk that overlooked the living room, which was the height and width of the front of the cabin. The facade was nearly all windows, long panels that reached the roof.

One full wall was Barbara's stone fireplace, made from boulders quarried in the mountains and trucked to the lake site. The foundation was made from the same rocks. As Barbara bragged to friends with newly acquired chauvinism, "All that's not from the mountains are the kitchen appliances and ourselves."

Michael moved the station wagon behind the house and unpacked the groceries, carrying the bundles in through the back door and stacking the bags on the butcher-block table. He filled the refrigerator first with perishables and the several bottles of white wine he planned to have evenings with his meals. His own special present to himself at the success of the book.

Packing the refrigerator gave Michael a sense of belonging. With that simple chore, he had taken possession of the place and the cabin felt like home.

He had thought of leaving the staples until Barbara arrived—she would have her own notion of where everything should go—but after the satisfaction of filling the refrigerator, Michael decided to put the staples away, beginning with the liquor.

He carried the box into the living room and knelt down behind the bar and opened the cabinet doors. Inside, growing along the two empty plain wooden shelves, was gray fungus. It grew thick, covering the whole interior of the cabinet, and the discovery frightened Michael, like finding an abnormality.

"My God!" A shiver ran along his spine.

He filled several of the empty grocery bags with the fungus. It pulled off the shelves easily and was removed in minutes. Then he scrubbed the hard pine boards with soap and water and put away the bottles of liquor.

It was the dampness of the house, he guessed, that had caused the growth. The house had stood empty and without heat since it had been finished. He knew fungus grew rapidly in damp weather, but still the spread of the candle-gray patch was alarming.

He returned to the kitchen and apprehensively opened the knotty-pine cupboards over the counter. The insides were clean, with the smell about them of sawdust. He ran his hand across the shelves and picked up shavings. Michael closed the door and sighed.

Barbara had given him a list of chores to do in the house before the weekend. The beds in the guest rooms should be made, the windows needed washing, and the whole house, from top to bottom, had to be swept. Also the living-room rug had arrived and was rolled up in the corner. It had to be put down and vacuumed.

First, however, Michael decided to have breakfast. On Sundays in the city he always made breakfast, grand ones of Eggs Doremus, crepes, or Swedish pancakes with lingonberries. Lately Barbara had begun to invite friends over for brunch. His cooking had become well known among their friends and his editor had suggested that he might write a cookbook about Sunday breakfasts.

Michael unpacked the skillet, and turning on the front burner melted a slice of butter into the pan. He took a bottle of white wine, one of the inexpensive California Chablis, uncorked it, and added a half-cup to the skillet. The butter and wine sizzled over the flame and the rich smell made Michael hungry.

He broke two eggs into the skillet, seasoned them with salt and pepper, and then searched the shopping bags for cayenne, but Barbara hadn't packed the spices. He could do without but made a mental note to pick up cayenne and more spices when he drove to the village later that morning.

Michael moved easily around the kitchen, enjoying the space to maneuver. In their apartment in the city, only one of them could cook at a time. Here, they had put in two stoves and two sinks, and enough counter space for both to work at once.

Michael glanced at the eggs. The whites were nearly firm. He took the toaster and plugged it in, noticing with satisfaction that the electrical outlets worked. That was one less problem to worry about. He dropped two pieces of bread into the toaster and then, going back to the bar, took the vodka, opened a can of tomato juice, and made himself a Bloody Mary.

He was working quickly now, sure of the kitchen. He cut the

flame under the skillet, crumbled Roquefort cheese and sprinkled it on the eggs; then he buttered the toast and unpacked a dish and silverware. He smiled, pleased. He was going to enjoy cooking in this kitchen.

Perhaps, he thought, he should move full time to the mountains. He could write more, he knew, if he lived by the lake, away from interruptions and distractions. He fantasized a moment. He could see himself going down on cool, misty mornings to the lake. He could smell the pine trees and the water as he crossed the flat lake to bass fish before sunup. He could see the boat gracefully arching through the calm water as behind it a small wave rippled to the shore. He sipped the Bloody Mary and let the pleasant thought relax him.

Then he remembered the eggs and he slipped them from the skillet onto the buttered toast, and carrying the plate and his drink walked out onto the oak deck. The deck was a dozen feet wide and built along the length of the east wall to catch the early morning sun. It was Barbara's idea that they could have breakfast on the deck.

The sun had cleared the mountains and touched the house. It had dried the puddles of rainwater and warmed the deck so Michael was comfortable in shirt-sleeves.

They had not yet purchased deck furniture, so he perched himself on the wide banister and finished the eggs. He could see the length of the front lawn from where he sat. It sloped gracefully down to the shore and the new pier.

The pier he had built himself during the winter. One weekend he had come up to the village, bought 300 feet of lumber, hired two men from a construction firm, and driven out to the lake in four-wheel-drive jeeps. Along the shore of the lake they found twelve sassafras trees that they cut and trimmed and pulled across the ice to Michael's property. They chopped holes in the thick ice and sledgehammered the poles into place to make the foundation. Then they cut two-by-eights into four-foot lengths and nailed them between the poles to make the pier.

Michael's hands blistered and his back ached for a week, but he was proud of his hard labor, and proud, too, of the pier which went forty feet into the water and could easily handle his two boats.

At first he could not see the pier because a late morning mist clung to the shore. It rolled against the bank like a range of low clouds. But as he sat finishing the eggs and drink, the rising sun burned away the mist and the thin slice of pier jutting into the mountain lake came slowly into view like a strange gothic phenomenon.

"What the . . ."

Michael stood abruptly and the dish and his drink tumbled off the railing. He peered down, confused. The whole length of the pier was covered with gray fungus. He looked around for more fungus, expecting to see it everywhere. He scanned the landscaped lawn, the pine trees which grew thick to the edge of his property. He spun about and ran the length of the oak deck, leaned over the railing and searched the high rear wall of the cabin. He glanced at the trash heap of construction materials left by the builders. No sign of more mold.

Next he ran into the house and taking the steps two at a time raced to the second floor. He turned into the bathroom and flipped on the light. No fungus grew on the pine wall. He turned immediately and ran downstairs, boots stomping on the wooden stairs, and opened the cabinet doors below the bar. The bottles of liquor were stacked as he had arranged them.

Michael calmed down, gained control. He kept walking, however, through the house, opening closet doors, checking cabinets. He went again to the kitchen and looked through all the cupboards. He opened the basement door and peered into the dark downstairs. The basement had been left unfinished, a damp cellar. Still no fungus.

When he was satisfied there was no fungus in the house, he left the cabin and walked across the lawn to the toolshed and found a shovel. He began where the pier touched the shore, scraping away the fungus and dumping the growth into the water, where it plopped and floated away. He shoveled quickly. The flat tenacious flesh of the fungus ripped easily off the wood. It was oddly exhilarating work. In a matter of minutes he had cleaned the length of the pier.

He stuck the shovel into the turf and went again to the house where he found a mop and bucket, poured detergent into the bucket, filled it with hot water, and returned to the pier to mop the planks. The pier sparkled in the morning sun.

Then Michael locked the cabin, backed the station wagon out of the drive, and drove into the village.

The village was only a few streets where the interstate crossed the mountains. It had grown up on both sides of a white river, and adjacent to railroad tracks. The tracks were now defunct and the river polluted. The few buildings were weather weary and old. The only new construction was the service station at the interstate, and a few drive-ins. When Barbara first saw the town, she wouldn't let him stop.

But the hills and valleys beyond the place were spectacular and unspoiled and when they found five acres of woods overlooking the lake they decided that in spite of the town, they'd buy.

"I looked down at the pier and the whole goddamn thing was covered with fungus. It's a gray color, like someone's puke." Michael paced the architect's office. He had already told the young man about the fungus in the bathroom and beneath the bar. And without saying so, implied it was the architect's fault.

"I'm not a biologist." The young man spoke carefully. He was unnerved by Michael. The man had barged into his office shouting about fungus. It had taken him several minutes to comprehend what the problem was.

"You're from these hills. You grew up here, right? You should know about fungus. What's all this mountain folklore we keep hearing about?" Michael quit pacing and sat down across from the architect. He was suddenly tired. The anxiety and anger over the fungus had worn him out. "That's a new house out there. I sunk $50,000 into it and you can't tell me why there's fungus growing on the bathroom walls? Goddamnit! What kind of wood did you use?"

"The lumber was green, true, but I told you we'd have problems. It was your idea to build the place with pine off your land. Well, pine needs time to dry. Still . . ." The architect shook his head. The growth of fungus confused him. He had never heard of such a thing. But the man might be exaggerating. He glanced at Michael.

Michael was short and plump with a round, soft face, and brown eyes that kept widening with alarm. He wore new Levi's pants and jacket, and cowboy boots that gave him an extra inch of height. Around his neck he had fastened a blue bandanna into an ascot. He looked, the architect thought, slightly ridiculous.

"Who knows about this fungus?" Michael asked. He had taken out another blue bandanna to wipe the sweat off his face. In his exasperated state, the sweat poured.

"I guess someone at the college . . ."

"And you don't think it's any of your concern? You stuck me for $10,000 over the original estimate and now that you've got your money, you don't give a damn."

"I told you before we started construction that we'd get hit by inflation. We could have held the costs close to that first estimate if your wife hadn't wanted all the custom cabinets, those wardrobes, and items like bathroom fixtures from Italy . . ."

Michael waved away the architect's explanations. He was mad at the kid for not solving the problem of the fungus. "Where's this college?" he asked.

"Brailey. It's across the mountain."

"How many miles?" Michael stood. He had his car keys out and was spinning them impatiently.

"Maybe thirty, but these are mountain roads. It will take an hour's drive. Why not telephone? You're welcome to use my phone." He pushed the telephone across the desk.

Michael fidgeted with his keys. He didn't want to let the

architect do him any favors, but he also didn't want to spend the morning driving through the mountains.

"Okay. You might be right." He sat down again and, picking up the receiver, dialed information.

It took him several calls and the help of the college switchboard operator before he reached a Doctor Clyde Bessey, an associate professor at the state university. Dr. Bessey had a thin, raspy voice, as if someone had a hand at his throat. He said he was a mycologist in the Department of Plant Pathology.

"Do you know anything about fungus?" Michael asked.

"Why, yes." The doctor spoke carefully, as if his words were under examination. "Mycology is the study of fungi."

"Then you're the person I want," Michael replied quickly. Then, without asking if the man had time, he described the events of the morning.

"*Peniophora gigantea,*" Doctor Bessey replied.

"What?"

"The species of fungi you've described sounds like *Peniophora gigantea.* It's more commonly called *Resin Fungus.* A rather dull-colored species that spreads out like a crust on the wood. You say the edges are serrated?"

"And it's lumpy . . ."

"Rightly so! *Peniophora gigantea.* Sometimes laymen mistake this species of crust fungi for a resinous secretion of the conifer."

"Does it grow like that? That fast?"

"No, what you've described is odd." He sounded thoughtful. "Fungi won't grow that extensively, unless, of course, a house has been abandoned. And certainly not that fast. We did have a damp winter and spring, still . . . you said the cabin was built with green lumber?"

"Yes, I'm afraid so." Michael glanced at the architect.

"Still . . ."

"Well, how in the hell do I stop it?" Michael was sharp, because the laborious manner of the professor was irritating.

"I don't know exactly what to tell you. Your situation sounds a bit unusual. Fungi doesn't grow as rapidly as you've described. In laboratory conditions, we've had fungus cover the surface of a three-inch-wide culture dish in two days. But that's ideal conditions. Without competition from other fungi or bacteria. But, generally speaking, fungi does thrive better than any other organism on earth." He said that with a flourish of pride.

"Doctor, I'm sure this is all just wonderful, but it doesn't help me, you see. I'm infested with the crap!"

"Yes, of course . . . If you don't mind, I'd like to drive over and take some cultures. I'll be able to tell more once I've had the opportunity to study some samples."

"You can have all you want."

"You've cleaned up the fungi, I presume. . . ."

"With soap and water."

"Well, that should destroy any mycelium, but then we never can be sure. One germinating spore and the process begins again. Rather amazing, actually."

"Let's hope you're wrong. It's a $50,000 house."

"Oh, I'm sure there's no permanent problem, just a biological phenomenon. Fungi are harmless, really, when they're kept in control. Your home will suffer no lasting effects." He sounded confident.

"Maybe you're right." Michael was cautious. Still, Doctor Bessey had eased his mind. Michael hung up feeling better.

"Do you mind if I make another call?" he asked the architect. "Our phone hasn't been installed at the cabin. . . ." The young man gestured for Michael to go ahead. Actually, he wasn't that bad, Michael thought, dialing Barbara in the city.

"I'm sure it's nothing serious," Barbara said when Michael told her about the fungus. "The wet weather and all . . ." Her mind was elsewhere, planning for the weekend. "Did you have time to make the beds?"

"The whole pier was covered, like a tropical jungle. *Peniophora gigantea* . . . that's what the mycologist called it."

"The who?"

"Dr. Bessey. He studies fungi."

"Well, if it's that well known, then it can't be any problem. . . . Have you had a chance to wash the windows? Perhaps I should come up earlier . . ."

"Don't worry about getting the cabin clean. I'll do that!" Michael snapped at her. He was upset that she hadn't responded. Barbara had a frustrating habit of not caring about a household problem unless it affected her directly. "I'll clean the windows, make the beds, and sweep the goddamn floors once I get rid of this fungus!"

"And the rugs . . ."

"And the rugs!"

"Michael dear, there's no need to be upset with me. I have nothing to do with your fungus."

"Yes, dear, but you wanted the place built from our lumber, our *green* lumber."

"And you said it would make the place look more authentic."

"The lumber's green!"

"I don't see where that's my fault!"

"It might mean that we'll have to live with this goddamn fungus!" Michael knew he was being unreasonable, but he couldn't stop himself. He was mad at her for not taking the fungus seriously.

"I'm sure you'll think of something," Barbara pampered him and then dismissed the whole issue. "You'll remember the windows . . . ?" She sounded like a recording.

Before leaving the village, Michael went to the general store and shopped for the week. He did not want to leave the lake again for errands. He bought Windex, the spices Barbara had forgotten, a new mop, a second broom. He bought two five-gallon cans of gas for the boats and more fishing tackle. He bought a box of lures; good, he was told by the store owner, for mountain lakes. He picked up a minnow box, a fishnet and a filet knife. He would need them if he planned to do any serious fishing.

But he understood himself enough to realize also that this impulse buying was only a compensation for the upsetting morning. Now that he had the money, he spent it quickly, filling the station wagon like a sled of toys. And it worked. Driving back to the cabin, his good mood returned.

He would not clean the cabin that morning, he decided, nor would he make the beds. Instead, he'd take out the flat-bottomed boat and fish for bass in the small lagoon of the lake. And he'd pan fry the catch that evening for dinner. He'd just have the fish and some fresh vegetables, asparagus or sliced cucumbers, and a bottle of the Pinot Noir.

Michael pictured himself on the deck frying the bass. The cloud of smoke from the coals drifting off into the trees, the late sun catching the glass of wine, the pale yellow color like tarnished gold. He'd cover the fish a moment, stop to sip the wine, and look out over the lake as the trees darkened on the other shore, and a mist formed. He'd get a thick ski sweater and put it on. When the darkness spread up the lawn to the house, he'd be the last object visible, moving on the deck like a lingering shadow.

Michael turned the station wagon off the county road and onto his drive and the crunch of gravel under the wheels snapped him from his daydream. He touched the accelerator and the big car spun over the loose stones. On that side of the property the trees grew thick and close and kept the house from view until Michael had swung the car into the parking space and stopped. Then he saw the fungus, a wide spread growing across the rock foundation like prehistoric ivy.

He ran from the car to the wall and grabbed the fungus. The mold tore away in large chunks. With both hands, frantically, he kept ripping away. Now it was wet and clammy, like the soft underbelly of fish.

Michael left the fungus on the ground, left his new fishing

tackle and other supplies in the car, and ran into the house. He pulled open the cabinet doors. The gray growth had spread again across the two shelves. It covered the liquor, grew thick among the bottles like cobwebs.

In the bathroom upstairs the patch of mold was the width of the wall. It stretched from floor to ceiling and had crept around the mirror, grown into the wash bowl, and smothered the toilet. He reached out and pulled a dozen inches away in his fingers. The waxy flesh of the fungus clung to his hand. Michael fell back exhausted against the bathroom door and wiped the sweat off his face with the sleeve of his jacket.

It was hot in the cabin. Michael took off his jacket and pulled off the blue bandanna ascot, then he started on the bathroom fungus. He filled five paper bags with fungus and dumped them into the trash heap behind the house. He went to the bar and removed the liquor and scraped the shelves clean again. He took the fungus to the trash pile and going back to the car got one of the cans of gas, poured it on the fungus, and started a blaze.

The wet fungus produced a heavy fog and a nasty odor, like the burning of manure. Michael watched it burn with pleasure, but when he returned to the kitchen to put away the supplies, he found that the fungus had spread, was growing extensively in all the cupboards and beneath the sink. It even lined the insides of the oven and grew up the back of the refrigerator.

Michael needed to stand on a kitchen chair to reach the fungus that grew at the rear of the cupboards, but he had learned now how to rip the mold away in large pieces, like pulling off old, wet wallpaper. Still, it took him longer; the fungus was more extensive and nestled in all the corners of the custom-made cupboards.

He went outside and found the wheelbarrow and carted away the fungus, dumping it into the fire behind the house. The gray smoke billowed into the trees. The mountain air stank. He swept the kitchen clean and washed the cupboards, the bathroom, and the cabinets beneath the bar. It was late afternoon when he had the house finally in order and he went upstairs and flopped into bed, feeling as if he hadn't slept in weeks.

He woke after seven o'clock. It was still daylight, but the sun was low in the sky and the bedroom at the back of the cabin was shaded by trees. He woke in the dark.

He had been deeply asleep and came awake slowly so it was several minutes before he remembered where he was and what had happened. When he did remember, he realized at the same time that the fungus would have returned, that it was growing again in the bathroom, beneath the bar, and in all the cupboards of the kitchen.

But he did not know that now the fungus had spread further and was growing along the green pine walls of the bedroom, had spread over the bare oak floors, and even started down the stairs, like an organic carpet. Michael sat up and swung his bare feet off the bed and onto the floor. His feet touched the lumpy wet fungus. It was as if he had been swimming in the lake and had tried to stand on the mucky bottom. His toes dug into the slime.

He shoveled the fungus off the floor and threw it out the bedroom window. The shovel tore into the rough-hewed floor, caught between the planks, and he had ruined the floor when he was done. He took a rake from the shed and used it to pull the fungus off the walls. He cleaned the bathroom again and shoveled the fungus off the stairs. Repeatedly, he filled the wheelbarrow and dumped it outside. The fire burned steadily.

It took Michael three hours to clean the cabin and only when he was done, resting in the kitchen, sitting at the butcher-block table and drinking a bottle of beer, did he first see the fungus seeping under the cellar door. It grew rapidly before his eyes, twisting and turning, slipping across the tile floor like a snake. Michael grabbed the shovel and cut through the fungus at the door. The dismembered end continued across the tile with a life of its own.

He jerked open the cellar door to beat back the growth, but

the gray fungus had filled the cellar, was jammed against the door, and when he opened the door it smothered him in an avalanche of mold.

Now it was everywhere. The cupboards burst open and the fungus flopped out and onto the counter. A tide of it pushed aside the food and shoved cans to the floor.

In the living room it grew along the rock fireplace and tumbled down the stairs. It spread across the floor, came up between the cracks in the oak floors. It grew around the tables and chairs and covered all the furniture with a gray dustcover of mold. It oozed from the center of the rolled-up rug, like pus from a sore. There was fungus on the ceiling, crawling towards the peak of the cabin. It was under foot. Michael slipped and slid as he ran from the house.

The fungus crawled along the rock foundation. It filled the deck, and under its weight the wooden supports gave way and the deck crashed to the ground. The pier again was covered and the gray mold came off the wood and across the new lawn, ripping the sod as it moved. It raced towards Michael like a tide.

Michael got the other can of gas from the station wagon. He went inside the house again and poured gas through the living room, splashing it against the wooden stairs, the pine walls. He ran into the kitchen and threw gas in a long, yellow spray at the cupboards, emptying the last of the can on the butcher-block table. When he dropped the can to the floor it sank into the thick fungus with a thud.

He was breathless, panting. His fingers shook and fumbled as he found matches, struck and tossed them at the gas-soaked mold. Flame roared up, ate away at the fungus, caught hold of the pine and oak and walnut with a blaze. In the living room he tossed matches into the liquor cabinet and set fire to the bar. He lit up the stairs and the flame ran along the steps. He tore through the fungus covering the furniture and ignited the couch.

The fungus had grown deep and billowy. It was as if Michael

was trying to stand on top a deflating parachute. He kept slipping and falling as the lumpy surface changed directions and expanded. The floor was a sea of mold. The front door was almost blocked from view. Gray smoke began to choke him. He tumbled towards the door and fungus swelled under foot and knocked him aside.

Michael found the shovel and used it to rip through the layers of wet mold. He cut a path, like digging a trench, to the outside. He ran for the station wagon. The fungus had reached the parking space and lapped at the wheels of the car.

Behind him the cabin blazed. Flames reached the shingled roof and leaped up the frame siding. The house burned like a bonfire. He spun the car around. The wheels slid over the slick mold like the car was caught on a field of ice, but he kept the station wagon on the gravel and tromped on the gas. The car fishtailed down the drive and onto the safety of the county road. Michael drove for his life.

"It's a total loss?" Barbara asked again, still confused by Michael's tale. Her blue saucer eyes looked puzzled.

Michael nodded. "In the rearview mirror I could see most of it in flames. I didn't have the courage to go back and check." He spoke with a new honesty and sense of awe.

"But to burn down our own home! Wasn't there some other way . . . ?" She stared at Michael. It was unbelievable. He had arrived at the apartment after midnight, trembling and incoherent. She had wanted to call a doctor, but he raged and struck her when she said he needed help. She cowered in the corner of the couch, shaking and frightened, as he paced the room and told her about the fungus and the fire.

"I tried to keep cleaning it with soap and water, but it kept . . ." He began to cry, deep, chest-rending sobs. She went quickly to him and smothered him against her breasts. She could smell the smoke in his hair, the bitter smell of wood that had smoldered in the rain.

"A smoke?" Barbara suggested. "It will calm you down." She rolled them a joint. Her hands were trembling with excitement. It was the first time in years that he had hit her, and the blow had both frightened and excited her. Her skin tingled.

They passed the joint back and forth as they sat huddled on the couch, like two lone survivors. Michael, again, and in great detail and thoroughness, told about the fungus, and why he had to burn the cabin.

"I know you were absolutely right," Barbara kept saying to reassure him, but in the back of her mind, growing like a cancer, was her doubt. To stop her own suspicious thoughts and his now insistent explanations, she interrupted, "Darling . . ." And she reached to unbutton his shirt.

They did not make it to the bedroom. Michael slipped his hands inside her blouse, then he pulled her to the floor and took his revenge and defeat out on her. It was brief and violent and cathartic.

Michael held her tenderly, arms wrapped around her, hugging her to him. He turned her head and kissed her eyes. It was all right, she whispered. He was home and safe and she would take care of him.

Yes, Michael thought, everything was all right. He was home in the city and they would forget the mountains and the second home on the lake. He had his writing and he had her, and that was all that mattered. And then his lips touched the candle-gray fungus that grew in a thin, irregular patch more than twelve inches wide across her breasts like a bra.

ROBERT R. McCAMMON

Makeup

Stealing the thing was so *easy*. Calvin Doss had visited the Hollywood Museum of Memories on Beverly Boulevard at three A.M., admitting himself through a side door with a hooked sliver of metal he took from the black leather pouch he kept under his jacket, close to his heart.

He'd roamed the long halls—past the chariots used in *Ben Hur*, past the tent set from *The Sheik*, past the *Frankenstein* lab mock-up—but he knew exactly where he was going. He'd come there the day before, with the paying tourists. And so ten minutes after he'd slipped into the place he was standing in the Memorabilia Room, foil stars glittering from the wallpaper wherever the beam of his pencil flashlight touched. Before him were locked glass display cases: one of them was full of wigs on faceless mannequin heads; the next held bottles of perfume used as props in a dozen movies by Lana Turner, Loretta Young, Hedy Lamarr; in the next case were shelves of paste jewelry—diamonds, rubies and emeralds—blazing like Rodeo Drive merchandise.

And then there was the display case Calvin sought, its shelves holding wooden boxes in a variety of sizes and colors. He moved the flashlight's beam to a lower shelf, and there was the large black box he'd come to take. The lid was open; within Calvin could see the trays of tubes, little numbered jars and what looked like crayons wrapped up in waxed paper. Beside the box was a small white card with a couple of lines of type:

Makeup case once belonging to Jean Harlow.
Purchased from the Harlow Estate.

All right! Calvin thought. That's the ticket. He zipped open his metal pouch, stepped around behind the display case to the lock and worked for a few minutes to find the proper lockpick from his ample supply.

Easy.

And now it was almost dawn, and Calvin Doss sat in his small apartment with kitchenette off Sunset Boulevard, smoking a joint to relax and staring at the black box that sat before him on a card table. There was nothing to it, really, Calvin thought. Just a bunch of jars and tubes and crayons, and most of those seemed to be so dry they were crumbling to pieces. The box itself wasn't even attractive. Junk, as far as Calvin was concerned. How Mr. Marco thought he could push the thing to some LA collector was beyond him; now, those fake jewels and wigs he could understand, but this? No way!

The box was chipped and scarred, showing bare wood beneath the black lacquer at three of the corners. The lock was unusual: it was a silver claw, a human hand with long, sharp fingernails. It was tarnished with age but seemed to work okay. Mr. Marco would appreciate that, Calvin thought. The makeup looked all dried out, but when Calvin unscrewed some of the numbered jars he caught faint whiffs of strange odors: from one a cold, clammy smell, like graveyard dirt, from another the smell of candle wax and metal; from a third an odor like a swamp teeming with reptilian life. None of the makeup carried a brand name nor any evidence where it had been bought or manufactured. Some of the crayons crumbled into pieces when he picked them out of their tray, and he flushed the bits down the toilet so Mr. Marco wouldn't find out he'd been tinkering with them.

Gradually the joint overpowered him. He closed the case's lid, snapped down the silver claw, and went to sleep on his sofa bed thinking of Deenie.

He awakened with a start. The harsh afternoon sun was streaming through the dusty blinds. He fumbled for his wristwatch. Oh God! he thought. Two-forty! He'd been told to call Mr. Marco at nine if the job went okay; panic flared within him as he went out to the pay phone at the end of the hall.

Mr. Marco's secretary answered at the antique shop on Rodeo Drive in Beverly Hills. "Who may I say is calling, please?"

"Tell him Cal. Cal Smith."

"Just a moment, please."

Another phone was picked up. "Marco here."

"It's me, Mr. Marco. Cal Doss. I've got the makeup case, and the whole job went like a dream."

"A dream?" the voice asked softly. There was a quiet murmur of laughter, like water running over dangerous rocks. "Is that what you'd call it, Calvin? If that's the case, your sleep must be terribly uneasy. Have you seen this morning's *Times?*"

"No, sir." Calvin's heart was beating faster. Something had gone wrong; something had been screwed up royally. The noise of his heartbeat seemed to fill the telephone receiver.

"I'm surprised the police haven't visited you already, Calvin. It seems you touched off a concealed alarm when you broke into the display case. Ah. Here's the story, section two, page seven." There was the noise of paper unfolding. "A silent alarm, of course. The police think they arrived at the scene just as you were leaving; one of the officers even thinks he saw your car. A gray Volkswagen with a dented left rear fender? Does that ring a bell, Calvin?"

"My . . . Volkswagen's light green," Cal said, his throat tightening. "I . . . got the banged fender in the Club Zoom's parking lot."

"Indeed? I suggest you begin packing, my boy. Mexico might be nice at this time of year. If you'll excuse me now, I have other business to attend to. Have a nice trip—"

"Wait! Mr. Marco! Please!"

"Yes?" The voice was as cold and hard as a glacier.

"So I screwed up the job. So what? Anybody can have a bad night, Mr. Marco. I've got the makeup case! I can bring it over to you, you can give me the three Gs, and then I can pick up my girl and head down to Mexico for . . . *What is it?*"

Mr. Marco had started chuckling again, that cold mirthless laughter that always sent a chill skittering up Calvin's spine. Calvin could envision him in his black leather chair, the armrests carved into the faces of growling lions. His broad, moonlike face would be almost expressionless: the eyes dull and deadly, as black as the business end of a double-barreled shotgun, the mouth slightly crooked to one side, parted lips as red as slices of raw liver. "I'm afraid you don't understand, Calvin," he finally said. "I owe you nothing. It seems that you stole the wrong makeup case."

"*What?*" Calvin said hoarsely.

"It's all in the *Times*, dear boy. Oh, don't blame yourself. *I* don't. It was a mistake made by some hopeless idiot at the museum. Jean Harlow's makeup case was switched with one from the Chamber of Horrors. Her case is ebony with diamonds stitched into a red silk lining, supposedly to signify her love affairs. The one you took belonged to a horror-film actor named Orlon Kronsteen, who was quite famous in the late thirties and forties for his monster makeups. He was murdered . . . oh, ten or eleven years ago, in a Hungarian castle he had rebuilt in the Hollywood hills. Poor devil. I recall his headless body was found dangling from a chandelier. So. Mistakes will happen, won't they? Now if you'll forgive me—"

"Please!" Cal said, desperation almost choking him. "Maybe . . . maybe you can sell this horror guy's makeup case?"

"A possibility. Some of his better films—*Dracula Rises*,

Revenge of the Wolf, London Screams—are still dredged up for late-night television. But it would take time to find a collector, Calvin, and that makeup case is very hot indeed. *You're* hot, Calvin, and I suspect you will be cooling off shortly up at the Chino prison."

"I . . . I need that three thousand dollars, Mr. Marco! I've got plans!"

"Do you? As I say, I owe you nothing. But take a word of warning, Calvin: Go far away, and keep your lips sealed about my . . . uh . . . activities. I'm sure you're familiar with Mr. Crawley's methods?"

"Yeah," Calvin said. "Yes, sir." His heart and head were pounding in unison. Mr. Crawley was Marco's "enforcer," a six-foot-five skeleton of a man whose eyes blazed with blood lust whenever he saw Calvin. "But . . . what am I going to *do?*"

"I'm afraid you're a little man, dear boy, and what little men do is not my concern. I'll tell you instead what you aren't going to do. You aren't going to call this office again. You aren't going to come here again. You aren't ever going to mention my name as long as you live . . . which, if it were up to Mr. Crawley, who is standing just outside my door at this moment, would be less than the time it takes for you to hang up the phone. Which is precisely what *I* am about to do." There was a last chuckle of cold laughter and the phone went dead.

Calvin stared at the receiver for a moment, hoping it might rewaken. It buzzed at him like a Bronx cheer. Slowly he put it back on its cradle, then he walked like a zombie toward his room. He heard sirens and panic exploded within him, but they were far in the distance and receding. What am I going to do? he thought, his brain ticking like a broken record. *What am I going to do?* He closed and bolted his door and then turned toward the makeup case on the table.

Its lid was open, and Calvin thought that was odd because he remembered—or thought he remembered—closing it last night. The silver claw was licked with dusty light. Of all the stupid screwups! he thought, anger welling up inside. *Stupid, stupid, stupid!* He crossed the room in two strides and lifted the case over his head to smash it to pieces on the floor.

Suddenly, something seemed to bite his fingers and he howled in pain, dropping the case back onto the table; it overturned, spilling jars and crayons.

There was a red welt across Calvin's fingers where the lid had snapped down like a lobster's claw. *It bit me!* he thought, backing away from the thing.

The silver claw gleamed, one finger crooked as if in invitation.

"I've got to get rid of you!" Calvin said, startled by the sound of his own voice. "If the cops find you here I'm up the creek!" He stuffed all the spilled makeup back into it, closed the lid and tentatively poked at it for a minute before picking it up. Then he carried it along the corridor to the back stairway and down to the narrow alley that ran behind the building. He pushed the black makeup case deep inside a garbage can, underneath an old hat, a few empty bottles of Boone's Farm and a Dunkin Donuts box. Then he returned to the pay phone and, trembling, dialed Deenie's apartment number. There was no answer, so he called the Club Zoom.

Mike the bartender picked up the phone. "How's it goin', Cal?" In the background the Eagles were on the jukebox, singing about life in the fast lane. He asked if Deenie was there. "Nope, Cal. Deenie's not comin' in today until six. Sorry. You want to leave a message or something?"

"No," Calvin said. "Thanks anyway." He hung up and returned to his room. Where the hell was Deenie? he wondered. It seemed she was never where she was supposed to be; she never called, never let him know where she was. Hadn't he bought her a nice gold-plated necklace with a couple of diamond specks on it to show her he wasn't mad at her for stringing along that old guy from Bel Air? It had cost him plenty too, and had put him in his current financial mess. He slammed his fist down on the card table and tried to sort things out.

Somehow he had to get some money. He could hock his radio and maybe collect an old pool-hall debt from Corky McClinton, but that would hardly be enough to carry Deenie and him for very long in Mexico. He had to have that three thousand dollars from Mr. Marco! But what about Crawley? That killer would shave his eyebrows with a .45!

What to do, what to do?

First, Calvin reasoned, a drink to calm my nerves. He opened a cupboard and brought out a glass and a bottle of Jim Beam. His fingers were shaking so much he couldn't pour, so he shoved the glass aside and swigged out of the bottle. It burned like hellfire going down. Damn that makeup case! he thought, and he took another drink. Damn Mr. Marco—another drink. Damn Crawley. Damn Deenie. Damn the idiot who switched those lousy makeup cases. Damn me for even taking on this screwy job. . . .

After he'd finished damning his second and third cousins who lived in Arizona, Calvin stretched out on the sofa bed and slept.

He came awake with a single terrifying thought: *the cops are here!* But they weren't, there was no one else in the room, everything was okay. His head was throbbing, and through the small, smog-filmed windows the light was graying into night. What'd I do? he thought. Sleep away the whole day? He reached over toward the Jim Beam bottle, on the card table beside the makeup case, and saw that there was about a half-swallow left in it. He tipped it to his mouth and drank it down, adding to the turmoil in his belly.

When his fogged gaze finally came to rest on the makeup case he dropped the bottle to the floor.

Its lid was wide open, the silver claw cupping blue shadows.

"What are you doin' here?" he said, his speech slurred. "I got rid of you! Didn't I?" He was trying to think. He seemed to remember taking that thing to the garbage can, but then again it might've been a dream. "You're a jinx, that's what you are!" he shouted. He struggled up, staggered out into the hallway to the pay phone again and dialed the antique shop.

A low, cold voice answered: "Marco Antiques and Curios."

Calvin shuddered; it was Crawley. "This is Calvin Doss," he said, summoning up his courage. "Doss. DOSS. Let me speak to Mr. Marco."

"Mr. Marco doesn't want to speak to you."

"Listen, I need my three thousand bucks!"

"Mr. Marco is working tonight, Doss. Stop tying up the phone."

"I just . . . I just want what's comin' to me!"

"Oh? Then maybe I can help you, you little punk. How's about two or three .45 slugs to rattle around in your brainpan? I dare you to set foot over here!" The phone was dead before Calvin could say another word.

He put his head in his hands. Little punk. Little man. Little jerk. It seemed someone had been calling him those names all his life, from his mother to the juvenile home creeps to the LA cops. I'm not a little punk! he thought. Someday I'll show them all! He stumbled to his room, slamming his shoulder against a wall in the process. He had to turn on the lights before darkness totally filled the place.

And now he saw that the black makeup case had crept closer to the table's edge.

He stared at it, transfixed by that silver claw. "There's something funny about you," he said softly. "Something reeeeallll funny. I put you in the garbage! Didn't I?" And now, as he watched it, the claw's forefinger seemed to . . . move. To bend. To beckon. Calvin rubbed his eyes. It hadn't moved, not really! Or had it?

Had it?

Calvin touched it, then whimpered and drew his hand away. Something had shivered up his arm, like a faint charge of electricity. "*What are you?*" he whispered. He reached out to close the lid; this time the claw seemed to clutch at his hand, pull it down into the box itself. He shouted "*Hey!*" and when he pulled his hand back he saw he was gripping one of the jars of makeup, identified by the single number nine.

The lid dropped.

Calvin jumped. The claw had latched itself into place. For a long time he looked at the jar in his hand, then slowly, very slowly, unscrewed the top. It was grayish stuff, like greasepaint, with the distinct odor of . . . what was it? he thought. Yes. *Blood.* That, and a cold, mossy smell. He dabbed a finger in it and rubbed it into the palm of his hand. It tingled, and seemed to be so cold it was hot. He smeared his hands with the stuff. The feeling wasn't unpleasant. No, Calvin decided; it was far from unpleasant. The feeling was of . . . power. Of invincibility. Of wanting to throw himself into the arms of the night, to fly with the clouds as they swept across the moon's grinning face. Feels good, he thought, as he smeared some of the stuff on his face. God, if Deenie could only see me now! He began to smile. His face felt funny, filmed with the cold stuff but different, as if the bone structure had sharpened. His mouth and jaw felt different, too.

I want my three thousand dollars from Mr. Marco, he told himself. And I'm going to get it. Yesssssss. I'm going to get it right now.

After a while he pushed aside the empty jar and turned toward the door, his muscles vibrating with power. He felt as old as time, but filled with incredible, wonderful, ageless youth. He moved like an uncoiling serpent to the door, then into the hallway. Now it was time to collect the debt.

He drifted like a haze of smoke through the darkness and slipped into his Volkswagen. He drove through Hollywood, noting the white sickle moon rising over the Capitol Records building, and into Beverly Hills. At a traffic light he could sense someone staring at him from the car beside his; he turned his head slightly, and the young woman at the wheel of her Mercedes froze, terror stitched across her face. When the light changed he drove on, leaving the Mercedes sitting still.

Yessssss. It was definitely time to collect the debt.

He pulled his car to the curb on Rodeo Drive, two shops down from the royal blue and gold canopy with the lettering

MARCO ANTIQUES AND CURIOS. Most of the expensive shops were closed, and there were only a few window shoppers on the sidewalks. Calvin walked toward the antique shop. Of course the door was locked, the blind pulled down, and a sign read SORRY, WE'RE CLOSED. I should've brought my tool kit! he told himself. But no matter. Tonight he could do magic; tonight there were no impossibilities. He imagined what he wanted to do; then he exhaled and slipped through, around the doorjamb like a gray, wet mist. Doing it scared the hell out of him and caused one window shopper to clutch at his heart and fall like a redwood to the pavement.

Calvin stood in a beige-carpeted display room filled with gleaming antiques: a polished rosewood piano once owned by Rudolph Valentino, a brass bed from the Pickford estate, a lamp with a shade shaped like a rose once belonging to Vivien Leigh. Objects of silver, brass and gold were spotlit by ceiling track lights. Calvin could hear Mr. Marco's voice from the rear of the shop, through a door that led back into a short hallway and Marco's office. ". . . That's all well and good, Mr. Frazier," he was saying. "I hear what you're telling me, but I'm not listening. I have a buyer for that item, and if I want to sell it I must make delivery tomorrow afternoon at the latest." There were a few seconds pause. "Correct, Mr. Frazier. It's not my concern how your people get the Flynn diary. But I'll expect it to be on my desk at two o'clock tomorrow afternoon, is that understood?"

Calvin began to smile. He moved across the room as silently as smoke, entered the hallway and approached the closed door to Marco's office.

He was about to turn the doorknob when he heard Marco hang up his telephone. "Now, Mr. Crawley," Marco said. "Where were we? Ah, yes; the matter of Calvin Doss. I very much fear that we cannot trust the man to remain silent in the face of adversity. You know where he lives, Mr. Crawley. I'll have your payment ready for you when you return."

Calvin reached forward, gripped the doorknob and wrenched

at it. He was amazed and quite pleased when the entire door was ripped from its hinges.

Marco, behind a massive mahogany desk, his three hundred pounds wedged into the chair with the lion faces on the armrests, gave out a startled squawk, his black eyes almost popping from his head. Crawley had been sitting in a corner holding a *Hustler* magazine; now, like a released coil, he sprang up to a towering height, his eyes glittering like cold diamonds beneath thick black brows. Crawley's hand went up under his checked sports coat, but Calvin froze him with a single glance.

Marco's face was the color of spoiled cheese. "Who . . . who are you?" he said, his voice trembling. "What do you want?"

"Don't you recognize me?" Calvin asked, his voice as smooth and dark as black velvet. "I'm Calvin Doss, Mr. Marco."

"Cal . . . vin?" A thread of saliva broke over Marco's double chins and fell onto the lapel of his charcoal gray Brooks Brothers suit. "No! It can't be!"

"But it is." Calvin grinned and felt his fangs protrude. "I've come for my restitution, Mr. Marco."

"*Kill him!*" Marco shrieked to Crawley. "KILL HIM!"

Crawley was still dazed, but he instinctively pulled the automatic from the holster beneath his coat and stuck it into Calvin's ribs. Calvin had no time to leap aside; Crawley's finger was already twitching on the trigger. In the next instant the gun barked twice, and Calvin felt a distant sensation of heat that just as quickly faded. Behind him, through the haze of blue smoke, were two bullet holes in the wall. Calvin couldn't exactly understand why his stomach wasn't torn open right now, but this was indeed a night of miracles; he grasped the man's collar and with one hand flung him like a scarecrow across the room. Crawley screamed and slammed into the opposite wall, collapsing to the floor in a tangle of arms and legs. He skittered past Calvin like a frantic crab and ran away along the corridor.

"*Crawley!*" Marco shouted, trying to get out of his chair. "DON'T LEAVE ME!"

Calvin shoved the desk forward as effortlessly as if it were a matter of dreams, pinning the bulbous Marco in his chair. Marco began to whimper, his eyes floating in wet sockets. Calvin was grinning like a death's head. "And now," he whispered, "it is time for you to pay." He reached out and grapsed the man's tie, slowly tightening it until Marco's face looked like a bloated red balloon. Then Calvin leaned forward, very gracefully, and plunged his fangs into the throbbing jugular vein. A fountain of blood gushed, dripping from the corners of Calvin's mouth. In another few moments Marco's corpse, which seemed to have lost about seventy-five pounds, slumped down in its chair, its shoulders squashed together and the arms up as if in total surrender.

Calvin stared at the body for a moment, a wave of nausea suddenly rising from the pit of his stomach. He felt light-headed, out of control, lost in a larger shadow. He turned and struggled out to the hallway, where he bent over and retched. Nothing came up, but the taste of blood in his mouth made him wish he had a bar of soap. *What have I done?* he thought, leaning against a wall. Sweat was dripping down his face, plastering his shirt to his back. He looked down at his side, to where there were two holes in his shirt, ringed with powder burns. That should've killed me. Why didn't it? How did I get in here? Why did I . . . kill Mr. Marco like that? He spat once, then again and again; the taste of blood was maddening. He probed at his gums with a finger. His teeth were normal now, everything was back to normal.

What did that makeup case turn me into? He wiped the sweat from his face with a handkerchief and stepped back into the office. Yep. Mr. Marco was still dead. The two bullet holes were still in the wall. Calvin wondered where Marco kept his money. Cal figured, since he was dead, Marco wouldn't need it any more. Right? Calvin leaned over the desk, avoiding the fixed stare of the corpse's eyes, and started going through the drawers. In a lower one, beneath all kinds of papers and other junk, was a white envelope with the name CRAWLEY printed on it. Calvin looked inside. His heart leaped. There were at least five thousand dollars in there—probably the dough Crawley was going to be paid for my murder, Calvin thought. He took the money and ran.

Fifteen minutes later he was pulling into the parking lot beside the Club Zoom. In the red neon-veined light he counted the money again, trembling with joy. Fifty-five hundred bucks! It was more money than he'd ever seen in his whole life.

He desperately needed some beer to wash away the taste of blood. Deenie would be dancing in there by now. He put the money in a back pocket and hurried across the parking lot into the club. Inside, strobe lights flashed like crazy lightning. A jukebox thundered from somewhere in the darkness, its bass beat kicking at Calvin's unsettled stomach. A few men sat at the bar or at a scattering of tables, drinking beer and watching the girl on stage who gyrated her hips in a disinterested circle. Calvin climbed onto a bar stool. "Hey, Mike! Gimme a beer! Deenie here yet?"

"Yeah. She's in the back." Mike shoved a mug of beer in front of him and then frowned. "You okay, Cal? You look like you saw a ghost or something."

"I'm fine. Or will be, as soon as I finish this off." He drank most of it in one swallow, swishing it around in his mouth. "That's better."

"What's better, Cal?"

"Nothing. Forget it. Jeez, it's cold in here!"

"You sure you're okay?" Mike asked, looking genuinely concerned. "It must be eighty degrees in here. The air conditioner broke again this afternoon."

"Don't worry about me. I'm just fine. Soon as I see my girl I'll be even better."

"Uh huh," Mike said quietly. He cleaned up a few splatters of beer from the bar with a rag. "I hear you bought Deenie a present last week. A gold chain. Put you back much?"

"About a hundred bucks. It's worth it, though, just to see that pretty smile. I'm going to ask her to go down to Mexico with me for a few days."

"Uh huh," Mike said again. Now he was cleaning up imaginary splatters, and finally he looked Calvin straight in the eyes. "You're a good guy, Cal. You never cause any trouble in here, and I can tell you're okay. I just . . . well, I hate to see you get what's coming."

"Huh? What do you mean by that?"

Mike shrugged. "How long have you known Deenie, Cal? A few weeks? Girls like her come and go, man. Here one day, gone the next. Sure she's good looking; they all are, and they trade on their looks like their bodies are Malibu beachfront properties. You get my drift?"

"No."

"Okay. This is man to man. Friend to friend, right? Deenie's a taker, Cal. She'll bleed you dry, and then she'll kick you out with the garbage. She's got about five or six guys on the string."

Calvin blinked, his stomach roiling again. "You're . . . you're lying!"

"God's truth. Deenie's playing you, Cal; reeling you in and out like a fish with a hooked gut—"

"You're lying!" Calvin's face flushed; he rose from his seat and leaned over toward the bartender. "You've got no right saying those things! They're lies! You probably want me to give her up so *you* can have her! Fat chance! I'm going back to see her right now, and you'd better not try to stop me!" He started to move away from the bar, his brain spinning like a top.

"Cal," Mike said softly, his voice tinged with pity, "Deenie's not alone."

But Calvin was already going back behind the stage, through a black curtain to the dressing rooms. Deenie's room was the third door, and as Calvin was about to knock he heard the deep roll of a man's laughter. He froze, his hand balled into a fist.

"A diamond ring?" the man said. "You're kidding!"

"Honest to God, Ray!" Deenie's voice, warmer than Calvin had ever heard it. "This old guy gave me a diamond ring last week! I think he used to work for NBC, or ABC or one of those

Cs. Anyway, he's all washed up now. Do you know what he wears in bed? Socks with garters! Ha! He said he wanted me to marry him. He must've been serious because that ring brought six hundred bucks at the pawn shop!"

"Oh yeah? Then where's my share?"

"Later, baby, later. I'll meet you at your place after work, okay? We can do the shower thing and rub each other's backs, huh?"

There was a long silence in which Calvin could hear his teeth grinding together.

"Sure, babe," Ray said finally. "You want to use the black one or the red one tonight?"

Calvin almost slammed his fist through the door. But instead he turned and ran, a volcano about to erupt in his brain; he ran past the bar, past Mike, out the door to his car. I thought she loved me! he raged as he screeched out of the parking lot. She *lied!* She played me for a sucker all the way! He floored the accelerator, gripping the wheel with white-knuckled hands.

By the time he locked himself in his apartment, turned his transistor radio up loud and flopped down on his sofa bed, the volcano had exploded, filling his veins with the seething magma of revenge. *Revenge*—now there's a sweet word, he thought. It was Satan's battle cry, and now seemed branded into Calvin's heart. How to do it? he wondered How? How? *Why am I always the little punk?*

He turned his head slightly and gazed at the black makeup case.

It was open again, the silver claw beckoning him.

"You're a jinx!" he screamed at it. But he knew now that it was more. Much, much more. It was weird, evil maybe, but there was power in those little jars: power and perhaps also revenge. *No!* he told himself. No, I won't use it! What kind of nutcake am I turning into, to think that makeup could bring me what I want? He stared at the case, his eyes widening. It was unholy, terrible, something from Lucifer's magic shop. He was aware of the roll of money in his back pocket, and aware also of the bullet holes in his shirt. Unholy or not, he thought, it can give me what I want.

Calvin reached into the makeup case and chose a jar at random. It was numbered thirteen, and when he sniffed at the cream he found it smelled of dirty brick, rain slick streets, whale-oil lamps. He dabbed his finger into the reddish-brown goop and stared at it for a moment, the odor making him feel giddy and—quite mad.

He smeared the makeup across his cheeks and worked it into the flesh. His eyes began to gleam with maniacal determination. He scooped out more of it, rubbing it into his face, his hands, his neck. It burned like mad passion.

The lid of the box fell. The claw clicked into place.

Calvin smiled and stood up. Stepping to a kitchen drawer, he opened it and withdrew a keen-bladed butcher knife. Now, he thought. Now, me Miss Deenie Roundheels, it's time you got your just deserts, wot? Can't have ladies like you runnin' about in the streets, prancin' and hawkin' your sweet goods to the highest bidder, can we, luv? No, not if I've got a bit to say about it!

And so he hurried out of the apartment and down to his car, a man on an urgent mission of love's revenge.

He waited in the shadows behind the Club Zoom until Deenie came out just after two o'clock. She was alone, and he was glad of that because he had no quarrel with Ray; it was the woman—it was Woman—who had betrayed him. She was a beautiful girl with long blond hair, sparkling blue eyes, a sensual pout in a lovely oval face. Tonight she was wearing a green dress, slit to show silky thighs. A sinner's gown, he thought as he watched her slink across the parking lot.

Stepping out of the darkness, he held the knife behind him like a gleaming gift he wanted to surprise her with. "Deenie?" he whispered, smiling. "Deenie, luv?"

She whirled around. "Who's there?"

Calvin stood between darkness and the red swirl of neon. His eyes glittered like pools of blood. "It's your own true love, Deenie," he said. "Your love come to take you to Paradise."

"Calvin?" she whispered, taking a backward step. "What are you doing here? Why . . . does your face look like that?"

"I've brought something for you, luv," he said softly. "Step over here and I'll give it to you. Come on, dearie, don't be shy."

"What's wrong with you, Calvin? You're scaring me."

"Scaring you? Why, whatever for? I'm your own dear Cal, come to kiss you goodnight. And I've brought a pretty for you. Something nice and bright. Come see."

She hesitated, glancing toward the deserted boulevard.

"Come on," Calvin said. "It'll be the sweetest gift any man ever gave you."

A confused, uncertain smile rippled across her face. "What'd you bring me, Calvin? Huh? Another necklace? Let's see it!"

"I'm holding it behind my back. Come here, luv. Come see."

Deenie stepped forward reluctantly, her eyes as bright as a frightened doe's. When she reached Calvin she held out her hand. "This had better be good, Cal—"

Calvin grasped her wrist and yanked her forward. When her head rocked back he ripped the blade across her offered throat. She staggered and started to fall, but before she did Calvin dragged her behind the Club Zoom so he could take his own sweet time.

When he was finished he looked down at the cooling corpse and wished he had a pencil and paper to leave a note. He knew what it would say: You have to be Smart to catch Me. Smart like a Fox. Yours from the Depths of Hell, Cal the Ripper.

He wiped the blade on her body, got in his car and drove to Hancock Park, where he threw the murder weapon into the La Brea Tar Pits. Then a weak, sick feeling overcame him and he sank down into the grass, clutching his knees up close to his body. He was wracked with shudders when he realized there was blood all over the front of his shirt. He pulled up handfuls of grass and tried to wipe it away. Then he lay back on the ground, his temples throbbing, and tried to think past the pain.

Oh God! he thought. What kind of a makeup case have I gotten my hands onto? Who made the box? Who conjured up those jars and tubes and crayons? It was magic, yes, but evil magic, magic gone bad and ugly. Calvin remembered Mr. Marco saying it had belonged to a horror-flick actor named Kronsteen, and that Kronsteen was famous for his monster makeups. Calvin was chilled by a sudden terrible thought: how much was makeup and how much was real? Half and half, maybe? When you put on the makeup the . . . essence of the monster gripped you like some kind of hungry leech? And then when it had fed, when it had gorged itself on evil and blood, it loosened its hold on you and fell away? Back there in Marco's office, Calvin thought, I really was part vampire. And then, in the Club Zoom's parking lot, I was part Jack the Ripper. In those jars, he thought, are not just makeups; there are real monsters, waiting to be awakened by my desires, my passions, my evil.

I've got to get rid of it, he thought. I've got to throw it out before it destroys me! He rose to his feet and ran across the park to his car.

The hallway on his floor was as dark as a werewolf's dreams at midnight. What happened to the damned light bulbs? Calvin thought as he felt his way toward his door. Weren't they burning when I left?

And then a floorboard creaked very softly, down at the hallway's end.

Calvin turned and stared into the darkness, one hand fumbling with his key. He thought he could make out a vague shape standing over there, but he wasn't sure. His heart whacked against his rib cage as he slid the key home.

He knew it was Crawley a split second before he saw the orange flare from the .45's muzzle. The bullet hit the doorjamb which shattered, pricking his face with wood splinters. He shouted in terror, twisted the doorknob and threw himself into the room. As he slammed the door shut and locked it another bullet came screaming through the wood, about an inch from the left side of his skull. He spun away from the door, trying to press himself into the wall.

"Where's that five thousand bucks, Doss?" Crawley shouted from the hallway. "It's mine! Give it to me or I'll kill you, you little punk!" A third bullet punched through the center of the door, leaving a hole as big as a fist. Then Crawley began to kick at the door, making it shudder on its aged hinges. Now there were screams and shouts from all over the building, but the door was about to crash in and soon Crawley would be inside to deliver those two .45 slugs as promised.

Calvin heard a faint *click*.

He whirled around. The silver claw had unlatched itself; the makeup case stood open. He was shaking like a leaf in a hurricane.

The door cracked and whined, protesting the blows from Crawley's shoulder.

Calvin watched it bend inward, almost to the breaking point. Another shot was fired, the bullet shattering a window across the room. He turned and looked fearfully at the makeup case again. It can save me, he thought, that's what I want, and that's what it can do. . . .

"I'm gonna blow out your brains when I get in there, Doss!" Crawley roared.

And then Calvin was across the room; he grabbed a jar numbered fifteen. The thing practically unscrewed itself, and he could smell the mossy, mountain forest odor. He plunged a forefinger into it, hearing the door begin to split down the middle.

"I'm gonna kill you, Doss!" Crawley said, and with his next kick the door burst open.

Calvin whirled to face his attacker, who froze in absolute terror. As Calvin leaped he howled in animal rage, his claws stripping red lines across Crawley's face. They fell to the floor, Calvin's teeth gnashing at the unprotected throat of his prey.

Beneath him Crawley's body twitched and writhed. He bent over Crawley's remains on all fours, teeth and claws ripping away flesh to the bone. Then he lifted his head and howled with victory.

Calvin fell back, breathing hard. Crawley looked like something that had gone through a meat grinder, and now his twitching arms and legs were beginning to stiffen. The building was full of racket, screaming and shouting from the lower floors. He could hear a police siren fast approaching, but he wasn't afraid; he wasn't afraid at all.

He stood up, stepped over a spreading pool of blood and peered down into Orlon Kronsteen's makeup case. In there was power. In there were a hundred disguises, a hundred masks. With this thing he would never be called a little punk again. It would be so easy to hide from the cops. So easy. If he desired, it would be done. He picked up a jar numbered nineteen. When he unscrewed it he sniffed at the white, almost clear greasepaint and realized it smelled of . . . nothing. He smeared it over his hands and face. Hide me, he thought. Hide me. The siren stopped, right outside the building. Hurry! Calvin commanded whatever force ruled the contents of this box. Make me . . . disappear!

The lid fell.

The silver claw clicked into place with a noise like a whisper.

The two LAPD cops, Ortega and Mullinax, had never seen a man as ripped apart as the corpse that lay on the apartment's floor. Ortega bent over the body, his face wrinkled with nausea. "This guy's long gone," he said. "Better call for the morgue wagon."

"What's this?" Mullinax said, avoiding the shimmering pool of blood that had seeped from the slashed stiff. He unlatched the black box that was sitting on the card table and lifted the lid. "Looks like . . . theatrical makeup," he said quietly. "Hey, Luis! This thing fits the description of what was stolen from the Memory Museum last night!"

"Huh?" Ortega came over to have a look. "Christ, Phil! It is! That stuff belonged to Orlon Kronsteen. Remember him?"

"Nope. Where'd that landlady get off to?"

"I think she's still throwing up," Ortega said. He picked up an opened jar and smelled the contents, then dropped it back into the case. "I must've seen every horror flick Kronsteen ever starred in." He looked uneasily at the corpse and shivered. "As a matter of fact, amigo, that poor fella looks like what was left of one of Kronsteen's victims in *Revenge of the Wolf.* What could tear a man up like that, Phil?"

"I don't know. And don't try putting the scare in me, either." Mullinax turned his head and stared at something else on the floor, over beyond the unmade sofa bed. "My God," he said softly. "Look at that!" He stepped forward a few paces and then stopped, his eyes narrowing. "Luis, did you hear something?"

"Huh? No. What's that over there? Clothes?"

"Yeah." Mullinax bent down, his brow furrowing. Spread out before him, still bearing a man's shape, were a shirt, a pair of pants, and shoes. The shoelaces were still tied, the socks in the shoes; the belt and zipper were still fastened as well. Mullinax untucked the shirttail, noting bloodstains and what looked like two cigarette burns, and saw a pair of shorts still in place in the pants. "That's funny," he said. "That's damned funny. . . ."

Ortega's eyes were as wide as saucers. "Yeah. Funny. Like that flick Kronsteen did, *The Invisible Man Returns.* He left his clothes just like that when he . . . uh . . . vanished."

"I think we're going to need some help on this one," Mullinax said, and he stood up. His face had turned a pasty gray color, and now he looked past Ortega to the rotund woman in a robe and curlers who stood in the doorway. She stared down at the shredded corpse with dreadful fascination. "Mrs. Johnston?" Mullinax said. "Who did you say this apartment belonged to?"

"Cal . . . Cal . . . Calvin Doss," she stammered. "He never pays his rent on time."

"You're sure this isn't him on the floor?"

"Yes. He's . . . a little man. Stands about under my chin. Oh, I think my stomach's going to blow up!" She staggered away, her house shoes dragging.

"Man, what a mess!" Ortega shook his head. "Those empty clothes . . . that's straight out of *The Invisible Man Returns,* I'm telling you!"

"Yeah. Well, I guess we can send this thing back to where it belongs." Mullinax tapped his finger on the black makeup case. "You say a horror actor owned it?"

"Sure did. A long time ago. Now I guess all that stuff is junk, huh?" He smiled faintly. "The stuff dreams are made of, right? I saw most of that guy's flicks twice, when I was a kid. Like the one about the Invisible Man. And there was another one he did that was really something too, called *The Man Who Shrank*. Now *that* was a classic."

"I don't know so much about horror films," Mullinax said. He ran a finger over the silver claw. "They give me the creeps. Why don't you stay up here with our dead friend and I'll radio for the morgue wagon, okay?" He took a couple of steps forward and then stopped. Something was odd. He leaned against the shattered doorjamb and looked at the sole of his shoe. "Ugh!" he said. "What'd I step on?"

WILLIAM F. NOLAN

The Small World of Lewis Stillman

In the waiting, windless dark, Lewis Stillman pressed into the building-front shadows along Wilshire Boulevard. Breathing softly, the automatic poised and ready in his hand, he advanced with animal stealth toward Western Avenue, gliding over the night-cool concrete past ravaged clothing shops, drug and ten-cent stores, their windows shattered, their doors ajar and swinging. The city of Los Angeles, painted in cold moonlight, was an immense graveyard; the tall white tombstone buildings thrust up from the silent pavement, shadow-carved and lonely. Overturned metal corpses of trucks, buses and automobiles littered the streets.

He paused under the wide marquee of the Fox Wiltern. Above his head, rows of splintered display bulbs gaped—sharp glass teeth in wooden jaws. Lewis Stillman felt as though they might drop at any moment to pierce his body.

Four more blocks to cover. His destination: a small corner delicatessen four blocks south of Wilshire, on Western. Tonight he intended bypassing the larger stores like Safeway or Thriftimart, with their available supplies of exotic foods; a smaller grocery was far more likely to have what he needed. He was finding it more and more difficult to locate basic foodstuffs. In the big supermarkets only the more exotic and highly spiced canned and bottled goods remained—and he was sick of caviar and oysters!

Crossing Western, he had almost reached the far curb when he saw some of *them*. He dropped immediately to his knees behind the rusting bulk of an Oldsmobile. The rear door on his side was open, and he cautiously eased himself into the back seat of the deserted car. Releasing the safety catch on the automatic, he peered through the cracked window at six or seven of them, as they moved toward him along the street. God! Had he been seen? He couldn't be sure. Perhaps they were aware of his position! He should have remained on the open street where he'd have a running chance. Perhaps, if his aim was true, he could kill most of them; but, even with its silencer, the gun might be heard and more of them would come. He dared not fire until he was certain they had discovered him.

They came closer, their small dark bodies crowding the walk, six of them, chattering, leaping, cruel mouths open, eyes glittering under the moon. Closer. Their shrill pipings increased, rose in volume. Closer. Now he could make out their sharp teeth and matted hair. Only a few feet from the car . . . His hand was moist on the handle of the automatic; his heart thundered against his chest. Seconds away . . .

Now!

Lewis Stillman fell heavily back against the dusty seat-cushion, the gun loose in his trembling hand. They had passed by; they had missed him. Their thin pipings diminished, grew faint with distance.

The tomb silence of late night settled around him.

The delicatessen proved a real windfall. The shelves were relatively untouched and he had a wide choice of tinned goods. He found an empty cardboard box and hastily began to transfer the cans from the shelf nearest him.

A noise from behind—a padding, scraping sound.

Lewis Stillman whirled about, the automatic ready.

A huge mongrel dog faced him, growling deep in its throat, four legs braced for assault. The blunt ears were laid flat along the short-haired skull and a thin trickle of saliva seeped from the killing jaws. The beast's powerful chest muscles were bunched for the spring when Stillman acted.

His gun, he knew, was useless; the shots would be heard. Therefore, with the full strength of his left arm, he hurled a heavy can at the dog's head. The stunned animal staggered under the blow, legs buckling. Hurriedly, Stillman gathered his supplies and made his way back to the street.

How much longer can my luck hold? Lewis Stillman wondered, as he bolted the door. He placed the box of tinned goods on a wooden table and lit the tall lamp nearby. Its flickering orange glow illumined the narrow, low-ceilinged room.

Twice tonight, his mind told him, twice you've escaped them—and they could have seen you easily on both occasions if they had been watching for you. They don't know you're alive. But when they find out . . .

He forced his thoughts away from the scene in his mind, away from the horror; quickly he began to unload the box, placing the cans on a long shelf along the far side of the room.

He began to think of women, of a girl named Joan, and of how much he had loved her.

The world of Lewis Stillman was damp and lightless; it was narrow and its cold stone walls pressed in upon him as he moved. He had been walking for several hours; sometimes he would run, because he knew his leg muscles must be kept strong, but he was walking now, following the thin yellow beam of his hooded lantern. He was searching.

Tonight, he thought, I might find another like myself.

Surely, *someone* is down here; I'll find someone if I keep searching. I *must* find someone!

But he knew he would not. He knew he would find only chill emptiness ahead of him in the long tunnels.

For three years he had been searching for another man or woman down here in this world under the city. For three years he had prowled the seven hundred miles of storm drains which threaded their way under the skin of Los Angeles like the veins in a giant's body—and he had found nothing. *Nothing.*

Even now, after all the days and nights of searching, he could not really accept the fact that he was alone, that he was the last man alive in a city of seven million.

The beautiful woman stood silently above him. Her eyes burned softly in the darkness; her fine red lips were smiling. The foam-white gown she wore continually swirled and billowed around her motionless figure.

"Who are you?" he asked, his voice far off, unreal.

"Does it matter, Lewis?"

Her words, like four dropped stones in a quiet pool, stirred him, rippled down the length of his body.

"No." he said. "Nothing matters now except that we've found each other. God, after all these lonely months and years of waiting! I thought I was the last, that I'd never live to see—"

"Hush, my darling." She leaned to kiss him. Her lips were moist and yielding. "I'm here now."

He reached up to touch her cheek, but already she was fading, blending into darkness. Crying out, he clawed desperately for her extended hand. But she was gone, and his fingers rested on a rough wall of damp concrete.

A swirl of milk-fog drifted away in slow rollings down the tunnel.

Rain. Days of rain. The drains had been designed to handle floods so Lewis Stillman was not particularly worried. He had built high, a good three feet above the tunnel floor and the water had never yet risen to this level. But he didn't like the sound of the rain down here: an orchestrated thunder through the tunnels, a trap-drumming amplified and continuous. And since he had been unable to make his daily runs he had been reading more than usual. Short stories by Welty, Gordimer, Aiken, Irwin Shaw and Hemingway; poems by Frost, Lorca, Sandburg, Millay, Dylan Thomas. Strange, how unreal this present day world seemed when he read their words. Unreality, however, was fleeting, and the moment he closed a book the loneliness and the fears pressed back. He hoped the rain would stop soon.

Dampness. Surrounding him, the cold walls and the chill and the dampness. The unending gurgle and drip of water, the hollow, tapping splash of the falling drops. Even in his cot, wrapped in thick blankets, the dampness seemed to permeate his body. Sounds . . . Thin screams, pipings, chatterings, reedy whisperings above his head. They were dragging something along the street, something they'd killed no doubt: an animal—a cat or a dog perhaps . . . Lewis Stillman shifted, pulling the blankets closer about his body. He kept his eyes tightly shut, listening to the sharp, scuffling sounds on the pavement and swore bitterly.

"Damn you," he said. "Damn all of you!"

Lewis Stillman was running, running down the long tunnels. Behind him a tide of midget shadows washed from wall to wall; high, keening cries, doubled and tripled by echoes, rang in his ears. Claws reached for him; he felt panting breath, like hot smoke, on the back of his neck; his lungs were bursting, his entire body aflame.

He looked down at his fast-pumping legs, doing their job with pistoned precision. He listened to the sharp slap of his heels against the floor of the tunnel—and he thought: I might die at any moment, but my *legs* will escape! They will run on down the endless drains and never be caught. They move so fast while my heavy awkward upper-body rocks and sways above them, slowing them down, tiring them—making them angry. How my legs must hate me! I must be clever and humor them, beg them to take me along to safety. How well they run, how sleek and fine!

Then he felt himself coming apart. His legs were detaching themselves from his upper-body. He cried out in horror, flailing the air, beseeching them not to leave him behind. But the legs cruelly continued to unfasten themselves. In a cold surge of terror, Lewis Stillman felt himself tipping, falling toward the damp floor—while his legs raced on with a wild animal life of their own. He opened his mouth, high above those insane legs, and screamed.

Ending the nightmare.

He sat up stiffly in his cot, gasping, drenched in sweat. He drew in a long shuddering breath and reached for a cigarette, lighting it with a trembling hand.

The nightmares were getting worse. He realized that his mind was rebelling as he slept, spilling forth the bottled-up fears of the day during the night hours.

He thought once more about the beginning six years ago, about why he was still alive. The alien ships had struck Earth suddenly, without warning. Their attack had been thorough and deadly. In a matter of hours the aliens had accomplished their clever mission—and the men and women of Earth were destroyed. A few survived, he was certain. He had never seen any of them, but he was convinced they existed. Los Angeles was not the world, after all, and since he escaped so must have others around the globe. He'd been working alone in the drains when the aliens struck, finishing a special job for the construction company on B tunnel. He could still hear the weird sound of the mammoth ships and feel the intense heat of their passage.

Hunger had forced him out, and overnight he had become a curiosity. The last man alive. For three years he was not harmed. He worked with them, taught them many things, and tried to win their confidence. But, eventually, certain ones came to hate him, to be jealous of his relationship with the others. Luckily he had been able to escape to the drains. That was three years ago and now they had forgotten him.

His subsequent excursions to the upper level of the city had been made under cover of darkness—and he never ventured out unless his food supply dwindled. He had built his one-room structure directly to the side of an overhead grating—not close enough to risk their seeing it, but close enough for light to seep in during the sunlight hours. He missed the warm feel of open sun on his body almost as much as he missed human companionship, but he dare not risk himself above the drains by day.

When the rain ceased, he crouched beneath the street gratings to absorb as much as possible of the filtered sunlight. But the rays were weak and their small warmth only served to heighten his desire to feel direct sunlight upon his naked shoulders.

The dreams . . . always the dreams.

"Are you cold, Lewis?"

"Yes, yes, cold."

"Then go out, dearest. Into the sun."

"I can't. Can't go out."

"But Los Angeles is your world, Lewis! You are the last man in it. The last man in the world."

"Yes, but they own it all. Every street belongs to them, every building. They wouldn't let me come out. I'd die. They'd kill me."

"Go out, Lewis." The liquid dream-voice faded, faded. "Out into the sun, my darling. Don't be afraid."

That night he watched the moon through the street gratings for almost an hour. It was round and full, like a huge yellow floodlamp in the dark sky, and he thought, for the first time in years, of night baseball at Blues Stadium in Kansas City. He used to love watching the games with his father under the mammoth stadium lights when the field was like a pond, frosted with white illumination and the players dreamspawned and unreal. Night baseball was always a magic game to him when he was a boy.

Sometimes he got insane thoughts. Sometimes, on a night like this, when the loneliness closed in like a crushing fist and he could no longer stand it, he would think of bringing one of them down with him, into the drains. One at a time, they might be handled. Then he'd remember their sharp savage eyes, their animal ferocity, and he would realize that the idea was impossible. If one of their kind disappeared, suddenly and without trace, others would certainly become suspicious, begin to search for him—and it would all be over.

Lewis Stillman settled back into his pillow; he closed his eyes and tried not to listen to the distant screams, pipings and reedy cries filtering down from the street above his head.

Finally he slept.

He spent the afternoon with paper women. He lingered over the pages of some yellowed fashion magazines, looking at all the beautifully photographed models in their fine clothes. Slim and enchanting, these page-women, with their cool enticing eyes and perfect smiles, all grace and softness and glitter and swirled cloth. He touched their images with gentle fingers, stroking the tawny paper hair, as though, by some magic formula, he might imbue them with life. Yet, it was easy to imagine that these women had never *really* lived at all—that they were simply painted, in microscopic detail, by sly artists to give the illusion of photos.

He didn't like to think about these women and how they died.

"A toast to courage," smiled Lewis Stillman, raising his wine glass high. It sparkled deep crimson in the lamplit room. "To courage and to the man who truly possesses it!" He drained the glass and hastily refilled it from a tall bottle on the table beside his cot.

"Aren't you going to join me, Mr. H.?" he asked the seated figure slouched over the table, head on folded arms. "Or must I drink alone?"

The figure did not reply.

"Well then—" He emptied the glass, set it down. "Oh, I know all about what one man is supposed to be able to do. Win out alone. Whip the damn world singlehanded. If a fish as big as a mountain and as mean as all sin is out there then this one man is supposed to go get him, isn't that it? Well, Papa H., what if the world is *full* of big fish? Can he win over them all? One man. Alone. Of course he can't. Nosir. Damn well right he can't!"

Stillman moved unsteadily to a shelf in one corner of the small wooden room and took down a slim book.

"Here she is, Mr. H. Your greatest. The one you wrote cleanest and best—*The Old Man and the Sea*. You showed how one man could fight the whole damn ocean." He paused, voice strained and rising. "Well, by God, show me, *now*, how to fight this ocean. My ocean is full of killer fish and I'm one man and I'm alone in it. I'm ready to listen."

The seated figure remained silent.

"Got you now, haven't I, Papa? No answer to this one, eh? Courage isn't enough. Man was not meant to live alone or fight alone—or drink alone. Even with courage he can only do so much alone, and then it's useless. Well, I say it's useless. I say the hell with your book and the hell with *you!*"

Lewis Stillman flung the book straight at the head of the motionless figure. The victim spilled back in the chair; his arms slipped off the table, hung swinging. They were lumpy and handless.

More and more, Lewis Stillman found his thoughts turning to the memory of his father, and of long hikes through the moonlit

Missouri countryside, of hunting trips and warm camp fires, of the deep woods, rich and green in summer. He thought of his father's hopes for his future, and the words of that tall, gray-haired figure often came back to him.

"You'll be a fine doctor, Lewis. Study and work hard and you'll succeed. I know you will."

He remembered the long winter evenings of study at his father's great mahogany desk, poring over medical books and journals, taking notes, sifting and resifting facts. He remembered one set of books in particular—Erickson's monumental three-volume text on surgery, richly bound and stamped in gold. He had always loved those books, above all others.

What had gone wrong along the way? Somehow, the dream had faded; the bright goal vanished and was lost. After a year of pre-med at the University of California he had given up medicine; he had become discouraged and quit college to take a laborer's job with a construction company. How ironic that this move should have saved his life! He'd wanted to work with his hands, to sweat and labor with the muscles of his body. He'd wanted to earn enough to marry Joan and then, later perhaps, he would have returned to finish his courses. It all seemed so far away now, his reason for quitting, for letting his father down.

Now, at this moment, an overwhelming desire gripped him, a desire to pore over Erickson's pages once again, to re-create, even for a brief moment, the comfort and happiness of his childhood.

He'd once seen a duplicate set on the second floor of Pickwick's bookstore in Hollywood, in their used-book department, and now he knew he must go after them, bring the books back with him to the drains. It was a dangerous and foolish desire, but he knew he would obey it. Despite the risk of death, he would go after the books tonight. *Tonight.*

One corner of Lewis Stillman's room was reserved for weapons. His prize, a Thompson submachine gun, had been procured from the Los Angeles police arsenal. Supplementing the Thompson were two automatic rifles, a Lüger, a Colt .45 and a .22 caliber Hornet pistol, equipped with a silencer. He always kept the smallest gun in a spring-clip holster beneath his armpit, but it was not his habit to carry any of the larger weapons with him into the city. On this night, however, things were different.

The drains ended two miles short of Hollywood—which meant he would be forced to cover a long and particularly hazardous stretch of ground in order to reach the bookstore. He therefore decided to take along the .30 caliber Savage rifle in addition to the small hand weapon.

You're a fool, Lewis, he told himself as he slid the oiled Savage from its leather case, risking your life for a set of books. Are they *that* important? Yes, a part of him replied, they are that important. You want these books, then go *after* what you want. If fear keeps you from seeking that which you truly want, if fear holds you like a rat in the dark, then you are worse than a coward. You are a traitor, betraying yourself and the civilization you represent. If a man wants a thing and the thing is good he must go after it, no matter what the cost, or relinquish the right to be called a man. It is better to die with courage than to live with cowardice.

Ah, Papa Hemingway, breathed Stillman, smiling at his own thoughts. I see that you are back with me. I see that your words have rubbed off after all. Well then, all right—let us go after our fish, let us seek him out. Perhaps the ocean will be calm. . . .

Slinging the heavy rifle over one shoulder, Lewis Stillman set off down the tunnels.

Running in the chill night wind. Grass, now pavement, now grass beneath his feet. Ducking into shadows, moving stealthily past shops and theaters, rushing under the cold high moon. Santa Monica Boulevard, then Highland, then Hollywood Boulevard, and finally—after an eternity of heartbeats—the bookstore.

The Pickwick.

Lewis Stillman, his rifle over one shoulder, the small automatic gleaming in his hand, edged silently into the store.

A paper battleground met his eyes.

In the filtered moonlight, a white blanket of broken-backed volumes spilled across the entire lower floor. Stillman shuddered; he could envision them, shrieking, scrabbling at the shelves, throwing books wildly across the room at one another. Screaming, ripping, destroying.

What of the other floors? *What of the medical section?*

He crossed to the stairs, spilled pages crackling like a fall of dry autumn leaves under his step, and sprinted up the first short flight to the mezzanine. Similar chaos!

He hurried up to the second floor, stumbling, terribly afraid of what he might find. Reaching the top, heart thudding, he squinted into the dimness.

The books were undisturbed. Apparently they had tired of their game before reaching these.

He slipped the rifle from his shoulder and placed it near the stairs. Dust lay thick all around him, powdering up and swirling, as he moved down the narrow aisles; a damp, leathery mustiness lived in the air, an odor of mold and neglect.

Lewis Stillman paused before a dim hand-lettered sign: MEDICAL SECTION. It was just as he remembered it. Holstering the small automatic, he struck a match, shading the flame with a cupped hand as he moved it along the rows of faded titles. Carter . . . Davidson . . . Enright . . . *Erickson*. He drew in his breath sharply. All three volumes, their gold stamping dust-dulled but legible, stood in tall and perfect order on the shelf.

In the darkness, Lewis Stillman carefully removed each volume, blowing it free of dust. At last all three books were clean and solid in his hands.

Well, you've done it. You've reached the books and now they belong to you.

He smiled, thinking of the moment when he would be able to sit down at the table with his treasure, and linger again over the wondrous pages.

He found an empty carton at the rear of the store and placed the books inside. Returning to the stairs, he shouldered the rifle and began his descent to the lower floor.

So far, he told himself, my luck is still holding.

But as Lewis Stillman's foot touched the final stair, his luck ran out.

The entire lower floor was alive with them!

Rustling like a mass of great insects, gliding toward him, eyes gleaming in the half-light, they converged upon the stairs. They'd been waiting for him.

Now, suddenly, the books no longer mattered. Now only his life mattered and nothing else. He moved back against the hard wood of the stair rail, the carton of books sliding from his hands. They had stopped at the foot of the stairs; they were silent, looking up at him, the hate in their eyes.

If you can reach the street, Stillman told himself, then you've still got half a chance. That means you've got to get through them to the door. All right then, *move.*

Lewis Stillman squeezed the trigger of the automatic. Two of them fell under his bullets as Stillman rushed into their midst.

He felt sharp nails claw at his shirt, heard the cloth ripping away in their grasp. He kept firing the small automatic into them, and three more dropped under the hail of bullets, shrieking in pain and surprise. The others spilled back, screaming, from the door.

The pistol was empty. He tossed it away, swinging the heavy Savage free from his shoulder as he reached the street. The night air, crisp and cool in his lungs, gave him instant hope.

I can still make it, thought Stillman, as he leaped the curb and plunged across the pavement. If those shots weren't heard, then I've still got the edge. My legs are strong; I can outdistance them.

Luck, however, had failed him completely on this night. Near the intersection of Hollywood Boulevard and Highland, a fresh pack of them swarmed toward him over the street.

He dropped to one knee and fired into their ranks, the Savage jerking in his hands. They scattered to either side.

He began to run steadily down the middle of Hollywood

Boulevard, using the butt of the heavy rifle like a battering ram as they came at him. As he neared Highland, three of them darted directly into his path. Stillman fired. One doubled over, lurching crazily into a jagged plate-glass storefront. Another clawed at him as he swept around the corner to Highland, but he managed to shake free.

The street ahead of him was clear. Now his superior leg-power would count heavily in his favor. Two miles. Could he make it before others cut him off?

Running, reloading, firing. Sweat soaking his shirt, rivering down his face, stinging his eyes. A mile covered. Half way to the drains. They had fallen back behind his swift stride.

But more of them were coming, drawn by the rifle shots, pouring in from side streets, from stores and houses.

His heart jarred in his body, his breath was ragged. How many of them around him? A hundred? Two hundred? More coming. God!

He bit down on his lower lip until the salt taste of blood was on his tongue. You can't make it, a voice inside him shouted, they'll have you in another block and you know it!

He fitted the rifle to his shoulder, adjusted his aim, and fired. The long rolling crack of the big weapon filled the night. Again and again he fired, the butt jerking into the flesh of his shoulder, the bitter smell of burnt powder in his nostrils.

It was no use. Too many of them. He could not clear a path.

Lewis Stillman knew that he was going to die.

The rifle was empty at last, the final bullet had been fired. He had no place to run because they were all around him, in a slowly closing circle.

He looked at the ring of small cruel faces and he thought: The aliens did their job perfectly; they stopped Earth before she could reach the age of the rocket, before she could threaten planets beyond her own moon. What an immensely clever plan it had been! To destroy every human being on Earth above the age of six—and then to leave as quickly as they had come, allowing our civilization to continue on a primitive level, knowing that Earth's back had been broken, that her survivors would revert to savagery as they grew into adulthood.

Lewis Stillman dropped the empty rifle at his feet and threw out his hands. "Listen," he pleaded, "I'm really one of you. You'll *all* be like me soon. Please, *listen* to me."

But the circle tightened relentlessly around Lewis Stillman. He was screaming when the children closed in.

DAVIS GRUBB

The Siege of 318

In 1923 the family Pollixfen migrated from Eire to settle in the small Ohio River town of Glory, West Virginia. Sean Pollixfen was a big, florid boast of a man of common heritage. His wife, Deirdre, was a lady of gentle breeding; raised in a Georgian town house in Dublin's Sackville Street; she deplored Sean's harsh upbringing of their only child, ten-year-old Benjamin Michael.

The Pollixfen house was a rambling one-story structure with a great blue front door and slate flagstone set level with its threshold. Their nearest neighbor was a man named Hugger who dwelt a good three blocks up Liberty Avenue.

When the thing began, it was an autumn night at supper. Benjy abruptly laid down his knife and fork and tilted his ear, harking. "But for what?" Sean asked him.

"I was listening for the auguries of the war that's coming, sor."

"Wisht, now boyo!" cried Sean. "'Tis 1932. The Great War ended fourteen years ago this November. And surely there's not another one in sight."

Sean paused, reminiscing, smiling.

"Still, somehow I'd favor another war," he said. "I'm proud to be wearing the sleeve of this good linen jacket pinned up to me left shoulder. I lost that hook at First Ypres. Yet, despite that, it was a Glory."

Benjy made no reply, though a moment later he left the table, went to the bathroom, and threw up his supper.

Next morning at eight two men pulled up in a truck out front. Moments later they had laboriously borne a huge pine crate to the flagstone threshold and rung the bell. Sean, on his way to his position at the firm, answered their ring.

"Is this here the residence of Master Benjamin Michael Pollixfen?"

"It is that," Sean replied, rapping the crate with his malacca cane. "'Tis another gift for me boy Benjy from his Uncle Liam in Kilronan. He's always sending the lad a grand present, no matter what the occasion!"

That night when they had finished supper, Sean went to Benjy's room. He stared at the great crate's contents, all ranked round the room so thick that one could scarce walk among them. There were five thousand miniature lead soldiers—Boche, French, and English. There was every manner of ammunition and instrument of warfare, from caissons and howitzers to hangars and tarmac for the landing fields of the miniature aircraft of all varieties and types, from Gotha bombers for the Boche to DH-4's for the British and Breguets for the French.

"Now, Liam is showing good sense," Sean said. "Rocking horses were fine for you a year ago. But you're ten now, Benjy. 'Tis time you learned the lessons of life's most glorious game!"

Benjy stared at the little soldiers, cast and tinted down to the very wrinkle of a puttee, the drape of a trenchcoat. Moreover, no two soldiers wore the same facial expression. Benjy could read in these faces fear, zest, valor, humdrum, cravenness, patriotism, and sedition. And somehow each of them seemed waiting. But for what? For whom? Sean missed seeing these subtleties. Yet Benjy saw. Benjy knew. Aye, he knew all too well.

"They are green, dads," Benjy said. "Green as the turf of Saint Stephen's Green Park. The British officers are just days out of Sandhurst, the gun crews hardly a fortnight from the machine-gun school at Wisquies. They don't know the noise of a whizbang from a four-ten or a five-nine. Yet once they've been through a bloody baptism such as Hannescamps or the Somme they'll know. Aye, they'll know then."

"And what would *you* be knowing of Hannescamps or the Somme?" Sean chuckled.

Benjy made no reply.

And so the three strange weeks of it began. Benjy spent every waking hour working feverishly in the great black lot of nonarable ground beyond Deirdre's flower-and-kitchen garden. While about him all the world seemed filled with the sound of locusts sawing down the great green tree of summer.

Benjy carved out the laceries of trenches with his Swiss army knife. He found strips of lath and split them to lay down as duckboards. He sandbagged the trenches well in front. Beyond this he staked, on tenpenny nails, the thin barbed wire which had come on spools in the great crate. Some distance to the rear of both sides he set up his little field hospitals, and his hangars and the tarmac fields for the little fighter, reconnaissance, and bombing planes.

At the kitchen door Sean would watch the boy and listen as Benjy chanted songs that Sean and his men had sung at Locrehof Farm or Tronc Woods once they'd billeted down for a night in some daub-and-wattle stable. He could fairly smell the sweet ammoniac scent of the manure of kine, lambs, and goats, and the fragrance as well of the Gold Flake and State Express cigarettes they smoked, saving only enough to barter for a bottle or two of Pichon-Longueville '89 or perhaps a liter of Paul Ruinart.

Strange to relate, it had not yet begun to trouble Sean that the boy knew of these things, that he sang songs Sean had never taught him and sometimes in French which *no one* had ever taught him. As for Benjy he soon began to show the strain. Deirdre's scale in the bathroom showed that in ten days he had lost twelve pounds. He seldom finished supper. For there was that half-hour's extra twilight to work in. Sean gloated. Deirdre grieved.

"Why in Saint Brigid's blessed name don't you put an end to it?" she would plead.

"No, woman, I shan't."

"And why not then?"

"Because me boyo shall grow up to be what I wanted for meself—a soldier poet more glorious than Rupert Brooke or the taffy Wilfred Owen."

"And them dead of their cursed war, dead before they could come to full flower of Saint Brigid's sacred gift."

"So much the better," Sean replied icily one night. "We must all die one day or another. And no man knows the hour. Death, it has no clocks. Moreover, we are Pollixfens. Kin on me father's side to Eire's glory of poets—William Butler Yeats."

"But Yeats died in no war," Deirdre protested.

"Better he had," Sean said. "'Twould have increased his esteem a thousandfold."

Deirdre went off to bed weeping.

Next night in Benjy's room, Sean spoke his dreams out plain.

"'Tis stark truth, old man," he said. "Real war is a rough go. But there is that Glory of Glories in it."

Benjy said nothing.

"Don't you understand me, boyo? Glory!"

"I see no Glory," said the child. "I see poor fools butchering each other for reasons kept secret from them. Oh, they give reasons. King and Country. They leave out, of course, Industry. No, dads, there are no fields of honor. There are only insane abattoirs."

Sean colored at this, got up and strode from the boy's room. Yet a minute later, unable to contain himself, he was back.

"Now, boyo!" he cried out. "Either you shed from yourself these craven, blasphemous, and treasonable speculations or I shall leave you to grow up and learn war the hard way. As did I."

"And what might that mean, sor?"

"It means that I shall go to Al Hugger's ga-rage and fetch home three ten-gallon tins of petrol and douse the length and breadth of your little no-man's-land of toys and then set a lucifer to it."

"That would be a most fearsome mistake, sor. For on the morning when the little armies came they were mine. Now I am Theirs. And so, poor dads, are you."

"That does it then! 'Tis petrol and a lucifer for all five thousand of the little perishers!"

Benjy smiled. Sadly.

"But 'tis no longer a skimpy five thousand now, man dear. 'Tis closer to a million. Perhaps more. Even files-on-parade could not count their hosts."

"Wisht, now! How could that be? Did Liam send you another great crate?"

"No, sor. There's been conscription on both sides. And enlistments by the million. A fair fever of outrage infects every man and boy of the King's Realm from Land's End to Aberdeen since Lord Kitchener went down in one of His Majesty's dreadnaughts off the Dolomites. Then there's Foch and Clemenceau and Joffre. They've whipped up the zest of Frenchmen to a pitch not known since the days of Robespierre and Danton in the Terror. In Germany the Boche seethe at every word from Hindenburg or Ludendorf or Kaiser Willie."

Benjy chuckled, despite himself.

"Willie—the English King's cousin! Willie and Georgie! Lord, 'tis more of a family squabble than a war!"

He sobered then.

"No, sor," Benjy said. "Cry havoc now and let loose the dogs of war!"

Sean stared, baffled.

"Tell me, boyo. If you loathe war so, why do you go at your little war game with such zest?"

"Why, because there's twins inside me, I suppose," Benjy replied, and press him as he might, Sean could elicit no more from the boy.

Sean's face sobered. He went off with a troubled mind to Deirdre in their goose-down bed. Lying there on his back he could hear Benjy singing an old war ditty, "The Charlie Chaplin Walk." Sean's batman, a Nottinghamshire collier, had used to sing that before the Somme. Sean was drowsy but could not sleep. Yet soon he roused up wide-waking from the drowsiness. Was it thunder he heard out yonder in the night? And that flickering light across the sill of the back window. Was it heat lightning?

He stole from Deirdre's sound-sleeping side and stared out the rear window. A river fog lay waist deep upon the land. Among the tinted autumn trees the cold sweet light of fireflies came and went as though they were stars that could not make up their minds. Yet the flashes and flames that flickered beneath the cloak of mists on the black lot were not sweet, nor cold.

Sean could hear the small smart chatter of machine guns. There were the blasts of howitzers, whizbangs, and mortars. Above the shallow sea of leprous white mists the Aviatiks and Sopwith Strutters swooped and dove and Immelmanned in dogfights.

Far to the rear Sean could see Benjy in his pj's, standing and watching. The child's wild face was grievous and weeping. He had flung out his spindly arms as if transcendentally to appease the madness to which he bore such suffering witness.

Sean crept shivering back into the bed. He lay awake, again thinking of Liam's great gift that had come to life, proliferated, and had now taken possession both of himself and Benjy.

And it went on thus. For another two weeks. Then one morning all was changed. Pale, half staggering from lack of sleep and haggard-eyed from poring over the war map thumb-tacked to his play table beneath the gooseneck lamp's harsh circle of illumination, Benjy—almost faint—came down to breakfast all smiles.

"What does that Chessy cat grin on your face mean, boyo?" Sean asked.

"*C'est la guerre, mon vieux, c'est la guerre!*" cried Benjy. "But last night news came through—"

"*C'est la guerre* and so on," Deirdre intervened. "And what might that alien phrase mean to these poor untutored ears?"

"'Tis French," Sean said. "That's war, old man, that's war."

"But now, tomorrow night at midnight, it will be over!" Benjy cried brightly.

"Tomorrow night and midnight be damned!" Sean exclaimed. "*Tonight* at midnight it shall end. I am unable to endure another night of it, and so I have determined to end it all meself! Benjy, I swear now by the holy martyred names of the Insurrection of Easter '16—Pearse, Casement, John Connolly, and the O'Rahilly—that I shall not let this thing possess the two of us for even one night more! I shall end it with me petrol and me lucifer at midnight tonight!"

"Lord save us, dads, you mustn't talk so!" cried Benjy. "Word has been flashed to all forces up and down the lines that the cease-fire is set for tomorrow's midnight. Already the gunfire is only token. Already the men crawl fearlessly over sandbags and under the barbed wire and march boldly into the midst of No-Man's-Land to embrace each other. They barter toffees and jars of Bovril and tins of chocs for marzipan and *fastnacht-krapfen* and strudels and *himbeer kuchen!* They show each other sweat-and-muck-smeared snapshots of mothers, sweethearts, and children back home. Men who a day ago were at each other's throats!"

Deirdre watched and listened, helpless, baffled, appalled.

"No matter to all the sweet sticky treacle of your talk!" Sean cried. "I'll not let this madness take possession of our home! So 'tis petrol and a lucifer to the whole game tonight at the strike of twelve! And a fiery fitting end to it all!"

"Bloody ballocks to that!" shouted Benjy, outraged.

"Go to your room, boy," Sean said, struggling to control himself. "We have man's words to say. Not words for the hearing of your mum."

A moment later Sean was strutting the length and breadth of Benjy's bedroom like a bloated popinjay. His swagger stick was in his hand; it seemed to give him back some of his old lost valor, some long mislaid or time-rotted authority. As he walked he slapped it in vainglorious bellicosity against his thigh.

Benjy watched him solemnly, sadly. "They'll not let you do this thing," he said. He paused. "Nor shall I."

Sean whirled, glaring.

"Ah, so it has come to that then!" he barked out in the voice of a glory-gutted martinet. "'Tis they shan't and I shan't and you shan't, eh? Well, we shall see about that! I am King of this house. And I am King of all its environs!"

"No," Benjy said, his face above the war map tacked to his table. "You are no King. You are a King's Fool. Though lacking in a King's Fool's traditional and customary wisdom and vision."

Sean broke then. In a stride he crossed the room and slashed the boy across the face with the swagger stick.

A thin ribbon of blood coursed down from the corner of Benjy's mouth. A droplet of it splattered like a tiny crimson starfish or a mark on the map to commemorate some dreadful battle encounter.

"King, I say! King!" Sean was shouting, pacing the room again. There was a livid stripe across the child's cheek where the leather had fallen. But there was even more change in Benjy's face. And even something newer, something darker in the mind behind that face. The boy smiled.

"Come then," Benjy said softly. "Let us sit a while and tell sad stories of the Death of Kings."

The next day neither child nor father spoke nor looked each other in the eye. When occasionally they would be forced to pass in a corridor it was in the stiff-legged, ominous manner of pit-bulls circling in a small seat-encircled arena. Deirdre, sensing something dreadful between them, was helplessly distraught. For what did she know of any of it, dear gentle Deirdre?

Benjy did not appear for supper. Sean ate ravenously. When he was done he drove his car into town and came back moments later with the three ten-gallon tins of petrol. He ranked them neatly alongside the black lot's border.

At nine Sean and Deirdre went to bed. For three hours Sean lay staring at the bar of harvest moonlight which fell across the carpet from the windowsill to the threshold of the bedroom door. Now and again half-hearted gunfire could be heard from the black lot. Soon Sean began speaking within himself a wordless colloquy. Fear had begun to steal upon him. Misgivings. He could not forget the thing he had seen in the boy's face after the blow of the stiff, hardened leather. He could never forget the strange new timber of the boy's voice when he spoke softly shortly after.

As the great clock in the hallway struck the chime of eleven-thirty, Sean decided to forego the whole headstrong project. Let the cease-fire come in its ordained time. What could another twenty-four hours matter? There was scarcely any war waging in the black lot anyway. Cheered by his essentially craven decision, he started, in his nightshirt, down the hallway toward Benjy's room to inform him of his change of mind.

Within ten feet of the boy's bolted door Sean came to a standstill. He listened. It was unmistakable. The tiny quacking chatter of a voice speaking from a field telephone. And Benjy's murmurous voice giving orders back. Only one phrase caught Sean's ear. And that phrase set beads of sweat glistering on his face in the pallid gaslight of the long broad hallway. The words were in French. But Sean knew French.

On a besoin des assassins.

Sean felt a chill seize him, shaming the manhood of him. We now have need of the assassins.

Shamed to the core of his soul, Sean fled back to the bedroom. With his one hand he turned the key in the door lock. With that same hand he fetched a ladder-back chair from against the wall and propped the top rung under the knob. Then he hastened to the bureau drawer where he kept the memorabilia of his old long-forgotten war and fetched out his BEF Webley.

The pistol was still well greased. It was loaded, the cartridge pins a little dark with verdigris but operable. Then Sean went and lay atop the quilt, shivering and clutching the silly, ineffectual pistol in his hand.

That was when he first heard them. Myriad feet; tiny footsteps and not those of small animals with clawed and padded paws. Boots. Tiny boots. The myriad scrape of microscopically small hobnails. Boots. By the thousands. By the thousands of thousands. And then abruptly above their measured, disciplined tread there burst forth suddenly the skirl of Royal Scots Highlanders' bagpipes, the rattle of tiny drums, the piercing tweedle of little fifes, the brash impudence of German brass bands.

Deirdre still slept. Even the nights of the war in the black lot had never wakened her. It was to Sean's credit that he did not rouse her now. For, as never before in his life, not even in the inferno of First Ypres of the Somme, had he so craved the company of another mortal. A word. A touch. A look.

Abruptly, just beyond the door, there was a command followed by total silence. Sean chuckled. They were not out there. It had been a fantasy of his overwrought mind. A nightmare—a *cauchemar* as the French call it. But his tranquillity was short-lived. He heard a tiny voice crying orders in German to crank a howitzer to its proper angle of trajectory. Another shouted command. Sean sensed, with an old soldier's instinct, the yank of the lanyard. He heard the detonation, felt the hot Krupp steel barrel's recoil, saw flame flare as the shell blasted a ragged hole in the door where the lock had been.

The impact flung the door wide and sent the chair spinning across the moonlit carpet. And now, in undisciplined and furious anarchy, they swarmed across the doorsill like a blanket of gray putrescent mud. Gone from them were the gay regimental colors, the spit-and-polish decorum of the morning of the great crate's arrival. Now they were muck-draped and gangrenous, unwashed and stinking of old deaths, old untended wounds. Some knuckled their way on legless stumps. Others hobbled savagely on makeshift crutches.

Sean sat up and emptied every bullet from the Webley into their midst. He might as well have sought to slaughter the sea, furious, impotent Xerxes, flogging the Aegean Sea. All of them wore tiny gas masks. A shouted command and small steel cylinders on miniature wheeled platforms were trundled across the doorsill and ranked before the bed. Another shout, and gun crews of four men each wheeled in, to face the bed, behind the gas cylinders, ten Lewis and ten Maxim machine guns.

At a cry from the leader, these now began a raking enfilade of Sean's body. He had but time to cross himself and begin a Hail Mary when the cocks of the little gas cylinders were screwed open and the first green cloud of gas reached his nostrils. Enveloped in a cloud of gas, the big man uttered one last choking scream and slid onto the carpet and into their very midst.

In a twinkling they swarmed over him like a vast shroud of living manure. They stabbed him with the needle points of their tiny bayonets, again and again. At last one of these sought out and found the big man's jugular vein. A shouted command again. The lift and fall of a bloody saber.

"All divisions—ri'tur'!"

And to a man they obeyed.

"All divisions—'orm rank!"

Again they obeyed.

"All divisions—quick 'arch!"

And with pipes skirling, drums drubbing, fifes shrilling, and brass bands blaring they went the way they had come. The siege was a *fait accompli.*

Awakened by all the gunfire and clamor at last, and at the very moment of the door's collapse, Deirdre sat up, watching throughout. First in smiling disbelief, then in fruitless attempt to persuade herself that she was dreaming it all, then in acceptance, and at last, in horror. Now as the first wisps of the chlorine stung her nostrils she went raving and irreversibly insane, sprang from her side of the bed, and hurtled through the side window, taking screen and all, to tumble onto the turf three feet below.

In the hushed autumn street of the night Deirdre, beneath the moon and the galaxies and the cold promiscuous fireflies, fled back into the hallucination of youth returned. She raced up and down under the tinted trees. She twirled an imaginary pink lace parasol as if doing a turn on a small stage. She chanted the Harry Lauder and Vesta Tilley ballads from the music halls of her Dublin girlhood.

Wakened by all this daft medly of unfamiliar songs, Al Hugger, the nearest neighbor, took down his old AEF Springfield rifle and came to the house to discover what calamity had befallen it.

When, at last, he stood in the bedroom doorway, he looked first at the monstrous ruin which had been Sean, humped in his blood on the carpet by the bed. Then Hugger saw the blasé and unruffled figure of Benjy, clad only in his pj's and sitting straight as the blackthorn stick of a Connaught County squire in the ladder-back chair now back against the wall. Almost all the gas had been cleared from the room by the clean river wind which coursed steadily between the two open windows.

"No one," Hugger said presently, more to himself than to the child, "shall likely ever know what happened in this room tonight. Better they don't. Yes, I hope they don't. Never. For there is something about it all—something—"

Benjy yawned. Prodigiously. He smiled hospitably at Al Hugger. He looked at the thing, like a great beached whale, on the carpet by the bedside. He yawned again.

"*C'est la guerre, mon vieux, c'est la guerre,*" he said.

RICHARD LAYMON

The Champion

"You're not going anywhere," said the man blocking the door.

He was smaller than Harry Barlow, with neither the bulk nor the muscle to make his words good. But he had a friend on each side. Though Harry figured he could take the trio, he didn't want to try. Like most big men, he'd been pestered all his life by people wanting to prove their toughness. He was tired of it. He wanted never to fight again.

"Please move," he said to the man.

"Not on your life, bud. You're staying right here. This is your big night."

The entire restaurant erupted with cheers. Harry turned slowly, studying the faces around him. Most belonged to men. Funny, he hadn't noticed that during the meal. He hadn't noticed much of anything, really, except his dinner of top sirloin.

When he first saw Roy's Bar and Steak House, he'd been surprised by the crowd of cars in its parking lot. The town, hidden in a valley deep in northern California's timber country, seemed too small to have so many cars. Once he tasted the rich, charcoal broiled steak, however, he realized that folks had probably driven miles for supper at Roy's. He was glad he'd stopped in.

Until now.

Now, he only wanted to leave. He took a step toward the three men barring his way.

"Hold up," someone called from behind.

Harry turned around. He'd seen this man before. During supper, the fellow had wandered from table to table, chatting and laughing with the customers; he'd even exchanged a few words with Harry. "I'm Roy," he'd said. "This your first time here? Whereabouts are you from? How's your beef?" He'd seemed like a pleasant, amiable man.

Now he had a shotgun aimed at Harry's midsection.

"What's that for?" Harry asked.

"Can't have you leave." Roy told him.

"Why's that?"

Except for a few scattered clinks of silverware, there was silence in the restaurant.

"You're the challenger," Roy said.

"What am I challenging?" Harry asked. He waited, feeling a tremor of fear.

"It's not a what, it's a who."

Harry heard a few quiet laughs. Looking around, he saw that every face was turned toward him. He rubbed his hands along the soft corduroy of his pants legs. "Okay," he said, "*who* am I challenging?"

"The champion."

"Am I?"

More laughter.

"You sure are. You ever hear of the Saturday Night Fights? Well, here at Roy's Bar and Steak House, we have our own version."

Cheers and applause roared through the restaurant. Roy held up his hands for silence. "The first man through the door after nine on Saturday night, he's the challenger. You walked in at nine-o-three."

Harry remembered the group of seven or eight men who had been standing just outside the door, talking in quiet, eager voices. A few had looked at him oddly as he stepped by. Now he knew why they were here: they'd arrived at nine, and had to wait until a chump went inside.

"Look," Harry said, "I don't want to fight anyone."

"They never do."

"Well, I'm not *going* to."

"We had a guy about two years back," Roy said. "Some kind of chicken pacifist. He wouldn't fight the champion. Just wouldn't do it. Made a run for the door." Roy grinned and waved the barrel of his shotgun. "I cut him down. I'll cut you down, if you make a run."

"This is crazy," Harry muttered.

"Just our way of having a good time." Roy turned his attention to the crowd. "All right, folks. For any newcomers to the Saturday Night Fight, I'll tell how she works." A waitress stepped up to his side, holding a fish bowl stuffed with red tickets. "We got a hundred tickets in the bowl. Each ticket has a three-second time period on it, going up to five minutes. Never had a fight go more than that. You pay five bucks for each chance. Winner gets the pot. Any tickets aren't sold by fight time, they belong to the house." He patted the arm of the woman holding the fish bowl. "Julie here, she's timekeeper. I'm referee. The fight's over when one or the other contestant's dead. Any questions?"

No questions.

"Buy your tickets at the counter. Fight starts in ten minutes."

During the next ten minutes, as customers filed past the cash register and drew their tickets from the bowl, Roy stood guard. Harry considered running for the door. He decided, however, that he would rather face the champion than Roy's shotgun. To pass the time, he counted the number of tickets sold.

Seventy-two.

At five dollars each, that came to $360.

Somebody'd be going home with a tidy prize.

"Fight starts in one minute," Roy announced. "Last call for tickets."

"Elmer?"

A thin, bald old man nodded and went out the rear door.

"The champion will be right in, folks. If a couple of you could help move these tables out of the way . . ."

Six tables from the center of the room were moved toward the sides, leaving a clear area that seemed awfully small to Harry.

The crowd suddenly cheered and whistled. Looking toward the rear door, Harry saw Elmer enter. A tall, lean man walked behind him.

"Ladies and gentlemen!" Roy called. "The champion!"

The champion scowled at the crowd as he hobbled toward the clear space. From his looks, he'd fought many times before. His broad forehead was creased with a scar. He wore a patch over his left eye. The tip of one ear was missing. So was the forefinger of his left hand.

Looking down, Harry saw the cause of the champion's strange, awkward walk: a three-foot length of chain dragged between his shackled feet.

"I'm not fighting this man," Harry said.

"Sure you are," Roy told him. "Elmer?"

The skinny old man knelt down. Opening a padlock, he removed the shackle from the right ankle of the champion.

Harry took a step backwards.

"Stand still," Roy ordered.

"There's no way you can make me fight this man."

"The fellas with low numbers'll be glad to hear that."

"Right!" someone yelled from the crowd.

"Just stand there," called another.

Others joined the shouting, some urging him to wait passively for death, some demanding that he fight.

Elmer locked the iron onto Harry's left ankle. The yard-long chain now connected the two adversaries.

"Time?" Roy called.

The yelling stopped.

"Ten seconds to starting," Julie said.

"Elmer?"

The old man scurried away. From behind the counter, he took a pair of matching knives.

"Five seconds," Julie said.

The knives had wooden handles, brass cross-guards, and eight-inch blades of polished steel.

"We won't do it," Harry said to the champion. "They can't make us."

The champion sneered.

Elmer handed one knife to the champion, one to Harry.

"Two seconds."

"Go!" said Julie.

Harry flung down his knife. Its point thunked the hardwood floor, biting deep. Its handle was still vibrating as the champion jabbed at Harry's stomach. Harry jumped away. The chain stopped his foot, and he fell backwards. The champion stomped on his knee. Harry cried out as his leg exploded with pain.

With a demented shriek, the champion threw himself down on Harry. Using both hands, Harry held back the knife that the champion was driving toward his face. The blade pressed closer. He blinked, and felt his right eyelashes brush the steel point. Turning his head, he shoved sideways. The blade ripped his ear, and stabbed the floor beside his head.

He smashed a fist upward into the champion's nose. Rolling, he got out from under the stunned man. He crawled away from the grasping hands, and stood.

"Enough!" he shouted. "That's enough! It has to stop!"

The crowd booed and hissed.

The champion, tearing his knife from the floor, leaped to his feet and swung at Harry. The blade sliced the front of Harry's plaid shirt.

"Stop it!"

The champion lunged, growling. He punched the knife

toward Harry's belly. Harry chopped down, knocking the hand away. The champion stabbed again. This time, the blade slashed Harry's blocking hand. It struck at his stomach. Spinning aside, Harry dodged the steel.

He gripped the champion's right arm at the wrist and elbow, and pumped his knee upward, breaking the champion's forearm with a popping sound like snapped kindling. Screaming, the champion dropped his knife.

But he caught it with his left hand, and thrust it wildly at Harry, who ducked out of the way.

Dropping to one knee, Harry grabbed the chain and tugged upward. The champion's leg flew high, and he tumbled backwards. Harry sprang onto him. With both hands, he clutched the champion's left hand, and pinned it to the floor.

"Give up!" he shouted into the champion's blood-smeared face.

The champion nodded. The knife dropped from his hand.

"That's it!" Harry raised his eyes to the crowd. "He gave up! He quit!"

Abruptly, the man sat up and clamped his teeth on Harry's throat. Blind with pain and enraged by the deception, Harry slapped the floor. He found the knife. He plunged it four times into the champion's side before the jaws loosened their grip on his neck. The champion flopped backwards. His head hit the floor with a solid thunk.

Harry crawled aside, feeling his wounded neck. He wasn't bleeding as badly as he'd feared.

Sitting on the floor, he watched Roy kneel at the champion's side.

"Is he dead?" someone shouted from the crowd.

Roy felt the pulse in the champion's neck. "Not yet," he announced.

"Come on!" someone yelled.

"Hang on, champ!" shouted another.

"Give it up!" called a woman's voice.

The crowd roared for a few seconds. Then silence fell.

Complete silence. All eyes were fixed on Roy kneeling beside the fallen champion.

"Gone!" Roy announced.

Julie clicked her stopwatch. "Two minutes, twenty-eight seconds."

"That's me!" a man yelled, waving his red ticket. "That's me! I got it!"

"Come on up and get your money," Roy said. Then he turned to his skinny old assistant. "Elmer?"

Elmer knelt between Harry and the body. He unlatched a shackle. Before Harry could move to prevent it, the metal cuff clamped shut around his right ankle. Elmer shut the padlock.

"Hey!" Harry cried. "Take 'em off! I won! You've got to let me go!"

"Can't do that," Roy said, smiling down at him. "You're the champion."

GAHAN WILSON

The Power of the Mandarin

Aladar Rakas gave a wicked grin and raised his brandy glass. "To the King Plotter of Evil. To the Prophet of our Doom. To the Mandarin."

I joined the toast willingly.

"May he never be totally defeated. May he and his vile minions ever threaten the civilized world."

We drank contentedly. Rakas leaned back, struck a luxurious pose, and wafted forth a cloud of Havana's very best.

"How many have been killed this time?"

Rakas tapped an ash from his cigar and gazed thoughtfully upward. I could see his lips moving as he made the count.

"Five," he said, and then, after a pause, "No. Six."

I looked at him with some surprise. "That's hardly up to the usual slaughter."

Rakas chuckled and signaled the waiter for more brandy.

"True enough," he said. "However, one particular murder of those six is enough to make up for hundreds, perhaps thousands, of ordinary ones."

His dark eyes glinted. He arched his thick, sable brows and leaned slowly forward.

"I have given the Mandarin a real treat this time, Charles," he said.

"You have, have you?"

I took a quick, unsatisfying puff at my cigarette and wondered what the old devil had been up to. I tossed out a guess.

"You haven't let him kill Mork?"

The brutish Mork. The only vaguely human emissary of the insidious Mandarin. He was, in his apish way, ambitious. Perhaps he had gone too far. It would be a shame to lose Mork.

Rakas waved the idea aside with an airy gesture.

"No, Charles. I have always liked Mork. Besides, he is far too useful as a harbinger of horrors to come. No, I would never dream of killing the dreadful creature."

Belatedly, a grim suspicion began to grow in me. Rakas was making quite a production out of this revelation. It would be something very much out of the ordinary.

"As a matter of fact," he continued blandly, covertly watching me from the corners of his eyes, "the only one of the Mandarin's henchmen to die in this particular adventure is a Lascar. A low underling hardly worth mentioning."

The suspicion hardened into a near certainty, but I tried a parry.

"How about the Inspector? Have you let him kill Snow?"

"Why bother? Inspector Snow. The poor blunderer. No, Charles, this murder is one of the first magnitude. This murder is the one which the Mandarin has burned to do since book one."

He looked at the expression on my face and grinned hugely.

"Of course you've guessed."

I gaped at him unbelievingly.

"You're joking, Aladar," I said.

He continued to grin.

He'd let the Mandarin kill Evan Trowbridge. I knew he'd let him kill Evan Trowbridge. I swallowed and decided to say it out loud and hear how it sounded.

"He's killed Evan Trowbridge."

It sounded like a kind of croak. Rakas gave a confirming nod and continued to grin.

I won't say that the room swam before my eyes, but I did wonder, just for a moment, if I was going to faint. I sat in my chair building up a nervous tic and thinking about Evan Trowbridge.

Who was it who stood between the malevolent Mandarin and his conquest of the world? I'll tell you who. Evan Trowbridge. Who was it who foiled, again and again, in book after book, the heartless fiend who plotted the base enslavement of us all? None other than Evan Trowbridge.

And now he was dead.

I wiped the palms of my hands carefully with my napkin and cleared my throat. I could think of nothing else to do, short of leaping over the table and crushing in the top of Aladar Rakas's skull.

He looked at me with some concern. I suppose I looked like a man trembling on the verge of a fit. I may have been.

He sighed.

"You must understand, Charles," he said. "If only you knew how often I have ached to let him do it."

"But why?"

His eyes shone dreamily.

"Evan Trowbridge," he said. "Pillar of the Establishment. Pride of the Empire."

He had turned deadly serious.

"Do you know where the strength of a Trowbridge lies, Charles? I'll tell you. It lies in his sublime conviction that he and his kind are superior to all other men. That anyone who is not both white and English is automatically not quite a human being."

He ground out his cigar forcefully, yet precisely, as if he were sticking it into a Trowbridge eye.

"It's different here in America," he said. "Do you know what it was like to be a poor Hungarian in London? Speaking with a foreign accent? Looking alien? Liking garlic and spicy foods?"

He looked down at his huge white hands and watched them curl into fists.

"I dressed like them. I even thought of changing my name. Then I realized I would only make myself more ridiculous in their eyes."

He looked at me, and then his expression softened and he chuckled.

"Wait until you read how the Mandarin kills him, Charles. It is a masterpiece, if I do say so myself. It takes up an entire chapter."

I bunched up my napkin and tossed it on the table.

"So what happens to the series, Aladar? Have you thought about that? Who the hell is going to fight the Mandarin?"

"Somebody will, Charles. The series will continue. We will continue. I have several possibilities in mind. I have thought, maybe a Hungarian. Maybe someone rather like myself."

We finished our coffee and parted in widely divergent moods.

I took the manuscript to my office, informed my secretary that I was strictly incommunicado, and read *The Mandarin Triumphant* from its first neatly typed page to its last.

I discovered, thank God, that it was good. Really one of his best.

I had been afraid that the hatred for Trowbridge which Rakas had just confessed would show through, and that he might turn him into some kind of villain, or, much worse, a quivering coward, but none of this had happened. The brave Britisher fought the good fight to the end. The Mandarin, after having committed what really was a masterpiece of murder, even spoke a little tribute to his redoubtable foe just before boarding a mysterious boat and vanishing into the swirling fog of a Thames estuary:

> "He was a worthy opponent," said the Mandarin in the sibilant whisper he adopted when in a thoughtful

mood, "In his dogged fashion, I believe he understood me and my aspirations as no man has done."

Slipping carefully from the plastic coverall which had protected him from the deadly mold, the towering man bent respectfully to the nearly formless heap which lay at his feet and, with great solemnity, he made an ancient oriental gesture of salutation to that which had once been Evan Trowbridge.

I closed the manuscript feeling much better.

After all, I figured, Rakas had managed to make the Mandarin series into a very successful enterprise with Trowbridge, and there was no reason why he couldn't go right ahead and carry on without him. It was the Mandarin who really counted, and if the heroic Englishman irritated the author all that much, I couldn't see why he shouldn't be allowed to go ahead and kill the bastard. There were a few bad moments with some of the other editors but, in the end, we all sat back with smug little smiles playing on our faces and waited to see how Rakas's newest champion fared in the struggle against the vast criminal campaign of the diabolical Mandarin.

One very comforting development was the unexpectedly large popularity of *Triumph*. The critics who had rejected the previous books as being too much, loved it. They liked the idea of the super hero getting horribly murdered. It moved the whole thing into a campy sort of area where they could relax and enjoy without being embarrassed.

We worked a series of TV and radio slots for Rakas, which was something we'd never done before, and he clicked. The public liked his sinister presence. They relished him in much the same way as they did Alfred Hitchcock. There is something very reassuring about a boogeyman who's willing to joke about his scareful personality. It eases all sorts of dim little fears and makes the dark unknown seem almost friendly. This sudden celebrity pleased Rakas.

"It is very nice," he told me. "I was walking down the street the other day and a beautiful woman came up to me. 'Are you Aladar Rakas?' she asked me. And I told her I was. A perfect stranger, and that very night we went to bed. I like this being famous."

I asked him how the new book was going.

"It's coming along nicely," he said. "My hero is a Hungarian, as I warned you he might be. I have not given him a name yet. I call him Rakas, after myself, for now. Later on I will figure out some name for him. I want it to be just right, of course.

"He is not a bullhead, like that Trowbridge. He is a man who thinks. The Mandarin will have his hands full with him, you will see. I think the only real problem will be to make sure that this new hero of mine doesn't finish him off in the first three chapters."

Then he laughed, and I laughed with him.

It was just about two weeks later, about four in the morning, when the telephone rang. I knocked over the alarm clock and upset a full ashtray before I managed to bark a hello into the receiver's mouthpiece. I expected to hear some fool drunk blurting apologies, but I got Rakas, instead.

"Charles," he said, "could I come over? I'd like to talk to you. Now. Tonight. I'm worried."

I told him he could. I slipped on a bathrobe and groped my way into the kitchen. I'd just finished brewing a pot of coffee when the doorbell rang.

He looked bad. He was pale and I think he'd lost weight. I noticed his hand shook a little when he lifted his cup.

"What's wrong, Aladar?"

"It's the book. Here." He had a manuscript in a folder and he passed it over to me. "It's not going well."

I considered giving him a little lecture about office hours and then decided to hell with it. I turned through the pages. Everything looked fine. A man killed by a poison dart on a misty wharf. The new hero narrowly missing death by scorpion-stuffed glove. A brief meeting with the Mandarin himself in a dark Soho alley.

> For an instant Rakas saw the huge forehead, the glittering eyes, the deep hollows of the cheeks, and then the light snuffed out, leaving only a skeleton silhouette.
>
> "You are confident, Rakas," came the harsh, icy whisper. "You consider me a puppet, a marionette."
>
> Suddenly Rakas felt his shoulder grasped by a merciless talon which seemed hard as steel. He grunted in pain and tried to twist free.
>
> "There are no strings on this hand, Rakas," continued the chill muttering of the Mandarin. "It kills when I want, and releases when I wish."
>
> Then the talon wrenched away, and Rakas found himself alone.

I lit a cigarette and read on happily. It was around the end of chapter eight when I saw the beginnings of the drift.

> The awful spasms of his dying had twisted Colonel Bentley-Smith's face into a grotesque grin, and this look of dead glee seemed to mock the perplexed frown of Aladar Rakas.
>
> "I don't understand. Inspector Snow," he snapped, "didn't you deploy your men as I asked you to?"
>
> "I did that, sir," replied the puzzled policeman, "but they got through to him without one of us having the foggiest."
>
> Rakas snarled and ground his teeth together.
>
> "Then we have sprung our trap upon a corpse!"

I looked up at Rakas.

"How did they get through?" I asked.

"That's just it," he said. "I don't know!"

He pulled out a cigar, started to unwrap it, and then shoved it back into his pocket.

"You've read it," he said. "In chapter seven I show how I, or rather I show how Rakas, has made absolutely sure that the Colonel's study is inaccessible. Every window, every door, all possible means of approach are under constant observation. There is no way, no conceivable method, for the Mandarin or his minions to have snuck in with the cobra."

He sat back and spread his hands helplessly. "And yet they do get in, *and* out, and no one the wiser."

I flipped an edge of the manuscript and looked at Rakas thoughtfully.

"Let me show you," he said, leaning forward and taking the folder from my hands. "Let me show you how it happens again." He thumbed through the pages. "Yes, here it is. Here is something just like it."

"Would you like some more coffee?"

"Yes. Sure. Here Rakas has rigged the mummy case in the museum so that there is no feasible way for anyone to open it and remove the body of the sorcerer. The slightest touch on the case's lid and an alarm goes off and cameras record the event. A fly couldn't land on the damned thing without setting off the apparatus. And yet the Mandarin does it. I don't know how, but he pulls it off."

I began, "Aladar—"

"No. Wait," he said, cutting me off. "That's not all. Here, in chapter fourteen, here's one that really gets me. I absolutely defy you to explain to me how he manages to poison the—"

This time I cut him off.

"Aladar, it's not my job to explain how he does it. I'm merely the reader. You, Aladar, are the one to explain it."

"But, how?" he asked me, flinging his hands wide. "I would like you to explain to me how?"

"Because it's a goddam story, Aladar, and because you're the goddam author. That's how."

It took him by absolute surprise. It seemed to stun him. He sat back in his chair and blinked at me.

"You are the one who's making this up," I said, waving at the manuscript which lay, all innocence, on the kitchen table. "You made up the Colonel and the Mandarin and the whole thing. It's you who decides who does what to who and how they do it. Nobody else but you."

He reached up and squeezed his forehead. He shut his eyes and sat perfectly still for at least a minute. Then he let his hand fall to his lap.

"You are right, aren't you," he said. He sighed heavily and reached out to touch the manuscript gingerly with his fingertips. "It's only a story, isn't it."

He looked up at the clock on the wall.

"My God," he said. "It's the middle of the night."

He took the manuscript in his hands and stood.

"I'm sorry, Charles. I'm a fool. I can't understand how I let myself be carried away like this."

"It's all right, Aladar," I said. "You just let yourself get too wrapped up. It happens."

We said a few more things, and then I walked him to the door. He opened it and stood there, looking dejected and foolish. I put my hands on his shoulder.

"Remember," I told him, "you're the boss."

He looked at me a little while.

"Sure. That's right," he said. "I'm the boss."

Then the preparation for that year's Christmas rush got underway, and I found myself up to my hips in non-books to lure the prospective festive shoppers. It is a busy time, this pre-Yule season, and Aladar Rakas got crowded out of my mind along with everything else except the confused and frantic matters at hand. At least that is my excuse for not getting in touch with him for a good month and a half.

In the end it was he who got in touch with me. I was plowing through a manuscript we'd bought on the archaeology of ancient Egypt, wondering what the copy editor was going to say about the author's ancient use of commas, when my secretary came in to tell me that Rakas was in the outer office. I went out, covered my shock at the way he looked, and walked him back to my sanctuary. He was so thin he had become gaunt.

"It has proven more difficult than you thought," he said. "I believed you, that night, but now I am not so sure."

He had an attaché case with him. He opened it and took out an enormous manuscript. He hefted it and then laid it on my desk.

"Is that the new book?" I asked.

"It is."

I squeezed its bulk, estimating the probable wordage.

"But, Aladar," I said, "the thing's easily three times as long as any of the others."

He smiled ironically.

"You are right, Charles," he said. "And it is not yet finished. If I go on like this I will end with a *Gone with the Wind* of thrillers."

I pulled the thing to me and went through the opening pages. It was obvious he had done a lot of work on them, the changes were considerable, but the story line remained exactly the same.

"You remember the scene where the Mandarin, or Mork, or whoever it is gets in and kills the Colonel?" he asked. "Well, it keeps on happening, Charles. No matter how I rearrange the constabulary of the good Inspector Snow, no matter if I, myself, remain on the premises, even in the room, itself, it keeps on happening. The Colonel always ends up being killed by the damn cobra."

"But that's mad, Aladar."

"Yes. Possibly it is because I am going mad. I sincerely hope that is the case. I was sure of it in the beginning. But now I am not so sure. The terrible possibility is that I may be sane and the thing may actually be happening."

I looked at him with, I think, understandable confusion. Rakas lit a cigar and I began to go through the manuscript quickly, skimming, turning several pages at a time when I felt I had the direction of the action.

"It goes that way all through the book," he said. "I increase the protection. I double and redouble the guards. It is all to no avail. The Mandarin wins. Again and again, he wins."

He had a weird kind of calm this time. He even seemed amused at his plight. He leaned forward and pointed at the manuscript with his cigar.

"At least a dozen times in there he could have killed me, Charles. Always he lets me go. Just in the nick of time, as we say in the trade." He paused. "But this last time, I am not so sure. I think he is getting tired of the game. I think he almost decided to do me in."

I turned quickly to the end of the manuscript. I found the scene easily.

> Despite the almost unendurable pain, Rakas could not move any part of his body, save his eyes. In particular, he could not move his hand. He stared at it, watching it become ever more discolored under the flickering ray from the Mandarin's machine. It felt as though a thousand burning needles were twisting in his flesh.
>
> The cadaverous form of the Mandarin arched over him, lit by the infernal rainbow of color emanating from the device. Rakas had the momentary illusion that the creature was not flesh and blood, at all, but a kind of carved architectural device, like a gargoyle on some unholy cathedral.
>
> "Your thoughts of rock images are most appropriate, Rakas," hissed the Mandarin, casually employing his ability to read men's minds. "Perhaps your unconscious is attempting to inform you that you, or at least your right hand, is undergoing a process unique in the history of living human flesh. It is turning into stone."
>
> Rakas stared in horror at the graying, roughening

> skin of his hand. When his bulging eyes traveled back to the Mandarin he saw that the face of the evil genius was now inches from his own. He could feel fetid breath coming from the cruel slash of a mouth.
>
> "Shall I turn you into a garden ornament now, Rakas? Or should I spare you for a time? What do you think?"

Rakas was smiling at me.

"Shall I show you my right hand, Charles?"

It had been hidden behind his attaché case. He pulled it out and held it before me. It was bluish, pale, and stiff.

"It is flesh, not stone," he said. "But it cannot move."

He touched the back of it with the lighted tip of his cigar.

"It cannot feel."

He removed the cigar and I saw that the flesh was still smooth and unbroken.

"It cannot burn."

He chuckled and slid his hand back behind the case.

"You see it is not as bad as in the story. Not yet. But it is getting close, is it not?"

I closed the manuscript without looking at it. Then I threw a part of my professional life out the window.

"Kill the son of a bitch," I said.

"What?"

"Kill the Mandarin. Get rid of him. End the series."

I took a deep breath.

"Look, Aladar, I'll admit the books made a nice bundle of money for us all, but to hell with them. They just aren't worth the damage they're doing to you. This hand business is awful but it's explainable. You can do things like that under hypnosis. But it's a goddamned frightening symptom."

I pushed the manuscript away from me. I didn't want to touch it anymore.

"I'm telling you as your editor, Aladar, that you have absolute carte blanche to slaughter the Mandarin and wrap up the whole business. As a friend, I suggest you do it quickly."

He chuckled again. It was a fair imitation of his usual one, but it didn't have the depth.

"You don't understand, do you, Charles?"

He took the manuscript back and put it into his case. He closed the case and brooded over it for a while.

"Don't you see? I am trying to kill him. Desperately."

He looked at me and his gaze made me uncomfortable.

"With Trowbridge it was altogether different. It was a sort of chess game. Check and countercheck. It was safe. Contained. But now I have removed Trowbridge, and the Mandarin is getting out. The only thing that kept that fiend in the books, I realize this now, was that blasted Englishman. Now I have killed him, and now there is nothing to stop the evil from slithering off the pages I have written."

"All right," I said. "Resurrect Evan Trowbridge. Bring him back from the dead. Conan Doyle did it with Holmes."

This time Rakas actually laughed.

"You have cited the perfect example why I cannot, Charles. Was Holmes ever really the same after Doyle killed him? No. Not except in the adventures Watson remembered from before the event. Even the most convinced Sherlockian must admit in his heart that Holmes never truly survived the tumble into the falls."

He rapped his knuckles on the case and frowned.

"You see, Charles, that is the thing. These creatures are real. They exist. I did not create the Mandarin. I came across him. Do we ever make anything up? I doubt it. I think we only make little openings and peer through them. And openings work both ways."

He stood.

"Doyle was infinitely wiser than I. He respected what he had created. He made bloody damned sure that Holmes took the devil with him when he died. Doyle knew that no one else, least of all himself, would have been able to stop him. And so we are presently safe from the baneful doctor. But I have loosed the Mandarin."

Then, without another word, he turned and left.

I don't know how long I sat there cursing myself for not having done something before, such as keeping in touch with Rakas after that early morning visit, before it occurred to me that sitting and cursing was hardly likely to help. I told my secretary to plead with Rakas to come back up if he decided to phone in, and then I left the office.

I figured the best possibility was that he'd head for his apartment. It was east off the park in the sixties. I knew he seldom took a cab but always walked if he had less than fifteen blocks to go. It was a good bet that he was walking now.

He might go up Fifth, and then he might cut over; there was no way of telling. I decided that a man in his state of mind would probably take the simplest route, the one that needed the least attention, so I crossed my fingers and bet on Fifth. I hurried along and when I drew abreast of the fountain in front of the Plaza, I saw him. He was heading into the park.

My first impulse was to dash right up to him, but then I realized I'd probably just dither, so I slowed to match his pace and tried to keep myself calmed down. He needed a doctor, he needed help, and it was going to take some fancy persuading. I followed him and mulled over possible gambits.

When he got to the zoo he began to walk idly from cage to cage, looking at the animals. I stopped by a balloon and banner man and bought a box of Cracker Jack. It helped me blend in, and I figured the taste of the homely stuff might bring me a little closer to earth. Rakas had stopped by a lion cage and, with slow turns of his head, was watching the beast walk back and forth.

I was standing there munching my Cracker Jack, creating and rejecting openers, when I caught a flicker of movement out of the corner of my eye and turned to see, or almost see, someone dart back under an archway. I stared hard at the empty place. The someone had been very squat and broad. His suit had been a kind of snake green.

I looked back to check on Rakas. He was still standing in front of the lion's cage. I backed, crabwise, to the arch, keeping one eye on it and the other on Rakas. When I reached the arch I darted through it and looked quickly to the left and right, and I got another glimpse of the squat figure.

He'd slipped around the corner of the monkey house. He'd done it so quickly I wouldn't have seen him if I hadn't been looking for him. I remembered a film strip I'd seen demonstrating the insertion of subliminal images. Just one frame, maybe two, edited in so that you weren't sure if it was something you'd really seen up there on the screen or a passing thought in your own mind.

Green clothes, apelike, and quick as a lizard.

Mork.

The Mandarin always sent Mork on before.

Then a kid's balloon burst and he gave out a squawk of fright and I found myself standing in Central Park zoo with a box of Cracker Jack in my hand.

I went back through the arch and saw that Rakas was no longer standing in front of the lion's cage. I looked in all directions, but he was nowhere to be seen. I wondered what Evan Trowbridge would have done in a situation like this, and then I shook my head and tossed the fool Cracker Jack into a Keep Our City Clean basket. Aladar Rakas had gone mad; it was important to remember that. He had gotten lost in his own lunatic fantasy.

I left the zoo and hurried along the path leading uptown. It was logical to assume he had gone that way. In spite of myself, I found I kept looking from side to side to see if I could spot Mork. Of course there were only young lovers walking, women pushing baby carriages, and old men lost in their smoking.

Then, as I stopped to catch my breath on the hill overlooking the pond where children sail their toy boats, I saw Rakas sitting on a bench. He had the manuscript open, resting on his case, and he was writing with furious speed.

I walked up to him carefully. He was absorbed in his work, and it was only when my shadow fell across the pages that he looked up and saw me.

"Charles! What are you doing here?"

"I was worried, Aladar."

"Oh?" He smiled. "That was very thoughtful of you. I am really quite touched."

He looked down at the manuscript.

"I am sorry to have left your office so rudely, Charles. But you know," he looked up at me suddenly, "just as I was leaving, I got an inspiration. A real inspiration. Sit down, please."

I did as he asked. I could see that he had several pages of close scribblings before him. He must have been writing at an incredible speed.

"I think I have figured out a way to get him, Charles. I really believe I know how to get the necessary leverage."

He smiled at me benignly.

"How do you propose to do it, Aladar?"

"Drag him out ahead of schedule. Manifest him before he is strong!"

I only looked at him blankly, but he was far too excited to notice.

"The Mandarin has been trying to get out, you see, attempting to push his way into life. He has been, you might say, pursuing me into existence. Well, I am going to turn and face him and pull him, willy-nilly, into reality. That should put him off his balance!"

He grinned and waved at the scene about us.

"I am going to write him into this actual location, Charles. And on my own terms!"

He rubbed his left hand over his stiff, pale right hand and cackled to himself.

"I began writing it, not on paper, but writing it nevertheless, while at the zoo, watching a lion prowl in his cage. I decided I would begin with Mork. I would not break the tradition of the stories. I had Mork pick up my trail there. I had him follow me," he pointed, "along that path."

I looked back at the path. It was, oddly enough, empty. Only dry leaves blew along it.

"Do you see that boulder?"

I did. It stuck out of the ground like the nose of a huge, gray whale.

"At this moment Mork is hiding behind it."

He tapped the manuscript.

"I have written it here. I have put it down in black and white. He cannot get away. He is trapped. He knows I know. It's all here."

He tapped the manuscript again.

"And now I am going to go over there and kill him, Charles."

He put the manuscript and the case on the bench beside him and then he stood. I opened my mouth, trying to think of something or other to say, but it all got stuck in my throat when I saw Rakas reach into his coat and calmly pull out the biggest revolver I had ever seen in my life. I hadn't known they made them that big. It was terrifying and, at the same time, ludicrous.

"I have been afraid for a long time now, Charles," he said. "Now wait here. I will be right back."

I sat and watched him walk over to the leaning rock. His black coat fluttered about him and the leaves swirled where he walked. He reached the rock, held the revolver straight before him, and walked out of sight.

I waited for the sound of the shot, but it never came. Eventually I stood and followed him. My legs felt rubbery. When I got to the rock I had to lean on it for support. I felt my way around the rock to its other side and saw him lying on the ground, partially covered with a drift of dirty city leaves. He looked up at me.

"How stupid," he said. "I couldn't bring myself to kill him."

Then he closed his eyes. I bent down, close to him. A thick, dark rivulet of blood ran from one of his ears. I brushed through the leaves until I found the revolver, and then I lifted it with both hands. I stood and walked around the rock and looked back toward the bench.

The Mandarin stood there, weirdly tall and thin, like the statue of a mourning angel in a graveyard. He held the manuscript clutched to his breast. Leaves scudded and broke at his feet. I began walking toward him.

"Not yet, you don't," I said.

I came closer.

"The manuscript isn't finished," I said, "not even if the author's dead."

I was closer. His eyes caught the gray autumn light and glinted.

"I'm the editor," I said. "It's my job, it's my right, to see that the book is properly finished. That's the way it's done."

A leaf blew through the figure's head. I was very close. I could see the long nails on his fingers.

I dropped the gun and held out my hands.

"That's the way it's done," I said.

And then I held the manuscript.

I turned away. Some playing children had discovered Rakas and they were shouting excitedly. I put the book into the case and took it away.

Now this, what I have written, is part of the book. I have added it to Rakas' terminal scribblings and now I am going to finish the book.

I have selected this place carefully. It is miles from any other habitation. Its destruction will not endanger any bystander.

I have soaked the walls and floors with gasoline. I have piled rags around my desk and the chair facing my desk and they are also saturated with it. Everything in this room is wet except for the folder of matches which lies beside me within easy reach. The matches are dry and ready.

Aladar Rakas discovered the Mandarin, but he couldn't quite believe in him. Even at the end he was unable to convince himself that such evil could really exist. He was too civilized a man. Too kindly and too generous.

But I am different. I have seen Rakas in the leaves and I, like Evan Trowbridge, believe in evil.

And I, like Evan Trowbridge and unlike Aladar Rakas, believe in and respect the power of the Mandarin. The devil may know what vile knowledge coils in that huge and unnaturally ancient brain, but I have only the faintest of glimmerings. I know only enough to realize that there is no question of my outwitting the monster.

I will attempt no subtleties. I will use the power I have as author to bring him here, and then I shall destroy everything, the entire hideous fabric of the pattern which made this situation possible. The book, the author and the creature spawned—all shall be burned cleanly away.

Now I am going to finish the book.

He is outside the door, now. He does not want to be but he must because I am writing it.

Now he has put his hand on the latch. Now he is opening the door. Now he stands there, in the twilight, looking at me with hatred in his eyes. That hatred takes a hater like myself to meet it.

He is here. Really and truly here. Not a near phantom, like the last time, but a solid, breathing being.

He is moving forward carefully, stepping high to avoid the soaked rags, but gasoline stains the hem of his gray, silken robe all the same.

Now he sits and glares at me.

He cannot move. He cannot budge, try as he may.

His eyes glow. They shimmer like fire seen through honey.

He cannot move.

Now I have lit a match and set the pack aflame.
He cannot

I hope I shall never forget the extraordinary expression of astonishment on Charles Pearl's face when he realized he had committed suicide to no purpose.

He remained conscious for a remarkable period of time, considering the damage the fire was doing to him, staring at me with utter disbelief as I gathered up the manuscript, including this last page torn from his typewriter.

The idiot had discovered Evan Trowbridge's strength, which was implacable hatred, but he had shared, and therefore missed altogether, his weakness, which was a lack of sufficient imagination.

Trowbridge always failed to bring me down altogether because he never quite managed to foresee the final trick of my science, the last fantastic ingenuity, the climactic trapdoor.

It would never have occurred to him, for instance, that I can live invulnerable in a pool of fire.

And so I, the hero of the series all along, have the opportunity to bring this final volume to, it pleases me to say, a happy ending.

RAMSEY CAMPBELL

Horror House of Blood

"Listen, I'm really sorry to bother you like this," the young man at the door said. "My name's David Lloyd and I'm a film director."

Marilyn drew back her foot, which she'd poised to kick should he try to stop the door. "You've been filming up the street," she said.

"Right, that's me. You've been watching us, right?"

"No, but you can't avoid being gossiped at in the shops round here. Anyway, come in, you're standing in a draft. I'm afraid you'll have to take us as you find us."

Lloyd surveyed the interior beyond the short entrance hall which was like an airlock: one large room reduced to an L by a partitioned-off kitchen; two settees surrounded by collages of Sunday newspaper sections; a man of about thirty with a chubby pink just-shaved face and a dressing gown, rising to his feet and swinging up his hand; a dining area next to the kitchen, a table and chairs of plain pale wood; a staircase leading up the pale blue wall on Lloyd's right to a landing and a door. "Knockout," Lloyd said.

"I'm Frank Taylor and this is my wife Marilyn," the man

said. "And you're a film director? Quiet on the set for Mr. Hitchcock, that sort of thing?"

"Right, that sort of thing. Not quite that big a name yet, maybe. In fact, that's what I want to talk to you about."

"If you're looking for extras I'm always telling Marilyn she should be in the movies. Go on, do 'Come up and see me sometime' for him. Well, maybe it's a bit early in the day. But you'd swear Mae West was in the room."

"Right on. It's not extras, actually, let me tell you what it is. This is my first film, right, and it just could be in line for a festival. I've got some money in it and so have some other people. We had budget problems but we thought we'd cracked them by shooting on location in the suburbs, right? Some friends of mine lived up your street here and we were using their house. But they got an offer in America and they just pissed off, sorry, you don't mind, good, they just pissed off after selling the house to these other people who won't let us film there. So zap, no film."

"All your work wasted," Marilyn said.

"A lot of people's six weeks wasted. I mean, you can understand that, Mr. Taylor, Frank, right on, call me Dave. So I don't have to tell you what's on my mind, you can see right through me. We're trying to duplicate the interior we were using and this is just knockout. Exactly the same. Not that you haven't done a lot with it, I mean you can tell it's your house and nobody else's. I'm just no good with words, you can tell that, right? But I want to believe I'm good with visuals. I really think I am. And by Christ I want those stairs."

"What were you thinking of doing with them?" Marilyn said.

"Can I show you?" Lloyd began to pace up the stairs, squinting through a rectangle of his fingers, swaying his head and fingers and body in slow complex syncopation. "It's just the suspense scenes we have to shoot. A lot of this film takes place on the stairs, it saves money and makes for claustrophobia. The paint's the wrong color but that's okay, we'll be shooting monochrome with a filter. Now here I am tracking up the stairs,

I'm the camera, right, I'm swaying a bit toward the wall so it feels as if it's closing in, I'm tracking in on the door, it's almost filling the screen and slowly, slowly, it opens—"

Slowly the door opened.

"It doesn't do that," Marilyn said.

"Yes, it has been," Frank said. "Last week it did, I forgot to tell you. I'll have to fix it."

"Well, we'll have someone inside to move it when we're shooting," Lloyd said. "But that shows you the sort of thing we'll be doing. We won't damage anything, I mean we won't even touch anything. And three days at the outside to pack up and go. I don't know what else to say except, you know, I'd be incredibly grateful."

"I don't see why not, do you?" Frank said.

"Not really, I suppose," Marilyn said. "Only it's a pity you won't be here. Don't expect a technical analysis every night when you come home."

"I only wish we could pay you, I mean except for the electricity," Lloyd said. "That's why the rest of the people we tried wouldn't have us. Anyway, listen, Mrs. Taylor, we won't be asking for anything, even bring our own flasks of coffee. Maybe we can take you out to lunch one day. Make a change from the housework, I mean, we guys don't know what it is to work."

"The boutique where I worked has closed," Marilyn said. "I'm just straightening things before I apply for another job."

"Looks like you've given us a wardrobe mistress, Frank," Lloyd said. "See you tomorrow, Mrs. Taylor, on the set of *Horror House of Blood.* Look, that door's rehearsing again."

When Frank arrived home on Tuesday night he found Marilyn hugging herself on the front lawn. "Have they thrown you out?"

"No, I'm standing guard so you don't spoil their film. That, and I've seen all I can stand."

"Yesterday you were fascinated."

"With the mechanics of it. It's the people I can't bear."

"The cast or the characters?"

"I can't tell. Perhaps both. Your friend Lloyd is an insufferable pig and his wife, if that's what she is in real life, is so meek it's terrifying. I can't see the point, but I know I don't like being in there with it. I don't care if it is only a film, it isn't pleasant to have two strangers in your home goading each other to violence by being what they are, and you not knowing what's going to happen."

"I think we're being invited in," Frank said. "David, would you and your wife like a cup of tea?"

"Love one," Lloyd said. "My wife's making dinner for the crew so you must excuse her. Listen, Frank, I'm sorry to be in your way when you come home. We've had to wedge your bedroom door because it's not cued to open yet, and I moved the phone behind the settee."

"Don't worry about it. I tell you what, though, we wouldn't mind hearing what the film is about. Only it's been disturbing my wife a bit in the wrong way, hasn't it, Marilyn. Not understanding, if you see what I mean."

"Right on. We've only got one more scene to shoot, Mrs. Taylor, so we won't be in your way after tomorrow. I mean, you've been fantastic, but I know you've got things to do. Let me tell you about this scene. I'm the husband, right, and I'm cracking up because my wife's possessed by this thing. She keeps becoming a real maniac, you know, violent, lots of aggro. So I go upstairs to her with a knife in case I need it. Then I hear her calling out and she sounds okay, so I leave the knife on the stairs. I go in and you hear us talking. You're staring at this door, right, your bedroom door, it's hanging there, it's all you can see, you know something's going to happen, the voices stop and there's dead silence, everything's still and it's like waiting for a snake to strike. Then you see her eyes, right? Straight cut in to close-up, these absolutely mad eyes—"

"Sorry to interrupt," Frank said, "but if I understand what

you're trying to do, wouldn't it be better to have it as a dinner scene? With her picking up a knife from the table and stabbing him, if that was your idea? I was just thinking that anyone who wouldn't accept the possession idea would go along with the wife losing her self-control. Right?"

"That's not bad," Lloyd said, peering between the treads of the stairs at the table. "That's good," gliding across the room and circling the table. "That's knockout!" zooming his face in on a knife. "Thing is, we've got the stairs now, and if we shifted to the table we'd have to reshoot some of the stuff in the can. And we could have done a lot with this fantastic low ceiling. Christ, what a film we could make if we had money."

"Yet you still expect it to be a success?" Marilyn said.

"I don't book films. It could make a second feature or it could make a festival where they like this sort of thing. It'll get me more work, that's where it's at. I'm sure you understand that, Frank."

When he'd left Marilyn pulled out the wedge from the bedroom door. She stood on the landing for some minutes, watching the hanging dormant wood and the immobile surrounding crack.

Marilyn was pulling out the dressing-table drawers and smiling at the hidden treasures in the corners—a cufflink, two Christmas cards left over from ten months ago, a plastic pawn—when she heard Lloyd downstairs saying "Yes, that might do. Christ, perfect!". She heard the stairs creak as he padded upward. She tensed, preparing a cold smile in case he should open the door. Then she giggled and turning her back to the door, pulled up her skirt and mimed dressing. But the creaks receded. Curious and determined not to talk herself out of it, she opened the door.

They'd switched off their lamps. She had gone upstairs partly to rest her eyes and her brain, for each time they switched off the glare the room and stairs looked dim and unreal, like a fading photograph, and she resented having to spend energy in adjusting. Lloyd and his cameraman were sandwiching the continuity girl on the couch, passing the script back and forth and scribbling on it with marker pens. Lloyd's wife was staring out of the window at a woman cleaning her car. The continuity girl's eyes met Marilyn's through the gesticulations on the couch. Marilyn smiled in sympathy with her expression, then almost tripped on a knife on the stairs.

It was her little sharp kitchen knife, scratched and discolored but still clean, which she used for cutting vegetables. One day her mother had let her use it, and that was the day she'd started to learn cookery. She remembered the warmth of the kitchen and the windows blurring, her mother laughing as Marilyn prised the knife from her fingers and her silent eye-corner supervision as Marilyn chopped the carrots, the single wind-troubled rose that swelled and dwindled on the blurred window like a red stain, and the almost inaudible hum as the coffin slid into the crematorium. "Who put this here?" she demanded.

"I did. It's for this last scene," Lloyd said. "I'm sorry, we didn't hear you coming down."

"This is my knife."

"Yes, but I mean you don't use it, do you? Really? Right, sorry. I'll tell you what it is. You know in horror films knives always look brand new, like it was an advertising film for steel or something. We want something nastier than that, something that looks real, a bit rusty and jagged, you know. It really would be a help if we could use it. Critics might, I know you can't predict critics any more than audiences, but they might think it was imaginative. I mean, imaginative details can add up to a good review.

Lloyd backed out of the bedroom and down the stairs, his whole body focused on an attempt to snatch up the knife before his wife caught sight of it. As he descended slowly, groping with his foot for the next step, his body began to stoop toward his right hand as if a weight were dragging it down. Then his wife's hand flew out and had the knife. She reared above him and stabbed. "Don't poke with it!" Lloyd shouted, his back to the camera. "Slice, you stupid bitch, slice! Imagine slicing off lumps of flesh with it! Imagine chopping slices off my cock!"

He plodded to the bottom of the stairs, mopping his forehead. "Jesus," he said. "Right, let's do it for real."

"I'm sorry, you mustn't use that," Marilyn said. "It's very sharp and you might have an accident."

"Oh come on. It's not coming anywhere near me. We'll be filming all the spouting blood next week."

"I'm sorry," Marilyn said.

"Wait five minutes," Lloyd said to his crew, and hurried out. Marilyn glanced round at them, but they avoided her eyes. Only Lloyd's wife met them for a moment. On the stairs as she'd tried to master the knife Marilyn had seemed to see a tiny fear scuttling inside her eyes, trying to hide and at the same time trying to escape. Now her eyes were as clear and blank as her skin and her dazzling silver hair. Marilyn looked away and stared at herself in the mirror, at the wrinkles around her eyes and mouth that Frank said smiled when she smiled.

Less than five minutes later the telephone rang. It was Frank. "Look, what on earth's the problem?" he said. "They aren't going to kill each other just for a film?"

"There's more to it than that," Marilyn said. "I don't want it in my house."

"I'd say that was a tribute to the film. Anyway, look, I was halfway through programming and it doesn't help to be interrupted. It's not as if they've just barged in, after all. I told them they could film and I don't think there's any reason to go back on that. And listen, he didn't have to go out to phone. For heaven's sake be a bit more hospitable."

When Lloyd returned he didn't look at her. "Go on; and remember, make it real," he told his wife. As he replaced the knife on the stairs the lamps blazed and glinted dully on the blade. Marilyn felt as if she were in a bunker in the desert, but she restrained herself from making for the kitchen. An urge recurred to snatch the knife and return it to the kitchen, but instead she snorted at herself and sat in a chair against the mantelpiece. "You won't mind if I watch, will you," she said.

"Right on. See how it grabs you." Lloyd was ascending the stairs slowly, hesitantly, listening to an absent voice and nodding and smiling, his face turned slightly to the camera that loomed at his back. He mimed planting the knife and the camera stooped to look at it. Marilyn heard the stairs creak long and deliberately beneath the camera's weight. They'd said it wasn't as heavy as it looked. She almost rose to her feet, then pressed her ankles together to restrain herself.

Lloyd had entered the bedroom. The camera was staring at the door. As it began to retreat, the cameraman's foot feeling for the edge of the stair, the stair emitting a prolonged throbbing creak, Marilyn heard Lloyd's voice beyond the door. "Let's see you do one good scene, right? I may not be Paul Newman but you sure as shit aren't Joanne Woodward. Now you grab that knife and cut great gobs of flesh out of me. Enjoy it, right?"

Slowly, slowly, the door opened. Lloyd emerged backwards like an insect from a hole, as if desperate for the moment at which he could turn and flee. One foot slipped on the edge of the staircase and his hand swung out, fingers frantic as the legs of an impaled spider. He slid his hand down the banister and then without warning ran down and made a grab for the knife.

His wife was quicker. She had the handle as he grasped the knife, and his fingers closed on the blade. His wife let go, and Marilyn cried out, for his hand came up with the blade still hanging from the folded cuts in his fingers. "Now then, real blood!" he shouted. "You felt it, right, like slicing butter! Go on, you stupid cow, you're over the shock, you're mad! Get the knife and slice, slice!" Then he fell back, his hand slithering down the wall in a trail of blood as she went to work on him.

"Get a sponge for the wall," Lloyd said to his wife, running water over his fingers. "That was knockout," he said. "Absolutely real."

As soon as Frank had closed the front door he said, "I'm sorry. I shouldn't have left you to put up with them by yourself."

"I think I managed perfectly well," Marilyn said.

Later they massaged each other before making love. His arms sometimes grew tense at the computer keyboard, and she freed them. Her neck and shoulders felt like a single plate of metal now the day had accumulated, although she understated this, not wanting it to seem a reproachful symbol or a further turn in the knot of half-felt but unspoken argument. Suddenly, as he kneaded her shoulders, she was moist and wide. For a moment she felt betrayed by her body, then she knelt forward and speared herself on him. At first his movements were slow and caressing, but as they continued he raised his thighs from the bed and thrust as if to impale her, helpless. He must have read the plea in her eyes not to turn her beneath him.

As they lay touching, their breath easing, they heard a creak on the stairs so loud as to be almost an explosion. Marilyn started, then ran to open the door. As she did so the top stair creaked back into shape.

"It was the camera," she said. "All that weight, the stairs couldn't take it. Poor stairs." She hurried into the bathroom and wiped herself. When she lay down beside him again she said "Frank, did that door really open before they came?"

"Yes," he said slipping an arm beneath her neck and stroking her cheek.

"Really?"

"Yes, of course."

"Really?"

"No, damn it! I don't know why I bothered trying to reassure you. It's you who have to stay at home with it."

She propped herself above him. "But what am I supposed to be frightened of?" she said.

Next morning at breakfast she said, "We haven't had a party for a while." Since Lloyd and his crew had left, the house felt like a vacuum, and all her reservations about the house returned: its anonymity, its oppressiveness, the sense of being threatened by a kind of middle-class commune where the front door was open to everyone else and their trivia. It's near London, she told herself. That's important.

They managed to call the party for Saturday. Marilyn was surprised how many people were free. Perhaps they were trying to ignore the suburbs too, she thought. She showed the latest arrivals where to throw their coats on the bed. Someone was already vomiting in the bathroom. It's going to be a good party, she thought.

Some of Frank's colleagues had congregated in the kitchen around the makeshift bar. "Oh, that old sod," one said. "Have you seen him since he came back from holiday? He's got himself a hairpiece. Either that or he's been sticking his head in a dungheap."

Frank picked his way upstairs through guests sitting on the staircase. A few were perched on the side of the bath. "Listen, you can use our bedroom," he said. "There's room in there even with all the coats."

Marilyn passed a group of wives casually poised on the edge of a settee, blowing out thin cones of smoke with a chorus of soft pops, and joined a poker game. "This is a hard school," one of the men said. "All right," Marilyn said, and won three pounds.

She went upstairs, patting her way among the heads and shoulders. She hadn't realized so many people would bring so many people. In the spare bedroom they were sitting shoulder to shoulder against the wall. Her and Frank's bedroom door was open, but the room was empty. She leaned into the spare room and said to whomever she was looking at, "There's a room next door as well."

"Oh no, not me," the girl said. "Try someone else."

Descending the stairs was like groping her way down a strewn hill in a mist. There was a ceiling of tobacco smoke halfway down. Marilyn coughed and nearly tripped, falling against the shoulders of a man who kneed the woman below him, and so on down the stairs. There were laughs and howls of protest.

"Listen, everyone," Frank said. "If we could shift some of you into our bedroom it would make things a good deal easier."

There was a silence. Then a friend said, "If that's a joke it's in appalling taste. Can we have our coats, please."

When he'd gone, taking with him half-a-dozen others and any hint of an explanation, the party seemed to arrange itself more comfortably. Corks popped and conversation welled. The subject of the bedroom sank at once and seemed not worth the rescuing. Nobody entered the room except to retrieve coats.

Swaying upstairs after turning out the downstairs lights, Frank found Marilyn standing outside their bedroom. "Shall I carry you across the threshold?" he said, steadying himself against the door frame

She saw herself caught up and borne into the darkness. "No thanks, you only just managed it the first time," she said laughing, and groped beyond his shoulder for the bedroom light switch. She felt her fingers almost touching the darkness. Then Frank sagged into the dark bedroom, taking her with him. A great gasp rushed into her, pummeling her chest. As she levered herself up from him she felt his body trembling. He was choking back laughter.

"Did you do that on purpose?" she demanded.

"Of course not," he said, roaring with laughter.

She lay in bed with darkness pressing on her open eyes. Just before she awoke the pressure of her eyelids built up a blaze of crimson. Then she was tiptoeing toward the bedroom. As she opened the door cautiously she leapt up from the bed, and her eyes were pools of blood.

On Sunday afternoon they walked in the nearby park. They walked until night and heavy rain began to fall. Marilyn ran to shelter beneath the awning of a deserted kiosk. The rain swung toward them, forcing water through their clothes, and then away. "I wish you hadn't hired out the house," she said finally.

"They had to get the film in the can somewhere."

"They had to what?" she said, peering at his lips.

"They had to make their film, right?"

At his last word she peered closer. His mind slipped out of synchronization, and his lips continued moving for a moment without words. "Oh come on," he said.

"It's not going to be the same."

"Don't tell me about it. You're capable of dealing with it yourself, you said so. If you don't need protecting, fair enough. It's a good job I didn't marry you for that, that's all."

She stared at his lips as he spoke. Because his shadow lay across her he couldn't see her eyes.

On Thursday afternoon he telephoned her. "I just thought you'd like to know that those notes I asked you to put in my trousers pocket last night aren't there."

"You're right. They were on the bedroom floor. You must have dropped them."

"Then it must have been the way you hung my trousers."

"Perhaps it was. I was just about to ring you, if we can talk about something else now. There's something here."

"Look, you don't want me to come home, do you? I've got two minutes to conference. Come up here if you must."

"Please don't disturb youself. It's nothing I can't deal with."

"Well, I'll have to try to improve. I should be able to take care of my own house, shouldn't I. After all, my place is in the home."

"Not necessarily. Not without efficiency."

At the door of the conference room he turned and rang the switchboard. "If my wife calls, call me," he said. Later, as he drove home, a frown kept shadowing his vision. I mustn't expect too much of her, he thought. After all, I'm three years older. I shouldn't be upsetting her except as a last resort. That's not what I'm for.

He pulled down the garage door and hurried along the path through the gardens, which most resembled a few scraps of green velvet among which were stuck lamps like white-headed pins. As he neared the back door his fist, raised to knock, sank. Through the frosted-glass panel of the door he could see on the white walls of the kitchen great blurs of dull crimson. A crimson trickle had seeped beneath the door and down the step.

He was stooping and almost touching the trickle with his fingers, while his mind tried to prepare itself to enter the house, when a pale blur opened the back door. It was Marilyn. She looked almost as if she were sleepwalking. "Mind where you walk," she said. "There's broken glass."

Indeed there was, and some of it still bore fragments of the ketchup label. "Why?" Frank said. "Don't answer that, I'm being stupid."

"Perhaps you are," she said, opening a cupboard and removing a mop and sponges.

"I'll do that. You sit down."

"No. After all, it's my job."

He took her arm gently and having led her to the settee, poured her a whisky. When he'd finished cleaning the kitchen she hadn't touched the drink. He'd counted the labels as he cleared up: at least four bottles. It seemed odd to him that she should have bought so many simply in order to express her frustration.

"Why did you buy so much ketchup?" he said, trying to trivialize.

"It's better than real blood, isn't it?" she said and then smiled sadly at him and frowned, hesitating. "To try to get it over with," she said.

On Friday night he was smiling behind a bouquet. He was happy to be home, to be with Marilyn all weekend: perhaps they could talk. A dull crusted trail of crimson hung down the back step. Must clean that, he thought.

Marilyn was cooking, but she turned and hugged him when she saw the flowers. "We've got a vase somewhere. I'll find it," he said. He found it beneath the sink. As he straightened up he saw the handle of a knife protruding from the kitchen bin. It was the small knife Marilyn used for chopping vegetables, its blade broken.

"Did you break this today?" he said.

"Yes, I broke it."

"I'll buy you another tomorrow."

"No. No thanks, I don't want one."

He arranged the flowers in the glass vase and stood it on the table. As he did so he caught sight of his hand refracted through the water, his fingers broken and warped. He pulled his hand away and glimpsed the knife hanging from the fingers, which were cut half through. They felt cold from the metal and exposure to the air that wedged itself icily into the gashes, yet warm with the blood that pumped up. The raw flesh and nerves seemed to be tasting the metal, for the cold flavor somehow seeped into his brain without relating to his tongue.

He had time to dread moving his hand in case the fingers flopped back against the knuckles before the moment passed. She's infecting me, he thought. No, that's unfair, it's a hangover from the film. That's right, that was the knife David Lloyd was going to use in the film. I wonder what he really did with it exactly. We'll have to wait and see the film. I hope it's soon. I'd like to see what he's made of our house. Although perhaps I'd better make sure it doesn't catch me in this sort of susceptible mood.

"Will you cut this for me?" Marilyn called.

She pointed to a French loaf on the breadboard. Suddenly he realized that she'd asked him to cut several things in the past few days: string, vegetables, meat. And the meals she'd made tended to involve little chopping and cutting. The only knives she used were the blunt saw-edged table knives. He frowned.

"I know it's my job," she said.

"Well, it is really."

"Perhaps I'll be better in a few days," she said. He saw her hands were shaking.

"Don't worry," he said. Her gaze sought his lips. He turned toward the breadboard, away from her, and tried to think of an approach to the subject that didn't sound like a cliché. There was no use in beginning with alienation. But he couldn't produce an opening, and while he was pondering he saw her reflected dimly in the glass doors of a cupboard. Her hands were calm. Turning suddenly, he said, "It's tension, we'll crack it," and saw her swiftly begin trembling her hands in evidence. Well, he thought, she's saying she needs me to protect her. That's what I've been saying all along, but out loud.

"I know what the tension is," he said. "Now listen and don't argue. It wasn't the film, it was you working. I could see it building up. Now you've given up work you don't know what to do with yourself. I tell you what I'll do. I'll come home for lunch every day. Then you won't have any excuse to get bored with the house. I think you feel it's still a bit unfamiliar, more than I do. But it is your house, you know, Marilyn. More even than mine. It's yours and you're stuck with it."

She was staring at the kitchen bin. He reached out to make her look up at him, but didn't touch her; she might simply withdraw further. "Now look, you know I'm right," he said. "Just think a bit and you'll see I am."

He sat down on one of the settees. A wedge of light from the front window fell across him. He felt spotlighted, held on a stage by the light. He heard Marilyn stirring soup, the unhurried purr of a mower on a lawn, a group of boys bouncing a football toward the nearby field. He felt the tensions of the day begin to seep out of him. Everything was all right, he thought, essentially.

A tongue of newspaper thrust through the letterbox, clacking then plopping to the floor. Frank shifted on the settee; he'd get the paper in a minute. Then he heard Marilyn moving behind him, near the stairs. "It's all right, don't bother," he said. "I'll get it." He glanced around to smile. Marilyn was not behind him.

For a retarded moment, during which the light seemed to

solidify about him, he had the irrational conviction that she was hiding below the back of the settee. He couldn't stop himself from looking to see. "I thought you'd come out of the kitchen," he called, picking up the newspaper. "Can't imagine why I'd think that."

He'd found an item in the newspaper that made him laugh and was rephrasing it in the terms he felt would amuse her most when his ears began to throb. His blood was thumping them like a shoulder against a door. All at once the sounds around him were snatched away, leaving him suspended in silence. He looked up, glaring. No, the sounds were there, but annoyingly muffled. He poked at his ears, swallowing. They felt as if a vacuum were pulling at them, he thought, and something was tugging at his nerves. He flapped the newspaper at himself angrily, tense, distracted. The light isolated him on its stage.

He'd smoothed out the paper again and was relaxing when he heard a vague muffled sound behind him, rolling down the stairs. More than anything else the muffled quality annoyed him, as if a projectionist had neglected to turn up the sound. What's she doing now? he thought irritably. He turned round and saw Marilyn in the kitchen, quickly nipping hot plates. But as he turned back to his reading he realized the edge of his eye or of his mind had retained another glimpse, of a red shape coming to rest at the foot of the stairs.

What have we got that's red? he thought, folding a page over. Red? he thought, trying to concentrate on the editorial, denying himself the relief of turning to look. Red? We haven't *got* anything that's red, he thought. "For God's sake!" he shouted, flinging down the newspaper and striding to the stairs.

There was nothing. Marilyn had run from the kitchen and was staring at him. "It's all right, it's all right," he said, gesturing her away. "It's nothing." She was still staring at him. "Nothing!" he shouted, frowning at her. He started upstairs. "Just off to the loo," he called to placate her, a motive he didn't bother to conceal.

He was almost at the top when the bedroom door swung

open. The top stair creaked loudly. As he stooped to examine it he felt a cold tickling sensation on his face, on his hands. He felt air cutting through his clothes, then through his flesh. Warmth leaked over his skin. He was still wondering what was happening when he felt his eyeballs part. He cried out and fell the length of the stairs.

At his cry Marilyn cried out too. She snatched the broken knifeblade from the bin and ran to the stairs. Frank was lying at the bottom. The shadow of a bruise was growing on his forehead, but he was otherwise unmarked. Heedless of the blood that filled the creases of her hand from her clumsy grip on the blade she stood over him, glaring defiantly up the stairs.

He regained consciousness minutes later, as she cradled him. She was about to help him to his feet when the bedroom door began to tremble. She grabbed the knifeblade from the pool of her blood, wondering if it were about to begin.

FELICE PICANO

Absolute Ebony

On a hot and stifling Roman night in the middle of the last century, a desultory tête-à-tête between two markedly different Americans was enlivened by a sudden barrage of knocking and shouting several floors below at the level of the Via Ruspoli.

The younger-seeming of the two men went to the wide ledge of the window and, peering down, reported that two rough *contadini* were attempting to gain admission to the *pensione.*

"Leave them, William," his friend remarked, with the same torpor and indifference he had displayed during their reunion dinner, fragments of which now littered the uncovered trestle table in the large, gloomy dining chamber. "The housekeeper, good Antonia, will see to them."

"Shall I go?" William asked. "Would you like to rest?"

"All I have is rest in this infernal city during this most dreadful summer. No. Stay. Your talk and natural high spirits bring me much comfort."

Although his companion had reason to doubt the exact veracity of these words, an acquaintance that extended some years to their childhood across the ocean obligated him to remain. Even before William had set forth on his European journey, he had known of his friend's various misfortunes, and the consequent disordered mental condition they had imparted.

A man in the prime of his life, Michaelis, as he called himself and was so known now, had been an artist of such extraordinary promise that a lifetime of the greatest renown and most elevated rewards had once appeared to be his natural birthright.

As a lad, his talent in draftsmanship and the application of *aquarelles* had been so precocious as to attract the attentions of the venerable Charles Willson Peale. Under such tutelage, an inherent genius for the plastic arts was both nourished and coordinated. Upon the death of the old master, the young heir to his artistic mantle had but one course left open to him; leaving the young Republic, he set off to conquer Italy, the art capital of the world.

Michaelis's arrival in Rome a decade previous had initially been embroidered with accolades and much patronage. He worked long hours, happily fulfilling many enterprises in the spacious fourth floor apartments of a palace on the Caelian, rented out by an indigent contessa obliged by penury to reside with more prudence outside the city gates. Nor was the young artist's life one only of toil, no matter how satisfying and conducive to others' admiration.

The handsome and confident youth was early sought out by representatives of the highest cultural circles the capital offered—not only artists and sculptors, but poets, musicians, and eventually scientists and philosophers of great subtlety and abstruseness. From these last intellects, Michaelis had learned the rarefied art of exploring the ideal; and from their examples he had conceived of the possibility of useful relations between the ideal and his own work.

There were lighter matters to counterbalance such sobriety in the young man's life: teas, salons, dinner parties, balls, riding every fair day, churches with frescoes to be studied, *palazzi* with paintings to be inspected. Nor was the fair sex absent or indifferent to Michaelis. Several women of various ages, ranks and nationalities had secretly given their hearts to the dashing artist upon first meeting. In turn, Michaelis had selected his lady from among the four handsome daughters of the Anglican minister, unofficial director of the English-speaking community in the city.

Because the young woman, although apparently sensible and reciprocal in her regard for the artist, was underage at the time of their meeting, nearly six years passed before their engagement could be consummated. When they did wed, Michaelis's happiness was unsurpassed. He had recently completed the commission of a large mural for the reception chamber of one of the most powerful prelates of the Roman church. His work was never in higher favor or greater demand. His fame, and that of his colleagues and circle of friends, spanned the continent. And his Charlotte was the flower of his existence.

Such extreme content was to last only eight months. On a trip to the *campagna,* the Signora Michaelis was suddenly taken with a fever. Fragile by constitution, she succumbed within a fortnight.

As was to be expected, Michaelis was utterly distraught. His great disappointment in Charlotte's death caused a melancholia which deepened long after the natural period of mourning had passed. His clerical father-in-law of so short a duration listened with much anxiety and little aid, to the young artist's words, which inclined dangerously to the heretical.

One year passed, then another, and Michaelis found himself still unable to renew his previous connections, nor, more importantly, to return to that labor which had once been the very mainspring of his life. Previously valued for his flights of fancy and unforced humor, he was now shunned by his friends for the various perorations of gloom he could evince on the least provocation. Former companions fell away or visited infrequently and only as a duty.

Michaelis's painting—at one time the joy of all who beheld it for its bright, noble evocation of youth and hope—underwent a transformation consonant with his altered sensibility. He began to espouse a new theory of art: that color itself was an aberration of the senses, a snare of illusion. He declared that all colors ought to be resolved to a more coherent system. Studying earlier theoreticians of chromatics, Michaelis found half-truths and errors to constitute the greater part of their writings. Finally, and by some never adequately explicated chain of reasoning, he decreed that only by a subtle yet complete mixture of the chromatic scale could color be true both to the mind and the senses.

When he picked up his brushes and palette at last, his tints began to darken; his hues became scarcely distinguishable from each other: reds diminished to deep indigoes, brilliant cobalts became muddied midnight navies. His skills were as evident as before—intensified, his more discriminating colleagues attested. But few sitters wanted portraits so dark, so evidently colorless that a brace of candelabra were needed to illuminate even the penumbral backgrounds, and where details of feature or attitude were transitory as a taper's flicker.

Patronage dwindled, and Michaelis's renown was distorted into that of an eccentric—or worse, a fraud. That his new work was mocked and scorned only confirmed his belief that he had found the hidden truth of art. He applied himself with renewed vigor to elaborating the darkening of his palette, the complex obscurity of his vision. Bitterness and poverty gradually seeped into his life. Voluntary loneliness and desolation of joy in human activities coarsened his courtesies. Mistrust and misanthropy and a growing sense of enmity silenced him.

So had William found his friend, and so Michaelis remained during his visit despite all efforts to elevate him by recollections of shared youthful joys and follies. Nor was William persuasive in suggesting alternative courses of action to a future that even Michaelis himself foresaw as one of deepening decline. The American pleaded that his friend return with him in some two weeks to the less somber environs of their mother commonwealth, and to the more wholesome memories and occupations that the voyage would surely entail; but the painter could not entertain the idea of leaving the locale of his greatest happiness and most utter devastation. William was to go on to Venice day after next, return to Rome, then embark alone for Boston. Sadly, William acquiesced, again scanning the haggard appearance which once had bloomed so vigorously, as though he too were an artist and wished to memorize each cruelly imposed distortion of feature for a future portraiture.

Micahelis's continued silence, and his companion's own resultant silence, became suddenly intolerable. William had just stood back from the table, signaling his intention to depart, when there was a knocking on the apartment doors, which, while less disturbing than that earlier heard, had a more portentous resonance due to the echoing of the high-ceilinged rooms.

His host bade William stay a minute more while he answered the summons. From the outer corridor, William heard the housekeeper's rapid sputter of Italian, followed by his friend's morose accents in that same tongue, soon intertwined with another, lighter voice, speaking a dialect of the language.

Michaelis reentered the room with an astonishing alteration and, energetically gesturing, ushered in the two grimy *contadini* William had seen outside. They gazed about them with hesitancy and awe at the apartment's size and elegance. The artist meanwhile cleared a space across half the table and asked the men to set down their parcel and open it.

When the molding cloths had been removed and each of the peasants served a flagon of wine, Michaelis touched and fondled a rough stone the size and shape of a three-pound loaf of freshly baked bread. William was as perplexed by his friend's sudden alteration of mood—hectic, ruddy enthusiastic now—as he was by the rock.

Taking up a small mallet such as marble-carvers use, the artist inserted an iron wedge into a hairline crack that ran along the top of the stone loaf and began to tap gently at it, all the while talking to his friend.

"These men, William, are from the countryside near L'Aquila in the Abruzzan Apennines, where lie the deepest charcoal pits in the peninsula: in all Europe, it is rumored. They assure me that what I am about to uncover is the finest, purest, blackest charcoal they or any they know have ever laid eyes upon.

"If they speak truthfully, then I have found at last the pigment I have been searching for these past three years; the inevitable yet almost ideal result of my studies and experiments; the base color I shall have ground and mixed to make a linseed oil to complete my most perfect masterpiece—there!, that large, shrouded canvas you beheld earlier and questioned me on, which I would not show you or any man, and which has lain incomplete, awaiting this final color.

"If these men speak truly, William, we have before us what I have dreamed of, what I have required to prove my theory. Then will I be vindicated within the fortnight, when the new salon of Rome opens and my painting walks off with the greatest acclaim."

Michaelis tapped a final soft blow on the wedge, and the stone gave off a sound soft as a sigh, before it fell sheerly onto the surrounding cloths. Within it, the size of a man's fist—of a man's heart—lay a mass of charcoal so black, so dense, that the *contadini* and William too were forced to gasp and draw back from it.

Michaelis stared, merely emitting a guttural murmur. "Ah, my beauty!"

William was unable to draw his eyes away from the dark mineral on the table. Its blackness was so intense that it seemed to recede from his vision, drawing his sight deeper within itself.

"What is it?" he asked.

"Only a fine chunk of charcoal now. But when it is made into a pigment, William, then it will be absolute ebony!"

William repeated the words, with growing discomfort.

"All colors composed of light mix to pure white," Michaelis explained. "Goethe proved that. But all colors composed of earthly material mix to black. Therefore I have painted a masterpiece in black so comprehensive as to make Rembrandt's darkest works seem like summer fripperies. We must see how this charcoal pulverizes. Good as its hue is, it must powder correctly or it will mix poorly."

So saying, he scraped one side of the wedge against the lump until a fine powder descended. This the artist held up on one finger, inspecting it by candlelight with great care and eventual satisfaction.

"It will do," the artist said, then sat down and sipped more wine, once more becoming pensive.

William believed the arrival of the *contadini* with the charcoal represented a turning point in his friend's life. He had never doubted Michaelis's skill or ingenuity, but he sensed disaster impending from this latest event. In applying to an all-black painting a pigment blacker still, the artist would surely seal his fate in Rome. His canvas would be completed, hung at the salon, scoffed at, made the butt of jokes and lampoons. Michaelis would be utterly crushed. Then William's arguments for a return to his homeland would be the only remaining alternative. Forced to consider his error like the virtuous and true man William knew Michaelis to be, the artist would return to a more moderately developed philosophy, to a life of light and color.

Yet the charcoal itself was strangely disturbing, and William was forced to busy himself in order to avoid having his eyes drawn to it. He paid the peasants out of his own pocket and, finding the housekeeper, sent her to fetch Castelgni the pigment maker for Signor Michaelis, who had urgent need of him.

The artist did not move from his seat. He sat regarding the charcoal with a concentrated attention, as though he foresaw more than vindication in it, as though he could envisage an entirely new universe potential in its depths.

So entranced was the artist, William had to shake him out of reverie to take his leave. Passing out the front door of the *pensione,* William was greeted by the pigment maker hurriedly ascending the wide, dim stairway to Michaelis's studio.

After the pigment maker had scraped a chip off the lump of coal, he ground it to a fine point, then swept the powder into an old bronze dish well aged with many previous mixings. Water was sprinkled in, then the binder added—a concoction Castelgni had learned from his father, his father from his, going back, it was said, to the days and to the very studio of the great Veronese himself. When he had done, Castelgni called Michaelis, who meanwhile had been busying himself uncovering what seemed to the old Roman guildsman a large, obscure canvas.

"How does the color look, old man?"

"*Nerissimo,*" the mixer replied. "Blacker than any black before it."

Indeed, the flat dish, barely coated with but a half inch of the new pigment, seemed to hold more than a pint of it, as though it had suddenly opened up to the size of a large flagon; as though ordinary laws of depth and foreshortening no longer held true.

"Chip and mix all of it—but carefully, mind you," Michaelis warned. "I'll need all of it. Bring it as soon as you're done."

He wrapped up the remainder of the charcoal, carefully sealing it back within its mantle of rock.

"As soon as you're done, you understand? No matter what the hour. Leave the dishful. I must test it."

When Castelgni had gone, the artist picked up the dish, looked once more into its depths, and brought it to the palette board, set up facing the uncovered painting.

Not even the Roman night was dim enough for the subtleties of darkness he had already committed to the canvas. The studio's arras were drawn double. Two dim candles in wall sconces were foreshaded by painted black baffles. Within this rare obscurity stood Michaelis's new painting, the summation of his life's work, unlike any work conceived of before.

It was a life-sized portrait of Michaelis himself, clad in the masquerade of a Spanish grandee of the previous era. In the painting, he stood half turned from the observer, as though he had been walking away and suddenly called to, had turned to face his caller—a most difficult view to achieve, even were it done with a model. For it to be a self-portrait was amazing, especially as Michaelis's care and technical skills insured that the portrait would be a compendium of every refinement of proportion and perspective.

But the unusual angle of the subject had another, more important purpose: to provide more than half the entire space of the canvas to one single area which he would fill in with the new pigment—the area of the full-length cape Michaelis wore. It fell heavily from his broad shoulders, plummeted leadenly, and swung slightly at the tops of his boots to reflect sudden movement as though by the exorbitant force of gravity.

This area was long prepared for the new color. For months he had covered it with a base of his own perfecting which would totally wed pigment to canvas. Once that had dried, the artist had painted over the area with lampblack, the darkest hue then available. To others, that might appear to be the end of the work. However Michaelis had looked on it with pain, knowing how far from his ideal the lampblack proved to be. Yet after it too had dried, and he had tediously scraped the entire area of the painted cape, he was pleased to discover how well his base had held. The razor he wielded was so thin it almost sliced through the canvas at certain points, a person's face could be clearly discerned behind its fragile surface, yet it was black; front and back; fully primed for the final application.

Michaelis decided on one further refinement—almost a jest He would leave a thin border of the lampblack to a half inch, outlining the new pigment with several more lines of lampblack as vertically flowing suggestions of folds. They ought to appear almost white against the new black.

He dipped a brush into the dish, careful not to miscalculate because of the curious depth. Emerging with a dab of utter darkness on the fine fat camel hair, he lifted it to the canvas.

The pigment almost sprang onto the portrait. Only a faint inkish stain remained on the brush. It was fully, instantly absorbed onto the prepared canvas, standing out against the other blacks like a spot of eternity.

Quickly, greedily, Michaelis dipped his brush and applied more of the pigment, broadening the spot, adding more, then more still, then all of it, until the dish was once more flat, and the pigment, to the size of a man's hand, covered the upper right-hand corner of the outlined cape.

"*Nerissimo.*"Michaelis whispered Castelgni's words. "Blacker than any black before it."

The artist pulled up a chair and sat staring at the canvas, pondering his work, admiring the new color, until it seemed that the hours of night were obliterated. When he finally left the studio in answer to his housekeeper's knocking, he was astonished to discover that it was already past dawn.

He slept briefly, fitfully, during the late morning and afternoon. Once he was partially awakened by William's voice outside: his friend seeking admittance and firmly turned away by the artist's protective housekeeper.

At dusk, Castelgni arrived, accompanied by an apprentice who helped carry a large covered vat. When Michaelis had the lid prized up, he saw the intense depths of the black pigment. It had mixed beautifully.

The guildsman apologized for his tardiness. His wife, the old man said, would not allow the block of charcoal in her house. The superstitious old fool had lighted candles and muttered litanies all day. Castelgni had been forced to ask space in the atelier of a fellow craftsman to complete the mixing.

Upon hearing this, the simple-minded young apprentice, already frightened by the intense blackness of the pigment, whined and begged leave to depart.

"But it was a very easy pigment to make," the phlegmatic old man said with a smile. "Almost as though it was eager to become a paint for the Signore."

"It is said that the great Frans Hals knew twenty-seven different shades of black, and when to use each one of them for perfect effect. Rembrandt himself provided twenty-nine different shades of black for the hats and doublets and backgrounds, to differentiate each of the doctors in his mass portrait *The Anatomy Lesson*. The Chinese have an entire school of ink painting where no colors are admitted. Their gradations range from grays so indistinct as to seem the smudge of a virgin's finger upon the petal of a white chrysanthemum, to that deepest of blacks, which is used to write but one word in their curious visual language—that signifying eternal rest. Their blacks number thirty.

"Already I have discovered one more shade than they. Intimate to me as to those mandarins are these various tints, as though each had a name and character. There exists a spectrum of six black hues with iron-oxide bases and the merest hint of scarlet, which seem to me the real colors of bloodlust in battle and the fevers of pestilences. Other tints of black, with browns and greens hinted at, are luxurious, as though embedded in velvet plush. Some blacks are the colors of certain practices of Roman courtesans I've heard whispered in my ears by masked women during lewd street celebrations, while other shades speak of quiet diplomacies, of saddened courtesies, of the final noble words spoken by high-born men and women meeting their ends by treacheries and the executioner's block. Other blacks are almost charming: one, with a hint of blue indigo, is as tart as a Parisian soubrette. Yet others are somber as widows' weeds, heavy as the unheard curses of decades-old prisoners in airless dungeons. I have acquainted myself with these varieties of despair and in turn invented new hues to reflect those new despondencies I have experienced.

"A pure lampblack from Liverpool is so black that in bright light it glitters almost white. But there! That only proves my point. What I've wanted was a pigment that would not reflect outward, by prismatics, but inward, by secret refinements upon nature."

Michaelis ceased to speak, and fell into a brooding silence. William could do nothing but sigh.

"Will you begin tonight?" he asked.

"The very minute you leave me. And I will work on until it is done."

"Then good night. Tomorrow morning I ride for Pisa and thence to Venice. But I will be returned before the exhibit opens its doors. Promise me that day to return with me to America."

"After the exhibit, I will not need to go anywhere," the artist said. "I will have arrived."

It was in the earliest hours of morning, the following day, when Michaelis applied the last dregs of the pigment to the final uncovered square inch of canvas. As with every previous brush-stroke, the paint seemed to leap off the brush onto the canvas, as though rejoining that portion of itself divided in the act of application.

During the exhausting labor the artist had scarcely glanced at the canvas before him, or if he had, it was only to ensure that the new pigment lay evenly alongside the lampblack outline he had devised for its entire perimeter.

Now, finished, he stood back to inspect his portrait, and instantly felt a catch in the back of his throat. It was precisely as he had forevisioned it: the figure in its unusual attitude against its dim background, his face half hidden by the gleaming lampblack domino he lifted with one black-gloved hand, the shadows, the thirty other individual shades of black he had used for the costume, shadings of silver blacks crosshatched to suggest the sheen of satin, golden blacks delicately embossed for the silken expanses of his doublet and trousers, blue blacks and indigo blacks in whorls and miniscule circles to intimate the textures of a throat ruffle, or shirt cuffs bursting from each dark sleeve, browner blacks in careful streaks for details of facial hair and for the highlights of the broad-brimmed hat he wore, all wrought so ingeniously as to offer a palette as rich and complex as the bright chromatics of David and Delacroix, his contemporaries.

And even if one were so myopic as to misapprehend these many dark subtleties, dominating the self-portrait was the new pigment: the immense and utter blackness of the cape.

Looking at it, Michaelis felt as though he were seeing through a portal into an entirely new dimension intrinsically opposed to any ever seen by man before. Where the lampblack edging ended and the new paint began, so sharp a delineation occurred that it seemed to signal another reality existed. The dark cape curved inward by some curious property of the pigment, drawing his vision into it, spiraling counterclockwise deeper and deeper within, until Michaelis felt weightless, unable to fix himself to any stable underpinnings of floor or walls or ceiling. Suddenly afraid that he would fall into the blackness of the cape, he pulled himself away from the canvas and meticulously sat himself down in an armchair at a fair distance from the easel.

That precaution availed little to dispel his impressions. From a dozen feet farther back in the room, the sense of the newly painted area being both more and less than a flat surface was intensified—as though he had assisted in representing the abysses of the heavens themselves, a starless heaven, one somehow pulsing alive with the very negation of matter.

A further curious side effect of the new pigment was that the large, gloomy studio seemed itself smaller, almost intimate, especially at that end of the chamber where the canvas was placed. One might infer that light itself could no longer exert its usual powers or properties in the same locale as that utter lack of light.

It was a bitter triumph, this ultra-black painting, yet it was a triumph Michaelis experienced. So entranced was he with his creation that he sat hours in front of it, before falling asleep on the rough studio cot.

When he awoke from his extended yet unrefreshing sleep, the day outside his windows was damp and gray and airless. He was still fatigued, chilled by the sudden wetness that held the city in thrall all that day, and he passed the afternoon and evening, enraptured by his masterpiece, discovering, within its maw of absolute black, echoes of all the suffering and despondency he had so long felt.

Those moments he was able to draw himself away from the canvas, and particularly from the yawning chasm of the cape, were filled with a vague sense of unease and restlessness. He picked at his solitary dinner, distractedly began, and then threw down unread a half dozen volumes of poetry and philosophy he had been wont to turn to as balm for his most melancholy hours before.

That night, as he began to slip into slumber, he thought he heard the distant approach of flood waters rising.

The consequent days were spent by Michaelis in an attempt to overcome a sense of weariness that strangely persisted. His housekeeper said she hoped he wasn't ill but as he could find no specific symptoms to complain of, the doctor that was sent for could find no matter wrong with the artist, and went off again baffled, prescribing rest.

Michaelis took advantage of this regimen to actively avoid all contact with others whose presence he had begun to find intolerable to his sensitivities. He asked that his food be set outside his apartment doors, where often enough Antonia would find it hours later untouched. He moved from sleep to waking through easier transitions than ever before, and a great deal more frequently during a single revolution of the hours. Soon it became difficult for him to fully separate these two states of consciousness with his prior conviction.

Instead, he began to inhabit an intermediate state, and in this he would find himself gazing out the windows for hours, or—more frequently—leaning against the studio doorjamb, his work chamber grown tiny to his eyes, except for the portrait looming immensely, its awesome depths flickering and breeding odd presentiments.

He began hearing soft sounds which seemed to derive from within the canvas: sounds like those he had first taken to be rising water, as though some liquid medium of great gravity had been stirred to life from an immense distance; and the movement caused a quiet yet distinct impression of a dark, viscous pond insistently, tediously lapping against the edge of the canvas.

He began to have inexplicable fantasies, sleeping or awake, of a small, misshapen creature—black as the blackness of the cape—who hid within the pigment, softly whimpering a dreadful because unfulfillable need.

Once that was heard, the delicate lapping ceased. But the whimpering continued, sometimes for hours; sometimes barely audible, at other times so loud he could not hear himself think. Nor could he escape it. He found he was unable to step beyond an invisible yet still-defined radius around the canvas without experiencing an unspecific though all-encompassing panic and actual physical pain in the form of megrims. At times he fancied the whimpering so near that it was within his very veins and arteries. He dared not nick himself, lest his lifeblood pour out not human scarlet, but absolute ebony too.

The childlike whimpering was approaching the door of his bedchamber. Although he slept and dreamed and knew he both slept and dreamed, it continued to advance through the precisely described dimensions and details of his bedchamber, black and small, almost viscous itself, moving slowly toward the edge of his bed. A fearful thing! He turned away, but could not awaken. It came to the bed's edge and slowly, viscously, climbed up onto the bedclothes, the whimper subsiding into a soft panting, not so much respiration as the inverse of breathing. Still unable to awaken or move away, he huddled further away from it within himself, dreading its approach, curling his body like an infant to avoid it. The maddening sound was in his ear now, the creature from within the canvas's chasm stretching itself slowly next to him, slowly, with infinitely, minute pressure leaning its viscous form against his back, his legs, his neck, as a freezing child would timidly approach a sleeping stranger for warmth, causing him to tremble, then shiver, then shake so intensely with the sense of living blackness and nothingness sapping warmth and color and life from him that he awakened with a start, leapt from the bed, and rushed out of the room.

In the dining-room cupboard he found a bottle of cognac and drank a cupful to warm and steady himself. Its half century of bottled spirits helped dispel the more immediate palpitations from the terrible nightmare, and he wrapped himself in his outdoors cloak and more deliberately sipped another cupful of the brandy until his hands no longer shook around the cup and his breath no longer frosted the cold edge of the metal. Yet he dared not fall asleep again, and passed the remaining hours before dawn huddled in the dining-room chair, peering alternately into the studio doorway, left half ajar and, anxiously, out the window for the first rays of the morning sun.

The nightmare had shaken him from his previous week and more of lethargy. He bathed and dressed rapidly, and even before Antonia could come to him, he went down to the ground floor for the first time since the pigment had arrived, and asked leave to breakfast at the common table she daily set for her family and several other pensioners.

After so long and so complete an absence, all were pleased to see Michaelis among them, and congratulated him upon his recovery as evidenced by the new prodigiousness of his appetite.

Cheered, he gathered up a wide-brimmed hat against the hot Roman sun and decided on a long morning walk. Antonia was free to clean and air out his apartments, a task she anticipated after being denied her housekeeping there for so long.

Michaelis returned to the *pensione* past noon. Already most of the Roman citizenry had escaped the debilitating heat of the outdoors for cool afternoon siestas. The artist felt renewed, his fears of the night dispelled by the benign morning sunlight. He had just settled himself at his table and was reading through his weekly *Corriere,* attempting to catch up on news of the town and anticipating the coming evening's dinner with his friend who was expected back, when Antonia appeared before him, the various implements of her trade in hand and an arch expression on her face.

"You have worked very hard, Signore. Too much. It is poor for your health. When you first appeared at our table this morning, we were convinced you were some baleful spirit."

Michaelis murmured the appropriate response.

"Never have I met such a persevering artist," she said, shaking her finger to scold him. "Why, you even paint in your sleep."

"How do you mean?"

"Come look," she said, leading him to the bedchamber. "What did I say. There! Those spots of black resisted all my efforts to remove them."

At the far side of the bed from where Michaelis slept, two spots of the new pigment lay on the floorboards. The artist wondered if he had been so distracted during the last stages of his work on the canvas that, unawares, he had tracked them into his bedchamber. He dismissed Antonia, assuring her he would ask the pigment maker for a solvent to remove them.

After she had gone, however, Michaelis returned to the side of the bed to look at the spots once more. Now they took on a more defined appearance. One was a mere half inch or so of smudge, the shape of an indistinct semicircle. But as he inspected them more closely, it struck him that the other mark could be nothing other than the pad and first three toes of a small foot: large, clear, the very impression that would be made by a child with paint on its feet leaning to climb onto the bed.

"I was certain the painting would be done by now," William protested. "You look as though you've worked on it without a minute of sleep since I've been away."

"Only one more night of work, then I am done," the artist replied, not unaware of his friend's vigorous health, almost a censure to his own appearance.

"Do you still mean to display it? The salón opens tomorrow."

"It will be done. Ready."

William was still to be appeased. "We were to celebrate its completion tonight. And also my return. We were to dine out. I have already accepted an invitation to a fête for us both at the Marchesa de B——'s."

"You must go alone. Tomorrow night, after the exhibit, we will celebrate. Have a little more patience with an old friend, I beg you."

"Tomorrow night for certain, then," William said brightly. "You'll have no way out, I assure you. I feel duty-bound to see you done with this canvas. Its last stages of work have taken a terrible toll of you, I fear."

Although exhausted and sad, Michaelis was calm, which William misperceived as the serenity of near-completion rather than the resignation it in truth signified.

"Let me only step into this pharmacy," the artist said. "I am promised a draught to sustain me during the last hours of labor."

William left his friend at the herbalist's shop. Michaelis received his prescription and ponderously took his way back to the *pensione*.

Arrived, he mixed the potent stimulants the pharmacist had prepared into a flagon of strong, hot espresso and, sighing, brought the cup with him into the studio.

Two large canisters sat in front of the shrouded canvas, delivered, on his orders, by the pigment maker and his apprentice. Michaelis pried up their lids, downing the first of a half dozen cups of the espresso and stimulants he would consume in the coming hours.

A great initial effort was required for him to dip a paintbrush into the vat in front of him, an even greater effort to lift the brush to the area of the canvas where the absolute ebony had only just dried. But Michaelis made his nerves iron. Only his heart was a waste of icy emptiness the moment he applied the brush to the canvas and began the destruction of his masterpiece with the purest, thickest, whitest zinc white pigment to come from Castelgni's workshop.

Perhaps it was because of the precautions he had taken before beginning his work—the dozens of candelabras with the brightest tapers illuminating the room as though the grandest party were in progress—perhaps for other, unknown reasons, but he had already emptied one large canister of the new pigment onto the canvas and had begun dipping into the second, when he began to sense the pulsing of the remaining black pigment.

He worked faster, dipping the brush more rapidly, applying the white in swaths over large areas of black.

He became aware of the lapping sound, at first so quiet he merely sensed it: at the tips of his hair, on the very surface of his facial skin. But it went on, growing stronger, louder, until Michaelis could hear nothing else and worked with greater dispatch to cover the remaining areas of the terrible black. Several times he felt the brush he used almost twisted out of his hands by some force from within.

When only a square foot or so of the original pigment remained, he changed over to a larger, rougher brush. Then the whimpering started up. Like the lapping sound before it, it too began, scarcely audible, but as the artist dipped his brush and raised it with more zinc white to the canvas, it became louder, growing to a crescendo of piteous, fierce moaning so encompassing he was certain all in the surrounding dozen streets and houses could hear it.

He filled his ears with wax melting off the many candles around him and, temporarily protected, worked on feverishly.

Now only a few inches or so remained of the black. But when he dipped his brush into the zinc white, it came up dry. The pigment was used up, gone. He frantically scraped enough from the sides of the canisters to cover a minuscule section, then cursed and kicked over the empty buckets.

The large canvas began bellying out, as though attempting to reject the application of the white—as though whatever existed within it was pushing through, to get out—at him.

Michaelis ignored its buffeting as best he could, shuddering, concentrating all his distracted attention to devise how he could cover the last spot of black. His heart beat wildly with the memory of last night's visitor and the footprint he had seen, with the whimpering that now pierced through the wax that stuffed his ears as though the sound derived from within his brain.

Not a thimbleful of the white remained. It was four in the morning: impossible to secure more pigment. How could he cover it?

Michaelis almost went mad then. He sensed a power within that tiny remaining spot of black pigment that had to be obliterated lest it annihilate all else. The canvas continued to shudder from top to bottom, sometimes vertically, other times diagonally, as though to shake off the new paint. It would. It would, he knew, unless he covered every last bit of black.

As though by inspiration, he suddenly recalled his own supplies, not looked into for the past several years since he had turned to dark colors. Ah, and there in the small cupboard it was, not a great deal, but still clean, clear, unsullied, a tube of the ancient zinc white he had used for children's dresses and maiden's hands. Deafened, near to maddened by the piercing whine, he worked to extract the pigment into a dish. Looking up, he saw the canvas blowing in and out as though it were the topmost sail of a clipper under a typhoon.

He managed to get enough white pigment mixed with water and binder, rapidly stirring until he supposed it thick enough to completely coat that last spot of black.

He dipped his thick brush into the paint, swirled it to soak up every particle of the liquid. But as he lifted the brush from the palette dish to the spot, the billowing canvas went utterly flat. From the remaining portion of absolute ebony the color seemed to emerge as though the black had taken on full life. Before Michaelis's terrified eyes, the pigment grew, forming itself into the grotesquely black lineaments of a small, unnaturally proportioned three-fingered hand reaching out.

He clenched his teeth to stifle an utterance of terror, then dabbed the brush at the fingers, covering them with lines, blotches, streaks of white. As he did, the hand pulled back; simultaneously a shriek emerged from the canvas's black core, so high pitched, so fraught with fear and pain, as to send him reeling back from it.

The shriek ended as suddenly. When his head stopped hurting from the sound, he approached the canvas again. All was silent: the whimpering gone, the canvas still. He painted over that last spot once more; then, calmed, he inspected the canvas and returned his brush over every possibility of insufficient white, no matter how thread thin the crevice, until he was satisfied that not an iota of the black pigment remained.

Exhausted, Michaelis slowly, arduously dragged himself from the studio, and swooned onto his bed.

"Arouse yourself, dear friend. It's past four o'clock in the afternoon."

Michaelis sat up in his bed and looked about as though he had awakened in a strange place.

"Have a cup of this *caffe latte.* It will help you awaken," William said. He sat in a chair near the bed, holding a cup out to Michaelis. Late afternoon daylight played over the floorboards through the uncurtained window.

"The exhibit has been open since midday," his friend went on. "You must rouse yourself and have some food before we go."

The artist sipped the insipid liquid, coming slowly awake as though from a long dream.

Suddenly he started. "The canvas. It must be brought to the salon."

"Relax, my friend. It is already done."

"Done?"

"Gone to the salon. This morning when I called on you, I found you sound asleep, the canvas finished and ready. I had it carted to the salon. You had wax in your ears, I supposed so as not to be disturbed by noise during your well-earned rest."

"Did you see it?" Michaelis asked.

"Alas, no. The men from the salon came in, covered it over and brought it out while I was trying to awaken you."

William insisted they eat at a popular *ristorante* nearby the exhibit, much attended by artists and other bohemians of all nationalities, and once Michaelis's own favorite haunt during his palmier days.

Several times during the course of their lunch, the artist was recognized by colleagues and acquaintances, but contented their curiosity by a single curt nod. As their dessert was served, Reigler, the noted art critic and prestigious historian, came to their table and requested a seat with them.

"I have seen your self-portrait on exhibit,' he said, taking Michaelis's hand in a warm clasp. "Allow me to be the first to congratulate you and to acclaim it a masterpiece."

Seeing Reigler not repulsed by the formerly misanthropic artist, others approached. All had either seen the portrait or heard of it. All were filled with congratulations and that unrestrained heartfelt pleasure that all true artists feel in a colleague's triumph over their recalcitrant materials and even more elusive muse. Champagne was ordered. Toasts were proposed to Michaelis and to his work. The dinner became a fête.

Soon the party spilled out into the piazza, and from there moved en masse toward the salon with great festivity. Michaelis had barely stepped over the threshold of the salon when a man who, for the past three years, had mocked him to all who would listen stepped forward to embrace the artist.

"You have been awarded the *Palma D'Oro*, the highest prize given to a work of art."

A cheer arose from the crowd. Others in the salon, hearing of the arrival of Michaelis, came to greet him. The president of the Art Society himself arrived, pinned the gold palm tree medal to Michaelis's jacket-front and launched into a speech of flowery laudation and great length.

The artist heard and witnessed all this with a scarcely hidden sneer and no satisfaction. What did these fools mean? The painting was an abortion, a mere whisper of a possibility of what he had intended, what he had idealized, what he had achieved—however briefly and perilously. Could these idiots not understand what he had done, what he had been forced to undo? Would they never know the depths of darkness he had plumbed, first in his imagination, then—when the pigment was made—in his art, in his life? If his undoing was the cause of so much honor, what would they have thought to see the painting as he had achieved it?

The president was done speaking. Applause was followed by more congratulations, more toasts and drinking of champagne. Michaelis was asked to speak, too, and demurred, but William—who, among all the others, the artist could believe was truly delighted in his friend's great success—persuaded him. So the artist talked, quietly, sadly, of his travails, of his search for new modes of expression, of his experimentation with new and old forms and themes and techniques, of how the ideal he had envisioned would live on, although the finished work would always be a mere copy, cipher, imitation of that ideal.

"Let us see this marvel of art," the president declared. "We have installed it at one end of the great salon, with no other paintings nearby, for all would suffer by comparison."

"The others are mere exercises," Michaelis heard his former enemy declare.

Nor was he the only man to utter such sentiments as the crowd, Michaelis in its center, flowed into the great salon, past one fine painting after another, each one ignored or subjected to abuse and invective from the onlookers.

When they had gathered and opened a space around the painter and his portrait, William read out the inscription: "Self-portrait in Absolute Ebony."

"Amazing, isn't it?" Reigler demanded.

"Astounding," several answered.

"Utter genius," another man said. "Who would have thought to outline the cape in lampblack."

"And the cape itself. Remarkable."

"Of course. Of course. The cape!" others chorused.

The president was speaking into Michaelis's ear during the sudden hubbub.

"When the canvas was first brought, we feared it had been damaged by the carters. Two tiny spots of white in the lower center of the cape seemed to mar it. Within minutes, they were gone. Almost as we watched."

Michaelis did not appear to listen, riveted as he was to the ground, his eyes completely filled by what he beheld: the portrait was exactly as he had finished it a week and a half before, the cape absolutely black.

"Why, you feel as though you could put your hand right into the pigment there," Reigler said, reaching out.

"Don't touch it!" Michaelis shouted.

"He meant no harm to it," William said.

"Don't touch it," Michaelis repeated more softly as if filled with anxiety. "Don't go near it."

"As though it were a window cut into yet another dimension," another man said. "One of utter blackness, naturally."

"Why, even the room appears smaller at this end," another viewer observed. "As though it were made smaller by the portrait."

"There's never been a painting like it," several agreed.

Michaelis turned away, grasping William's arm.

"We must go," he whispered.

"Go? Where?"

"To Boston. Tonight. Immediately."

"Why?" he asked. Then, seeing his friend's face: "But the barque doesn't leave until tomorrow afternoon."

"I must pack my neccessities tonight. Now. You will help me," the artist said, pulling William away from the crowd still gathered in wonder around the portrait.

"Why the sudden hurry? We were to celebrate tonight. Surely you don't want to leave Rome quite yet. It is a great success."

William had to repeat his question, then repeat it again.

Although Michaelis stared at him from only inches away, he could not hear his countryman. All he could hear was a soft, viscous lapping sound, then the awful familiarity of a barely audible whimpering that spoke of an unfillable abyss that would reach out slowly and draw him into the maw of absolute ebony.

GRAHAM MASTERTON

The Root of All Evil

I wouldn't even have known about it if the traffic hadn't been so goddamned clogged up on the Triboro Bridge that night. It was a wet Friday in November, rush hour, and I had to drive some fat, agitated Texan out to JFK. Like most of them, he'd left Manhattan with no time to spare, and after we'd spent twenty minutes creeping and nudging our way along FDR Drive, with the rain drumming on the roof of the cab and the meter clicking its way up to twelve dollars, he was bobbing up and down in his seat and cursing blue lightning.

I got him out to the airport in plenty of time to make his connection to Dallas, but the fat slob only tipped me a buck. As if it was *my* fault it was Friday. I drove around to the front entrance of the TWA building to see if I could pick up one of those nice courteous English people to take back into the city. One of those who sit there and say, "Dear me, what frightful weather you're having." I'd had enough of Texans in a hurry.

As it happened, I got some tall black guy in a camel's hair coat. Maybe a professor or something like that. Gucci suitcases, and a very Harvard way of talking. He told me to drive him to the Croydon, on East 86th Street, but first of all to stop at an address in Harlem, 113th Street, so that he could drop off a package.

Well, I kind of demurred at that. The last place I wanted to be on a wet Friday night was 113th Street, but the black guy said, "You'll be okay. It's my old neighborhood. Everybody knows me," and so I shrugged and told him I'd do it.

The bridge was clearer on the way back, but the weather wasn't. It was raining like all hell, and when I turned off the bridge into the side streets of Harlem, the taxi was splashing and bouncing through flooded potholes and brimming gutters. The radio was playing, "We're not as smart as we like to think we are—"

I could see the black guy peering out of the window as we drove along East 113th. The tenements were narrow and dilapidated, and the rain was glistening on the corrugated iron that covered half the windows and most of the stores. A few black kids were standing on the corner of 113th and 3rd, sheltering themselves under plastic trash bags and hooded windbreakers.

"Okay, it's here. Stop here," he said. I drew in to the side of the road.

"I'll give you five minutes," I told him. "If you're not back by then, I'm leaving. Take this card. If I'm gone, you can pick up your cases at the cab company."

He hesitated. Then his black hand, heavily embellished with gold rings, came through the partition. It was holding a neatly folded twenty. "I may be longer than five minutes," he said politely.

I took the twenty and tucked it into my shirt pocket. "All right. But make it quick, please. Even twenty isn't worth a mugging."

"I know."

He turned up the collar of his camel's hair coat and climbed out of the cab. I locked all the doors immediately and switched on my emergency flashers. Through the rain-spotted window, I could see the guy hurry across the garbage-strewn sidewalk and into a peeling entrance. He pressed a bell and waited. I tapped my fingers on the steering wheel. Judy, my wife, would be back from school by now and starting to cook dinner. I'd been driving since eleven this morning, and I could have eaten a radial tire, provided it had enough mustard on it.

The radio said, "This is WPAT, where everything is beautiful."

I thought, This is cab medallion no. 38603, where everything is tedious. I looked at the black-and-white mug shot on my license: a frowning twenty-nine year old with thinning hair, a droopy mustache, and heavy-rimmed glasses. Edmond Daniels. Architect, failed genius, and cabdriver. Just another member of that tired, irritable brotherhood of old men, Puerto Ricans, Jews and Chinese, the people who drive our battered yellow taxis around and keep our city moving.

My reverie was startlingly interrupted by a loud bang on the roof of the cab. I looked up in fright. But it was only the guy in the camel's hair coat. He was twisting his hand around to indicate that I should let down my window. He looked kind of agitated about something.

I put the window down two inches. Even then, the rain came drifting in. "What's the matter?" I asked him. "Did you deliver your package yet? I have to get going."

"You have to come inside," he said. His voice was high and strained. His eyes were very wide.

I said, "Mister, I'm not coming anywhere. And I'm not leaving my cab on this street."

"You have to. I need a witness. You don't understand."

I checked my driving mirror. The rain was so heavy now that even the kids on the street corner had sloped off. There was nobody else around, either. Nobody who looked like a potential car thief or a mugging artist.

"Okay," I agreed, wearily. "What is it you want me to see?"

I opened the taxi door and stepped out into the rain. He

immediately seized my arm and led me across to the doorway. The door was open now, and he pulled me into the dark hallway before I could say anything.

It stank in there. Of decay and rats and kids' urine. But the black guy led me quickly up the first flight of sagging stairs to the landing, and then down to an apartment at the front of the house. The apartment door was ajar, with a faint triangle of orange light crossing the floor, and a sound that I thought at first was a cricket, but which I soon recognized as a record player at the end of its record. Click-*hissss*, click-*hissss*, click-*hissss* . . .

"In here," he said. He was so scared that his face was the color of the sports pages at the back of the *New York Post.*

"I'm not sure I feel like going along with this," I said reluctantly. "I mean, I just drive people."

"You're the only one," he insisted. "I have to have a witness, and you're the only one. You saw that I came from the airport. You know how long I was in here. And you can see that I'm completely clean."

"Clean? What do you mean?"

"Take a look. I'm sorry, but it's necessary."

I tentatively pushed at the door with my fingertips. It swung open a little wider, then creaked to a stop.

"I hope you're sure about this," I told him.

He nodded.

Cautiously, with my heart beating in slow, suppressed bumps, I put my head around the door. There was a narrow room with a single lamp burning. The light was faint and orange because somebody had draped a knotted handkerchief over the shade. Probably soaked in cologne or after-shave, to mask the smell of grass. On the walls were all kinds of African souvenirs, like grinning wooden masks, and spears, and zebra-skin shields. And there was some kind of ebony effigy of a tall dark figure with slanting eyes and teeth like a piranha.

There was so much African stuff in there that I didn't notice the girl at first. But when I looked down toward the rug and actually made sense of the shape that was lying there, oh, Jesus, my hair prickled up and I felt as cold as a Thanksgiving turkey in a supermarket freezer.

She had to be dead. I hoped, for her sake, that she was dead. And for my sake, too, because if she was still alive I would have to touch her, try to bring her back to life. And the way she was right then, I didn't feel like touching her, you know? I was just too squeamish.

She was a black girl, young, with one of those cornrow hairstyles, all plaited and tied up in beads. Somehow, with some kind of maniacal strength and dedication, someone had impaled her on one of those bentwood hatstands, the kind Kojak tosses his hat onto when he walks into the office. *Impaled* her, right through her back and right through her stomach, so that her body had slid right down to the base, but her liver and spleen and long loops of her pale white guts had been left festooned around the hooks. There was blood all over the floor. More blood than I had ever seen in my whole life.

I wasn't sick. I don't know why. I was numb, as if my dentist had injected me all over with novocaine. I stepped back out of the room, and the guy held my arm, and I didn't know what to say or what to do.

"I'm sorry," he said, hoarsely. "I had to show you, just to prove to the cops that I couldn't have done it myself. I couldn't have done it, could I, not in three minutes, not without getting myself splashed all over with blood?"

"Who is she?" I whispered. "Was she someone you knew?"

He nodded. "Her name is Bella X. A very close friend. Or she was."

"A Black Muslim?"

"Yes."

I said, "We have to call the police."

"I know," he nodded. "That's why I needed a witness. My name's John Bososama, by the way. I work for Chase Manhattan Bank. African investments."

There was a telephone at the end of the hall, mercifully unvandalized. I dialed 911 and waited for the police to answer.

John Bososama stood beside me, still upset, but much more together than he had been before. They put me through to the local precinct and I told the duty officer what had happened; he instructed me to wait where I was and not to touch anything.

I said, "If you could see this mess, you wouldn't even want to touch it."

"All right," said the duty officer tiredly.

I put down the phone. I was still trembling. I said to John Bososama, "I'm going to wait in the street. Screw the rain. If I stay here any longer, I'm going to barf."

"Okay," he nodded.

The street smelled fresh by comparison. I leaned across the roof of my cab, while the rain fell in sparkling drops all around me, and I smoked a soggy Kool.

John Bososama stood a few paces away, his hands in the pockets of his camel's hair coat, his shoulders soaked with damp. "I was afraid this would happen," he said. His voice was deep and there was genuine sorrow in it.

I glanced at him. "You mean you knew in advance?"

"Not exactly. But it was one of the reasons I returned to Zaïre. One of the reasons I came here tonight with this."

He held up the brown paper package he'd been taking up to the girl's apartment.

"What's that?" I asked him. "Grass?"

He smiled sadly and shook his head. "A few charms that might have saved her."

I sucked at my cigarette. I could hear a police siren whooping and warbling in the distance.

"You mean she was superstitious?" I queried.

"In a way."

"In what way? Superstitious enough to worry herself about getting stuck through with a hatstand?"

John Bososama laid his hand on my shoulder. "You don't really understand. And maybe it's better that you don't."

I stared at him coldly. "Mr. Bososama, if I'm going to be your lonely and only witness, then I think I'm going to need to know what's going on here. I'm not about to swear anything until you fill me in."

The siren was louder now. Then, farther away, another siren joined in. An ambulance.

John Bososama bit his lip. He was silent for a moment, then he said, "You wouldn't believe me anyway. You're white."

"My great-grandmother was Cuban. Try me."

He cleared his throat. Then he said, "Very well. What you have seen tonight, as far as anyone can tell, is the work of Iblis."

"Iblis? What the hell's Iblis?"

"Just listen. The police will be here in a minute. Iblis is the most terrible of Islamic devils. Now, I don't care right this moment whether you believe in devils or not. Just think of what you've seen tonight and try to understand."

I flipped my cigarette into the flooded gutter. "Come on," I said. "I'm listening."

"Listening sympathetically, or listening skeptically?"

"What does it matter? I'm listening."

"Very well," said John Bososama. "In the culture of Islam, the legend goes that when Allah created man, he required all His angels to bow down before His new creation. The angel Iblis alone refused, saying that he despised man because man was made of nothing more than dust. So Allah cursed Iblis, and dismissed him from heaven.

"Iblis, however, persuaded Allah to postpone his final punishment until the Day of Judgment and to grant him freedom to roam the earth and lead astray all those who are not true servants of Allah. It was Iblis, concealed in the mouth of a serpent, who tempted Eve."

"What was this Iblis like?" I asked. I could see the red and white flashing lights of the blue-and-white police car, only three blocks away. The rain, softer now, prickled on my face.

"Hunched, cloaked, with a head like a camel, only with rows and rows of teeth. Legs and claws like a vulture. A creature without any kind of mercy or feeling."

"And you think what happened tonight . . . ?"

"You can believe me or not. But it was the work of Iblis."

I sniffed. "As a matter of fact, I don't believe you. You didn't really expect me to, did you?"

"No, I suppose I didn't," said John Bososama. He rubbed the glittering rain from his close-cropped hair. Then he added, almost sadly, "No, I guess not."

"I mean—how did he get here . . . to New York? This Iblis?"

John Bososama shrugged. "As far as I've ever been able to find out, a long time ago. In the days of the slave trade. The slave ship *African Galley* sailed to New Callebarr in the winter of 1700, looking for slaves and teeth. Among the slaves the ship took on board was a young man called Bongoumba, who was unnaturally strong and said to be mad, or possessed. He was brought over to the New World and sold, although his madness made it necessary for him to be kept in shackles twenty-four hours a day. One day, however, he broke out of his chains and raped a young black girl slave, who became pregnant from his assault. She bore a son, and the line of Bongoumba has descended through to the present day.

"It was only when present-day blacks started to become aware of their roots, however, that the inherited possession of the Bongoumbas began to express its true strength. And when the blacks turned to the religion most suited to them, Islam—well, it was then that the spirit of Iblis, which had remained dormant through all these generations, was regenerated. It was like defrosting a body from a cryogenic chamber."

"So where do you come into this?" I wanted to know. The police car was just pulling in to the curb and we didn't have any more time to talk.

John Bososama looked at me. There were glistening drops under his eyes that could have been rain, or tears. "There was a young man called Duke Jones. His hereditary name, his African name, was Bongoumba. He lived here, in this apartment, and that young girl you saw tonight was his wife. Bongoumba had felt the dark power of something terrible inside him ever since he joined the muslims. Something evil and vengeful and strange. Something that threatened to take him over completely.

"That was why I was bringing him this package. On a business trip to Saudi Arabia, I detoured to Zaïre, and acquired all the magic artifacts which the old-time juju doctors used to dismiss the spirit of Iblis. Magic tokens, lion's hair, charmed bones."

"Kind of primitive, isn't it?" I asked him.

He nodded, almost smiled. "Sure. But we're dealing with a very primitive devil. An evil spirit from way, way back. You see, I think we're learning that every religion has its demons, and that when you embrace a religion as ancient as Islam, you have to cope with its ancient perils as well."

"And you still believe in Allah and Mohammed?"

"More than ever. The more evidence I find of the existence of Iblis, the more I believe in the greatness and the power of Allah and His holy messenger. Doesn't Satan prove beyond any reasonable doubt the true existence of God?"

A cop in a leather windbreaker came up and said, "Are you the people who called the police? Something about a homicide?"

John Bososama nodded. "She's upstairs," he said gravely. "I'm afraid she's been dead for a long time."

I went through the whole routine of a police interrogation, and hours of hanging around the station house, but eventually the detectives let me go home, and I tiredly ate a plate of congealed lasagna and watched the late-night news before I went to bed. Judy was kind of pissed, but when I told her what had happened, she was very calm and sympathetic about it and she mixed me a strong old-fashioned to help me sleep.

I didn't tell her about any of that Iblis stuff. Apart from the fact that I didn't believe it myself, I didn't want to give her nightmares. It was bad enough thinking about that black girl's looped-up intestines without thinking some kind of multifanged camel-headed creature might have done it. I woke up two or three times in the night, listening to the sound of sirens along 12th Street, where we lived, and wondering what the hell this world was really all about. Was there a dark and frightening underworld, populated by devils and demons, or was it nothing more than a bad dream? I heard a scratching noise in the darkness, and I hoped to hell it was nothing worse than mice.

For two or three weeks, everything ran as usual. I woke up mid-morning, took the subway to taxi headquarters, picked up my hack and drove my tour of duty. I picked up businessmen, shoppers, old ladies with tired blood, executives, models, hookers and tourists. I drove uptown, downtown and across town. I waited in jams in Herald Square. I edged my way up Sixth Avenue. I drove to the airport and back. I wended my way through the falling leaves of Central Park. It was cold and snappy and there was always the smell of burned pretzels in the air.

Then, one morning, I checked in for work and my boss came out of that little overheated shack of his with pinups of Chesty Morgan on the walls and handed me a package.

"This is for you," he said. "Some black guy brought it around. I said you wouldn't be long but he didn't want to wait."

"A black guy?" I asked, feeling the package. Feeling softness and hardness and unwelcome lumps. "Tall, speaks like a professor? Camel-color coat?"

"That's the one. Looked sick."

"Okay," I said, uncertainly. "Thanks."

I sat in my vehicle and opened up the package. I peered inside and saw a loop of silvery-black hair, tied with raffia, two brownish bones and a small figure of a man made up of discs of copper, all wired together and painted. There was a short letter in the package, too. I unfolded it and scanned it quickly.

Dear Mr. Daniels,

You know that I wouldn't have passed this package to you unless it was a matter of life or death. But whether you believed what I told you or not, the spirit of Iblis has come alive again in Manhattan, and it is taking its revenge on "the sons of dust," those Muslims whose lapses in the observance of their religion makes them easy and legitimate prey.

I fear that it is after me, too, and that it has been tracking my movements. So all I can do is to pass this package to you and ask that if you read in the newspapers of my death, you *immediately* come to the morgue where my body is kept and perform with these enclosed artifacts the short ritual I have written down below. I know you are not a Muslim yourself, nor even black, but it is for that reason that Iblis will not suspect you at first and may allow you to approach my body unharmed.

For the sake of all those black people who were brought to this country in slavery—for the sake of Allah—please do what you can.

I remain your friend,

John Bososama

I tucked the letter back in the package. Your friend, huh. With friends like that, you wouldn't need enemies. You wouldn't even need crime on the streets. I started the cab's motor, and with an uneasy feeling of alarm and dread I drove out onto the streets. All that day, I avoided picking up black people. Even Chinese. Who the hell knew what kind of demons the Chinese had up their sleeves?

I slept badly for two or three nights. Judy was real worried and wanted me to call the doctor. But I didn't need to spend forty dollars to know what was wrong with me. I kept remembering the impaled girl on 113th Street, and the tall black guy in the camel's hair coat, and his stories about an ancient Islamic demon. It was nuts, I know. But there's something about driving through Manhattan day after day that makes you ready to believe anything. Do you know that one day in Queens I saw a girl sit in the roadway and set herself afire with gasoline? And the way people stood around and watched her, so casual and curious, I was only surprised that nobody came up with a wiener on a stick.

Then, the day before Thanksgiving, I got the word. Not in the newspaper, but over the radio when I was driving some insurance salesman home to Yonkers. "An official from the Chase Manhattan Bank has been found brutally murdered under the ramp where the southbound lane of Park Avenue joins 40th Street. Credit cards found on the body identified the corpse as John Bososama. The deceased was only a few blocks away from the Lexington Avenue branch of his bank. Police and bank officials say he was carrying no money and that the motive of the homicide was 'probably not robbery.' Bososama's head was jammed into a car door, and then his body was twisted around until his neck broke. His body was also slashed until, in the words of Detective Ernest Saparelli, 'it looked like hamburger.'"

I felt nauseated. My driving began to waver and my fare said, "Watch it, fella. I want to get home safe, if you don't mind." I managed to steer the cab straight until I dropped my passenger off, and then I sat behind the wheel and thought and thought and didn't know what in all hell to do.

I mean, why should I care about a bunch of Black Muslims? They'd never meant anything to me and as far as I was concerned, they were nothing but trouble. Look at all the sweat they'd given us over Iran. Look at that loudmouth Muhammad Ali. Look at Malcolm X, and all that stuff. If their devil had caught up with them at last, what business was it of mine? Especially if there was genuine danger involved.

Yet, in a way that I can hardly even tell you about, I felt

guilty. So the blacks had their problems. But *why?* Because they'd newly discovered their true religion and were trying to fight their way back to their own personal and religious identities. And why were they having to do that? Because they'd been denied their birthright for so long by the whites. Because, for centuries, they hadn't been allowed to know either the joys or the dangers of their beliefs.

I drove to the morgue. Don't ask me why. If I was in the same position again, I'd drive anyplace else but. Up to Buffalo maybe, or clear across to Cleveland. Anywhere but the midtown police morgue to look at some mutilated stiff.

Surprisingly, I didn't have much trouble getting in. I said that John Bososama had been an acquaintance of mine and that maybe I could help identify him. They took me along a narrow brown-tiled corridor until we reached the cold room. Then the morgue assistant slid out a drawer, and there he was, swathed up to the neck in a white sheet. The morgue assistant chewed gum and occasionally blew a green bubble.

"He wanted me to say a few words over the body," I said. "Do you think that's okay?"

"What kind of words?"

"He was a Black Muslim. Some kind of special ritual, you know?"

The morgue assistant turned to the uniformed cop who had accompanied me down there. The cop shrugged, and said, "Okay by me. Long as you don't take all night."

The two of them watched me as I fumbled with my brown paper package. I knelt on the cold wax-polished floor and took out all the magic artifacts: the hair, the bones, the little copper figure. The morgue assistant popped a bubble and shrugged at the cop in bafflement.

I spread out the paper that John Bososama had written out for me. The hair had to be arranged like the rays of the sun. The two bones had to point north and south. The little copper man represented human hope and had to be set down in the center of the hair.

I cleared my throat. It was totally silent in the morgue except for the uneven whirring of the cooling system. To tell you the truth, I felt like a real fool at that moment and I couldn't stop myself from blushing. But I'd decided to do it, so I went ahead with it.

"Iblis," I said, "evil angel of Islam, I recognize you."

The cop sniffed.

"Iblis," I repeated. "Evil angel of Islam, I recognize you and I am here to cast you out of this body and out of this world."

I stood up now, holding John Bososama's paper in front of me so that I could read it.

"You are to leave this true servant of Allah, and to continue your wanderings elsewhere. Yes, even unto the Day of Judgment itself. And you shall allow this servant of Allah to take his place in heaven, and you shall let him be."

The morgue lights, three fluorescent tubes, began to flicker. Then one of them dimmed and almost went out. The morgue attendant raised his head and looked around uneasily.

"Busted fuse?" suggested the cop.

"Iblis, I cast you out from this earthly body, and I expel you," I said, louder this time, maybe because I was getting a little scared. "I call upon all of your former brothers in Allah's heaven to lock you out."

The morgue was suddenly pitched into complete darkness. And then a wind blew up, a harsh, moaning wind. A wind that was not only abrasive and fierce, but *hot,* like a wind across the desert. I heard the cop say something indistinguishable, and the attendant say, "The lights, what happened to the goddamned lights?"

"Go, Iblis!" I shouted. "Go! Walk no more among these abandoned brothers of Africa! Let them be! Leave them to find their own way back to the true religion of Islam, untempted and untrammeled by your mischief! Go!"

A dim, pulsating glow lit the morgue. Only just enough for me to be able to distinguish the banks of drawers where the bodies lay stored. Only just enough for me to be able to see the face of John Bososama. His face glistened, as if he were sweating, and his eyes were wide open.

There was a sudden, terrifying bang. One of the upper drawers had slid open by itself. The morgue attendant said "Jesus" and his jaw dropped. The cop had his revolver out, but there didn't seem to be anything to shoot at. Just the wind and the darkness and the terrible moaning sound of a distant and ancient desert.

Then there was fire. Drawer after drawer banged open by itself and out of each drawer rose a corpse, sitting up as if it were alive. Gray-green corpses that had been dragged out of the East River, their flesh puffy with gas. White corpses that had bled to death in unknown doorways on Eighth Avenue. Corpses that were mauve from heart attacks, and corpses that were dark red with post-mortem lividity. Each one, as it rose out of its drawer, burst into flames. Spontaneous combustion. I saw their hair frizzle and their skin sizzle and smoke that was heavy with the smell of charred humanity filled the room like a fatty mist.

"Jesus," gibbered the cop. "Jesus *Christ.*"

But this horror didn't respond to appeals to Jesus, nor to any Christian God. And out of the dark and wind-blown smoke, impossibly tall and black as some kind of tattered crow, came the apparition of Iblis.

His head was more like that of a skeletal horse than a camel, and when he bared his teeth, I saw row upon row of dripping incisors. He was gigantic, hideous, terrifying. His eyes gleamed in the smoky gloom like the headlights of some dark and unstoppable truck. He roared, but it was more like a harmonic vibration than a roar. A sensation more than a sound. It set my teeth on edge and went right through my bones to my balls.

"Iblis!" I screamed. *"I expel you!"*

By the unsteady light of this roomful of blazing corpses, the devil twisted its head around in a gesture of contemptuous superiority.

"You cannot expel me, you fool," it roared, in that same subaudible rumble. *"Only those who think they believe in Allah can expel me. Only those who heed the word of the prophet Muhammad."*

"I act on behalf of such a man," I shouted. My voice was taut with fear. "This man here. John Bososama. He deputized me."

Iblis laughed. It was more like a subway train falling down a bottomless well than a laugh.

"You are not of his kind," he mocked me. *"You can do nothing."*

I stood my ground. Don't ask me why. But it seemed, just for a moment, that I had something to believe in. I could see at last, right in front of my eyes, the kind of evil that really made the world what it was. Iblis, like Satan, was a sham and a shyster, a trickster dealing in uncertainty and fear.

"I can do *everything!*" I screeched. "I can expel you because I respect my black brothers' belief in Allah and the prophet Muhammad! I can expel you because all men are equal, and because this country guarantees it so! I can expel you because I came to help this man John Bososama for no reason at all except his people ought to be free! I can expel you because I accept the responsibility for what the white people did to his people, and because both of our races have come to terms with history, and with what we are, and our religious and magical roots!"

I paused for breath. I was mad with rage and fear. *"Get out!"* I yelled. "Go! And leave our brothers alone!"

There was a moment when the air itself seemed to be under intolerable stress. When vision wavered, and an unbearable droning crowded the morgue.

Then the fiery bodies exploded. Chunks of blazing torso were hurled over my head. Skulls with eyes of fire. Hands that were heat-twisted claws. I dropped to the floor and kept my eyes shut tight, and prayed to God that this wasn't the end.

It was a long time, minutes, before I opened my eyes. Iblis had vanished. The morgue was blackened with smoke, choking, but more or less intact. Fragments of body were strewn all around. The cop got up from the floor, brushing human ashes from his clothes, and he seemed incapable of saying anything.

The morgue attendant was still lying on the floor, concussed.

Eventually, the cop said, "What the hell happened?"

I shook my head. My throat was dry and constricted. "I don't know. I think we won."

I looked down at John Bososama and his eyes were closed. He seemed to be peaceful enough.

I never heard any more about Iblis or the Black Muslims. Sometimes, in my cab, I pick up young black ladies with cornrow hairstyles, and I don't shy away from talking to them about their religion. It usually seems like they are happy and content and finding all kinds of exciting new openings in their lives. It seems like ill luck is leaving them alone.

I don't mix with black people any more than I used to. I don't even pretend to understand what they really want out of life, or out of society, or out of anything. But that experience with John Bososama and his Islamic devil taught me more than any other kind of experience could have that we're more than brothers under the skin. We're all Americans, we're all ordinary people, and we all have the obligation to stand up for each other when danger threatens, or when the ground starts falling away from under our feet.

You think I'm a sentimentalist? Judy thinks I am. But she and you can think what you like. As far as I'm concerned, there's a motto under our country's crest that reads E PLURIBUS UNUM, and it's practical enough to beat devils as well as men.

Someplace out there, in space or in time, there's a banished black devil called Iblis to prove it.

GARY BRANDNER

Julian's Hand

At first it was only an itch, an irritation of the skin under his left arm; nothing more.

Julian scratched idly at the spot while he shaved. Shaving was the only thing he still did naturally with his left hand. In all other actions he had been converted in early childhood to conform to a right-handed world.

He blew the whiskers out of his electric shaver and rinsed them down the sink drain, mopping the porcelain clean with a sponge. Before leaving the bathroom he turned sideways to examine the itch in the mirror. There was a slight reddening in a spot the size of a dime—an insect bite, or maybe some allergy. Julian dabbed medicated salve on the spot and rubbed it in. He finished dressing and went out to the kitchen.

Margaret, her bright little eyes watching him, sat at the table. Julian poured a cup of coffee from the electric percolator and carried it over to sit opposite her. It was bitter. After sixteen years of marriage he still missed sugar in his coffee. Margaret had shown him statistics that proved he was better off without it. It was easier to drink his coffee black and bitter than to argue with her.

She did have a point. It was a man's responsibility to his

family to take care of himself. At one time Julian had hoped his family would consist of more than just Margaret. A son would have been nice, but it wasn't Margaret's fault that she was not built for childbearing. Was it?

"Don't scratch yourself like that," Margaret said.

"Sorry."

"You look like an ape."

"I didn't realize I was doing it."

"Are you going to talk to Hugh Biggerstaff today?"

"Talk?"

"Don't play games. I mean talk about the opening in the Sales Department, as you know very well."

"I'll see him if I get a chance."

"Make the chance. He's not going to walk out there and hand you the job, you know."

"I suppose not."

"It may be too late now. You should have gone in to see him last week."

"We've been very busy."

"I'll bet. You just get in there today and tell Hugh Biggerstaff that you're the man for the job. The years you've been with that company, you should be making a lot more money than you are, and it's obvious you're not going to make it in Accounting. Sales is where the money is. And Sales is where they pick the top executives from."

"I'll talk to him today," Julian promised.

"You're scratching again."

Julian finished his coffee and rinsed the cup at the sink. He leaned down to kiss the air an inch from Margaret's face and left the apartment. He drove downtown to the high-rise office building where he worked, and parked in the subterranean garage. He stepped into the elevator and touched the button for the twelfth floor where the offices of Datatron Systems, Inc., were located.

The elevator stopped at the street-level lobby and the girls who worked in the building got on. Bright eyed and colorful, they chattered about their dates and their clothes and always made Julian feel good. They smelled of cologne and hair spray and soap. The heat of their firm young bodies warmed the elevator car, and for the short ride upward Julian savored the nearness of the girls. At each floor, as more of the girls got out, he felt a growing ache of loneliness. By the twelfth floor he was the only one left. He stepped out into the carpeted corridor and rubbed at the rash under his arm.

The first three hours were occupied with the regular entries, checks, and cross-checks that Julian made every day. He never found these tasks dull or routine. He enjoyed beginning his day in an orderly manner and then he would be ready for any new problems that arose in Accounting. On this day there were no new problems, and by eleven o'clock he had no further justification for not talking to Mr. Biggerstaff.

To stall just a little longer, Julian went into the men's room and combed his thinning hair, then reknotted his necktie. He scratched once more under his arm and walked down the hall to the oak-paneled office of Hugh Biggerstaff, ready to get it over.

Julian tapped lightly on the open door and stood there several seconds while the vice-president of Datatron Systems, Inc., finished what he was writing before he looked up to acknowledge Julian's presence.

"Come on in, Julian. Glad to see you." Hugh Biggerstaff had taken off his jacket and rolled up his shirt sleeves two turns, just like one of the fellows. Curly black hair spilled across his unlined forehead. "What can I do for you?"

Julian's throat tightened, and his voice squeaked out with even less authority than usual. "Um, I was just wondering if you've found someone to fill the opening in Sales yet."

"No, actually we haven't firmed up the decision. Why, is it causing some problem in Accounting?"

"Oh, no, nothing like that. It's, well, it's . . ." Julian had to stop and clear his throat. "I was thinking that I'd like to be considered for the position."

"You?" That was all, just the single questioning syllable.

"Ah . . . yes."

The young vice-president stared intently at Julian, who fought down the impulse to look away. Hugh Biggerstaff put a lot of stock in eye contact.

"Julian, do you have any kind of sales experience?"

"No, but I learn quickly. And I'm a diligent worker."

"I'm sure of that. I checked your record when the home office first sent me out here, and I've watched your work since. I don't mind telling you, Julian, you're one of DSI's most valued employees."

"Thank you."

"In fact, I'd really hate to have the job of replacing you. You may not know this, Julian, but men who can handle the kind of work you do are hard to find. I couldn't take some kid fresh out of business school and put him at your desk. No way. The Sales job, heck, I could find a dozen men to fit that, but to replace a first-class Accounting man . . . well, that's another story."

"Are you saying I'm not right for the Sales job?"

"No, I'm saying the Sales job is not right for you. I came up through Sales myself, and I can tell you it's not all long lunches and expense accounts. There's a lot of being nice to people you can't stand, and a lot of forcing yourself to be pushy and aggressive when you're not that way at all. Do you see what I mean?"

"Yes, I think I do."

"Good, good, I'm glad that's settled. Come around any time, Julian. We don't get together nearly enough, you and I." The vice-president shifted slightly in his chair, indicating that the interview was over.

"Thank you," Julian said, and backed out of the office.

Back at his own desk Julian let his fingers dance across the keys of his calculator. He hummed along with the clicking of the machine. His obligation was fulfilled, he had kept his promise and asked for the job. It was not his fault that the company found him more valuable here in Accounting.

He thought of Margaret, and his fingers stopped their dance. He rubbed at the renewed irritation under his arm. If only she would understand that things had worked out for the best.

Margaret understood nothing of the kind. That evening she made Julian repeat the entire conversation with Hugh Biggerstaff as nearly word for word as he could remember it.

"So you just thanked him and walked out," she said when Julian had finished his recitation. "You didn't even argue your case. Couldn't you see he was testing you to find out if you're forceful enough for the job? Don't you know you've got to pound on a desk sometimes to make people pay attention to you? Hugh Biggerstaff didn't get where he is by mumbling thank you, you can bet on that. He's a desk pounder."

The same theme was repeated with little variation for the remainder of the week and through the weekend. The next Monday morning when Julian stood shirtless before the mirror he saw that the rash under his arm had congealed into a lump; no bigger than an orange seed, but a definite lump. It no longer itched, and it was not painful. It was just . . . there—and growing.

Tuesday morning the lump was visibly larger—the size of a bean. By Wednesday it was as big as the end of his thumb, and Julian was frightened.

That afternoon he called his physician, Dr. Aaron Volney. The doctor was busy attending an AMA luncheon, but his receptionist made an appointment for Julian the following morning.

When Julian awoke Thursday the lump was as big as a walnut.

"Hurry up or you'll be late for work," Margaret said.

"I'm not going to work this morning. I'm going in to see Dr. Volney."

"Did the company give you time off?"

"They gave me time off."

"What's the matter with you?"

"Nothing. I just want the doctor to look at something."

"Pick up a quart of buttermilk on your way home."

At the age of fifty-three Dr. Volney was tanned and youthful, with a spring in his step and a twinkle in his eye, a model of good health for his patients to envy. Golf, tennis, boating, and leisurely vacations kept him that way.

"Well, well, Julian," the doctor beamed, "what brings you around between annual checkups? Looks like it wouldn't hurt you to put on a little weight. A lot of my other patients would like to hear that, I'll bet, ha-ha."

"I have this lump under my arm," Julian said. "It started last week. First there was a rash, then a lump. It's getting bigger."

"Well, let's get the old shirt off and have a look-see, shall we?"

Julian fumbled with the buttons.

"Now, don't get yourself all upset," the doctor said. "This could be any of a hundred different things. It doesn't have to be what you're worrying about."

"I wasn't worrying about anything in particular."

"Of course you were. These days the whole world is cancer-conscious. I'm not saying that's bad, mind you. It's just that people tend to get frightened to death over nothing."

Julian stripped off his shirt and undershirt and laid them aside. He raised his left arm to show Dr. Volney the swelling. The doctor touched the lump with his fingers and prodded the flesh around it.

"Have you been under a mental strain lately?"

"There was a problem at work."

The doctor was pleased. "There you are, it's just as I thought. This sort of thing is often caused by nothing more than a temporary nervous condition."

"But it's growing."

"Or it might be caused by some minor glandular disturbance."

"But, Doctor, isn't it just possible that I've got—"

"Cancer?" Sure, there's always that chance, but don't start shopping for a burial plot until we find out for sure, ha-ha. I'll just hack off a piece and we'll send it out to the lab."

Dr. Volney selected a gleaming scalpel from his instrument case and drew it lightly over the lump under Julian's arm. He wiped the small scraping of flesh onto one glass slide and sealed it with another, then returned to his desk with a smile of professional reassurance.

"I'm going to give you a prescription for a light sedative, something to help you relax. Call me on Friday. And give my best to Norma."

"Margaret," Julian said.

"Of course."

By Friday the lump had doubled in size. There still was no pain, but Julian could feel the thing with every movement of his left arm. He called Dr. Volney four times, but each time reached an answering service. The answering service could not locate the doctor.

Julian spent much of the weekend locked in the bathroom, staring into the mirror at the growth under his arm. The original lump now had its own tiny lumps—five of them. The foreign thing on his body horrified and fascinated him. Sometimes he fancied he could see it growing.

On Monday Julian finally got through to Dr. Volney. "I tried to get you all day Friday, Doctor."

"Yes, sorry, but I was tied up in court all day testifying for an old classmate. Some trumped-up malpractice suit. You wouldn't believe the way some people try to take advantage of us."

"Doctor, about the lump under my arm . . ."

"I've got good news for you about that. The results of the biopsy were negative. It's nothing."

"But the thing is still growing," Julian said. "It has little ones."

"Julian, you do *not* have cancer."

"I don't care what I have, the thing is ugly and getting uglier. I want it removed."

"As you wish." The doctor sighed. "I'll make the arrangements for you to have surgery at Queen of Mercy sometime next week. Check back with me in a few days."

The days passed and Julian did not check back with the doctor. At the end of the week Dr. Volney called him.

"I have you all set up, Julian. You'll sign into the hospital Sunday evening, I'll be in to see you Monday morning before you go to surgery."

"I changed my mind," Julian said.

"What's that?"

"I don't want any surgery. I'm all right."

"Of course you want surgery. I've made all the arrangements."

"Send me a bill," Julian said, and broke the connection before Dr. Volney could reply.

As soon as he hung up the phone Julian went back into the bathroom and locked the door. He pulled off his shirt and stared at what was growing under his arm. He recognized the thing now. It had assumed enough of a shape so anyone could tell what it was—a hand; a tiny baby hand.

Julian was not going to let Dr. Volney and his friends get a look at it. They would treat him like some kind of freak. He could imagine the sensation it would make. Those tabloids they sell in supermarkets would love it: MAN GROWS THIRD HAND. Julian leaned his forehead against the cool glass of the mirror and cried like a child.

In the following weeks the hand grew rapidly. In less than a month it matched the hand of a four-year-old child. After seven weeks the new hand was as large as Julian's own. There the resemblance stopped. The new hand was smooth and devoid of features. No nails, no lines, no knuckles, it looked rather like a rubber glove blown full of air. It was tough and resilient to the touch, and slightly cooler than body temperature.

The thing was also growing an arm. When the hand reached full size, a rubbery, tubelike appendage began to push it out from Julian's side.

As first the hand, then the arm grew, Julian had to make some changes in his life-style to prevent detection. The first thing he did when the thing became really noticeable was to stop sleeping with Margaret. The adjustment was not overly difficult, since both of them had long before ceased to enjoy sharing a bed. Margaret readily accepted Julian's plea of insomnia, and he moved to the living-room sofa.

He began wearing larger jackets to work, and kept them on all day. At home he would change immediately into a loose-fitting robe, which he wore until Margaret went to bed.

As time passed, familiarity with his new appendage made it appear less hideous to Julian. He began to experience a sensual pleasure in examining the hand and touching it. Holding the inert fleshy thing between his own two hands gratified him in a way he could not fully understand. He had a notion that somehow this made up for the son that Margaret would never give him.

Then the hand came to life.

For some time Julian had been aware of its developing sense of touch. He enjoyed placing various objects on the smooth palm. The feel of the different surfaces registered on his brain in an entirely new way. It became like a game as Julian introduced the hand to new textures and temperatures. Then one day it moved. Julian was delighted to find that by concentrating his will he could make the hand obey simple commands. After a few days of practice the fingers could bend individually and grasp objects, and the hand could move about on its flexible tube of an arm. Soon it was as adroit as Julian's original hands. He began to feel a paternal pride in its accomplishments.

The first indication that the hand had begun to act on its own came when Julian found small articles from the office unaccountably turning up in his pockets at night: a roll of stamps, a stapler, a plastic tape dispenser. Julian's first shocked reaction was to return the things the following morning. Then he asked himself, why should I? Everybody else in the office stole whatever they could get away with. Why not? Datatron Systems, Inc., had plenty of money.

Julian put the stolen items away in a desk drawer, then sat down and wrote several personal letters, using the office stamps. The experience was exhilarating.

His attitude toward the hand became that of an indulgent parent toward a mischievous son. Although he was amused by the hand's little escapades, Julian resolved to exert more control over its behavior.

The hand seemed content to obey him until one morning a week later in the elevator. The car stopped at the lobby, and the usual flock of secretaries got on. Julian moved as always to the rear of the car as the girls crowded in. Somewhere between the fifth and sixth floors the girl directly in front of him gasped and arched her back in surprise. Julian looked down and was aghast to see the hand protruding from beneath his jacket and fondling the girl in a way Julian himself would never have dared. Although he concentrated mightily to pull the hand away, it stayed where it was, sending the most delightful touch sensations back to his brain.

Deliberately the girl turned and speared Julian with her eyes. Only then did the hand let go and slip back out of sight. All Julian could manage was an apologetic shrug. The girl, a well-built brunette whom Julian had admired from a distance, lifted one expressive eyebrow and turned away.

For the rest of the day Julian kept his left arm pressed to his side to be sure the hand stayed under his jacket. His unusual posture drew some curious looks, but the hand remained hidden.

On the way home he stopped at a drugstore and bought a rolled bandage and a spool of adhesive tape. The next morning before leaving for work he wound the bandage around his upper body, binding the hand to his side, and made it fast with adhesive tape. It was not a comfortable arrangement, but Julian could no longer risk leaving the hand free.

Riding up in the elevator that morning he prayed that the brunette would not be among the girls who got on his car.

She was, of course.

He was too tall to lose himself among the other passengers, and to his acute embarrassment he found himself once again immediately behind the girl. He prayed that she would not turn around.

She did, of course. Julian was astonished to see that she was smiling.

"Hi," she said.

"Uh, hello."

"You're Julian Dunbar, and you work on the twelfth floor for DSI."

"How did you know?"

"I've known for a long time. I was curious about you and I asked somebody who you were. Aren't you curious about me?"

"Very much."

"I'm Tina Cross. I've worked on the sixth floor for months, and I was beginning to wonder if you'd ever speak to me." The girl laughed softly. "Well, you didn't exactly *speak*, but you did make contact—you did get in touch."

Julian could scarcely believe this was happening to him. He groped for something to say to the girl.

She said it for him. "I'm through work at five o'clock."

"So am I," Julian managed. "Will you have a drink with me after work?"

"I'd love it. Meet me in the lobby."

Julian spent the day in an agony of anticipation. This adventure was completely outside his experience. He even forgot about the discomfort of having the hand bound to his side. Before leaving, he went into the men's room to make sure the thing was still secure. It would never do to have it flop out on his first date with Tina.

The drink after work stretched into several drinks. Julian

found himself talking and laughing freely with a girl for the first time in years. He remembered, however, to keep his right side toward Tina. He did not want her to brush accidentally against the bulge under his left arm.

Later, when he took Tina home to her apartment, he kissed her. It was a short kiss, and light, but it promised that this was only the beginning.

The hand remained the only obstacle in the way of a satisfactory relationship. Although he had grown used to the thing, Julian could guess at the disgust it would arouse in others. To his immense relief, the problem was easily solved after all.

In the first place, Tina offered no objection to keeping the bedroom totally dark for their intimacies. She even found it amusing that he chose to wear a soft, loose-fitting shirt at all times. For his part, Julian became quite adept at moving his body just far enough so Tina's caressing hand would not encounter the thing taped to his side. With these minor adjustments, Julian gave himself over fully to the pleasure of the affair.

At home he no longer bothered to alibi his absences. Margaret complained bitterly at first but, confronted by Julian's new indifference, soon lapsed into puzzled silence. The situation might have continued indefinitely had not Julian failed one night to lock the bathroom door.

He had left Tina earlier than usual, and was standing naked in the front of the mirror letting the hand move about, free of its constricting bandage. Without warning, the door burst open and Margaret faced him, hands planted on her bony hips.

"What are you doing in here so long, washing off the smell of your girl friend? Oh, yes, I found out who she is and where she works. Right there in the same building. Very handy for you, I must say. It has been up to now, anyway. Tomorrow I'm paying a little visit to Miss Tina Cross, and I think things will change pretty sud—"

The speech died in Margaret's mouth as Julian turned to face her. Her eyes fastened in horror on the thing growing from his side. The hand rose on its tubular arm and stretched toward her like a fleshy snake.

When Julian regained control, the body of his wife lay half in and half out of the bathroom. Her upturned face was dark and swollen like an eggplant. The hand hung limp and heavy at his side. Julian stared down at it. How could he ever have accepted this monstrosity as a part of himself? It was clear now what he must do, what he should have done long ago.

Stepping over the corpse, he walked into the kitchen. From a wooden rack screwed into the wall he selected the heaviest of a set of carving knives. He honed the blade in the electric knife sharpener and tested the edge against his thumb. Satisfied, he spread newspapers across the tabletop and sat close in a chair.

He took hold of the hand and pulled it out across the newspapers. It lay docile in his grasp. Julian pulled in deep lungfuls of oxygen, trying to slow the hammering of his heart. He poised the knife in front of his face, his fingers gripping the bone handle. It had to be done in a single blow. He would never have the courage to hack at it a second time. Slowly he brought the edge of the blade against the rubbery skin at the point where the arm grew from his side.

The hand jumped in his grasp.

> . . . the deaths were labeled double homicide by detectives. Dunbar apparently tried to fight off the attacker with a kitchen knife, wounding himself in the attempt. A massive search is underway for the assailant, described by police as immensely powerful, based on evidence that he strangled the victims using only one hand.

JERE CUNNINGHAM

The Face

In this life there are only two choices: to see everything as strange or to see nothing as strange. There is no middle ground. I felt that to see nothing as strange was not only incorrect, but unbearably boring. I suppose that viewpoint was in itself the beginning of the secret.

My life was perhaps average, but not ordinary—no life is ordinary, no job is ordinary, and no house, no matter how typical, is ordinary. When in the red and purple dusky evenings I would drive the patient Toyota into the suburbs from my downtown office, I would love to see the warm lights in rectangular windows and porches. The poorer streets had houses closer together. Our street had houses slightly larger and slightly farther apart. The houses were no mansions, but I could feel the people inside them, breathing, alive, thinking, desiring, dreaming. I thought of the women in those houses. Every woman was in some way beautiful with her own human, female secretness. I had my own wife and house and car. In my wallet was an amulet of modern life, an American Express card, and as I walked into my house I felt that I had earned the right of tranquility.

In her sleep my wife breathed as if her nostrils were clipped together. She was very pretty when animated with consciousness, and so I watched her sleep with fascination, wondering at the increase of my desire now that she was temporarily limp and asexual. I closed my eyes and felt a gritty pain as if seeing her for the last time. I could feel the secret with us in the pale moonlight of the room. Before sleep came I was always afraid and excited, for something was growing, something was coming, and like weeds, images grew rapidly in the dark earth of my imagination.

Drowsing in my bed at dawn was a great pleasure. I could merely shift my limbs to feel my groin begin to glow. Often I would pretend still to be asleep, not wanting to be touched; at other times I would reach for the warm friendly body of the woman who had been my bed companion for so long. Happy that I still took her sensuality so seriously, she would respond with wonderful passion. That was when the secret, in its earliest phase, grew strongest.

Someone seemed to be with me, within me or very close by while I made love. Movies came into view, starring actresses from my own neighborhood. The most prominent stars were the teenage girl with blond bangs who lived next door and the tall, thin female bachelor attorney in the ranch-style house on the other side. The teenager often seduced me in childhood hiding places. Her body was incredibly resilient within its childish tenderness. The attorney was riper, as if delicately bruised; I could enjoy her with no guilt at any time, even at work when I surely appeared to be staring into space, deeply concerned with some company problem.

"What are you dreaming about?" my wife would ask at dinner or breakfast. I realized that my other mind was reaching beyond the bed.

"Remembering the wonderful sex we had the first year or two after we met in school," I could easily lie.

"The past year or two haven't been so bad either," she would answer, smiling, reaching to touch me.

✸ ✸ ✸

THE FACE ✱

The teenage girl was kicking a soccer ball one evening as I left my house to jog. I took part of her with me down the sidewalk. My compulsion to do this was becoming irresistibly strong. Something strange and wonderful, something very secret, was taking form. I was happy as I ran. I believed that every human mind or heart must keep at least one secret place, one intimate, private place in which to remain sane. I felt the secret then but did not know it. To me it was pure and inviolate like something told desperately in childhood to a very best friend in some dark closet, a leaf-isolated tree house or an attic rendezvous full of shadowy timeless things discarded by those who were gone.

I jogged that evening for a much longer time than was my habit; it was as if something had to be worked out. The shadows of the neighborhood in dusk were long and stretched; merging, the dark bars were constantly broken by my moving body. I ran evenly and steadily along that sidewalk, waiting for something, listening to the rhythm of rubber soles abrasive against concrete, and to the caustic animal reports of my body's breathing. I had passed the white neocolonial house on the corner and was on the next block for the fourth time when I was first aware unmistakably of something there besides myself.

An unfamiliar excitement ran through the flesh and short hair of my neck, and I put a hand there almost expecting to feel a scratchy sweater collar.

In broken stride I was glancing over my shoulder. There was no one. Nothing moved in the deepening shadows and yet, as I ran on again, steadying, I felt the sweat of my body changing character. It was both lust and fear; I felt objectless lust and was frightened. My fatigue lost its purity, became rancid with anxiety. I realized that I was running as fast as I could.

I stopped completely.

Panting on the shadowed sidewalk, I searched the line of houses. The night seemed to be coming down from the sky. The sparse streetlights seemed dim and weak and yellowish. The familiar outlines of my block were different, somehow strange. With self-ridicule I strove to collect myself. That was when I saw him step from behind the black wall of a hedge half a block down.

We stared at one another. He stood between my house and myself. I could not clearly see his face but his frame was like mine, his shape like mine. And his jogging clothes were the same. He stood looking at me exactly as I stood looking at him.

I remember running urgently, cutting through yards and circling the block with frantic speed. Over my shoulder I saw him following me, his arms pumping exactly like mine, the slap of his rubber soles in precise syncopation with my own.

Not until I was locked within the warm familiarity of my house was I able to lose enough of the strange sensations to feel foolish. I even told my wife about it. How I loved her at that moment. I felt myself destroying the secret forever. We had a great laugh.

"Joggers chase each other around the block," she kidded. She looked tired and drawn from her own day of work, but her eyes lit up as brilliantly as ever. God, how I loved her then, as she said, "It's like an Escher print: someone after him, him after you, you after someone else."

"There wasn't anybody in front of me," I heard myself saying.

She frowned, looking old again. "You said there was."

"I did?"

"We should call the police, I think."

"No."

"At least the neighborhood association?"

"No," I said.

We had had our good laugh; she had laughed, I realized, because she truly knew nothing whatever about me, this man she lived and slept with.

It was fall; the leaves were everywhere. I came home from work to find the teenage girl from next door raking our lawn.

Helplessly I put on mental film the small high rotation of her buttocks in faded cutoffs, her delicious motion with the rake, just the same as I had done with girls at the pencil sharpener decades before. When she had all the leaves stuffed into plastic bags I paid her more than my wife had contracted for—I was afraid for her, I realized. Why did I feel so damned guilty?

The next evening my wife met me at the door. She did not usually do so. In her own work she earned more money than I did, and got home later, often with prepared food from a restaurant. I expected no subordinate behavior, nor would I have respected her if she had shown any. We coexisted under civil, sexual, and emotional agreements. And so I should have been surprised and pleased to see the lovely, pallid oval of her face just inside the window next to the door.

Instead, I was afraid. I was afraid I knew something I could not know.

"Darling," I said, embracing her.

"The police didn't phone you at work?"

To shut her mouth I kissed her small lips, felt her teeth pressing through the warm flesh. Her breasts, small too and very high, flattened slightly against my chest. She thrust me back at arm's length.

"I told them to call you at your office," she said, irritated, obviously alarmed.

The girl next door had been raped that afternoon when she had come home from school to an empty house where someone had been waiting.

I did not jog that evening.

My free hours at home for the next few days were spent installing deadbolt locks on doors and window frames, and assuring my wife that a gun in our house would only endanger ourselves in a way worse than rape. Furious, and terrified of men in general, she fought this in her own way: fought the fear of men with lovemaking.

We made violent love. There was, for a time, a kind of rage when we were alone together. I welded myself to her and then, when she slept, I lay watching her beside me, her mouth gaping in sleep, the slightly wrinkled tissue of her lips bluish with moonlight through the gauzy muslin curtains she had chosen for our bedroom.

We were in bed together just that way the night I saw a shadow pass our bedroom window. It paused momentarily to block out the faded light of a distant streetlight. Its hair and its shoulders were familiar. Frozen, struggling as if up from the depths of an unspeakable dream, I managed to groan and then to cry out an obscenity. The shadow was gone. I lay beside my wife, awake and sweating.

At the office the next morning, I saw a small column in the newspaper that made my eyes feel tipped with glass: SECOND RAPE IN ANNESDALE AREA THIS MONTH. There had been two police cars in the driveway of the attorney's house next door to ours when I had left for work.

The police detective who came to see me at the office that day was a woman. She was not pretty, but there was something powerful about her, a kind of coarse confidence that meant aggression. My secretary, obviously impressed and intimidated, let the detective in without a warning, then retreated with an apologetic whine.

"Why did you leave your house so quickly this morning?" the detective asked me.

I realized that I had. Of course I had, I could *feel* what had happened in that house. . . .

"I was late," I said. Luckily, that was true.

She leaned forward toward me, "Did you know that a young girl living in the house just on the other side of yours was recently raped?"

"Yes," I said. "Why aren't you out looking for whoever did

those things instead of asking these damned questions in my office?"

That night my wife would not let me touch her. She kept looking at me in a funny way, as if she did not know me.

As I lay beside her after she fell asleep, listening to her breathe in the dark, I saw the attorney being raped. There was a growing tension. She was undressing as she wearily climbed her carpeted stairs. She did not sense anyone in the dark hall above as she reached for the light switch. The rag-filled hand was stuffing her mouth before she even thought to scream.

There was no pleasure in the things that came next, only lust and fear. Fear and a terrible satisfaction. I went into the bathroom and vomited.

On my knees, facing the slick, gleaming porcelain of the commode, I remembered a time when I had visited my wife's grandmother on a Sunday afternoon. There had been talk of a crazy woman, very old, who had helped raise my wife's grandmother from the time she was a child. This old woman had been thought strange but harmless. My wife's grandmother had said the old woman believed many weird things. Her basic philosophy was that for everything holy in this world there is an equal to it that is unholy, that joy and pain are as necessary to one another as are God and Satan, that evil is as needed as good. That Sunday afternoon had ended with talk of other superstitions and of mirrors.

On my knees, remembering my wife's grandmother on that distant Sunday afternoon, I realized that I had never, before this moment, understood myself.

I lay shivering in the bed beside my sleeping wife. There was a smell in the air, something I had smelled before: cheese and crushed flower petals? The aroma seemed half-real, burnt and cruel and delicious. I strove with all my mind not to sleep. I concentrated upon the nasal whang of my wife's breath. I would not let myself sleep.

The heaviness in every limb dragged me down. Images

floated brilliantly before my eyes and the film scenarios flowed together. The teen-age girl had been my secret and was again, but this time not in fantasy. I saw the attorney wearily reclimbing her stairs. And then I saw my wife, coming from the shower, the steam clinging to her damp heated body. I was coming through my own house. I was soundless. I was smiling. I was feeling very friendly.

There were screams.

I heard them as if from a great distance. They seemed stifled but to go on forever, very human, so afraid, with the scent of warm cheese and crushed petals, a drunken sensuality, satisfaction utterly without pleasure. Then it became truly obscene.

I awoke.

Beside me on the bed the heavy opaque shape lay ferociously and rigidly atop the female person with whom I had chosen to live and submit and survive.

I could not move.

The hair on the head of my secret was cowlicked exactly like mine, darker than the dark wall behind the bed. I kept hearing my wife's stifled cries of fear and pain, the black shadows of their limbs stark bars against that wall. Something within me tore. I fought to sit up, to lift my arms.

The face turned slowly to stare upon mine; its eyes gleamed with tears, trying to reach a focus with mine.

I kept hearing my wife cry out.

The face above her was locked with mine, its eyes dazzling with knowing, with an unmistakable hatred.

For the face was my own.